Snipped

A Cutting Comedy

Lee Gabel

FRANKENSCRIPT

Frankenscript Press
Box 717, #105 - 1497 Admirals Road
Victoria, BC, Canada   V9A 2P8

SNIPPED

Cover illustration and design by Lee Gabel

Cover images supplied by Shutterstock

Cover font (Harlow) by Letraset Canada Ltd.
Body font (ITC Galliard Pro) by International Typeface Corporation
Folios, heads and caps (Zapf Humanist 601) by Bitstream Inc.
Scissor Icon (Zapf Dingbats) by Bitstream Inc.

ISBN: 978-0-9918498-7-1 (ebook)
ISBN: 978-0-9918498-8-8 (paperback)

Want to join Lee's Reader Group or find out more
about Lee and the books he writes? Please go to:
LeeGabel.com
LeeGabel.com/facebook
LeeGabel.com/twitter
Or follow Lee at BookBub - LeeGabel.com/bookbub

Snipped

A Cutting Comedy

Titles by Lee Gabel

Detest-A-Pest Series
Arachnid 2.0 (Coming 2019)
Vermin 2.0

Standalone
Snipped
David's Summer
Tied

To all those men out there.
You know who you are.

Buster

I'M THE LUCKIEST son of a bitch on the planet, Ted thought as he lay naked on the bed, the sheets strewn over half his ass. The air still held the mingled essences of perfume and sex. From his prone position he took in the view over the Willamette River towards Portland's downtown core.

He heard bare feet pad back towards the bedroom. Ted turned his head around on the pillow. From his new vantage point, he could see past bare legs and into the hallway that led to the main bathroom, kitchen and living area. Leaning against the bedroom door frame stood Iris, the love of his life, her hair in a high ponytail tied with a red ribbon.

She wore a white, loose-fitting t-shirt with an image of a rocket taking off amid plumes of smoke. Beside it were the words "Launch Time." The hem of her shirt was just long enough to hide her panties from view.

If she's wearing any. The thought brought a warm smile to Ted's lips and he felt himself getting hard again. In front of him was still the woman he had imagined underneath that black business suit five years ago. Confident, intelligent, and sexy as hell. Business and pleasure: Ted had the best of both worlds.

Iris reached up with her left hand and pulled out her hair ribbon, one red inch at a time. With her left arm raised, the hem of her t-shirt lifted enough to offer Ted a glimpse of her white bikini-style panties, the ones with a small red bow on the waistband that he loved so much.

Like a present waiting to be unwrapped.

Iris licked her lips, anticipating Ted's desire. "Ready for round two?"

Before Ted could answer, Iris placed her hands together and dived *into* the bed, the covers rippling like water as she disappeared into the mattress.

"What the hell?" Ted propped himself up on his elbows and looked toward her point of entry. "Where did you go? Iris?"

"Hey lover-boy."

Ted followed the source of Iris's voice and found her underneath him. She kissed his chest. "Wait. How did you—"

As his last rational thought slipped out of his head, Iris appeared *behind* him, layering kisses on his back.

"Iris, how are you—"

"Shut up." Iris pushed Ted down onto the bed. She was no longer wearing her t-shirt as he could feel the hot skin of her breasts and nipples brush against the small of his back, buttocks, and thighs.

Iris disappeared under the sheets and spread Ted's legs apart. He closed his eyes and took in the warm, wet sensations as they traveled down his back and over his buttocks.

Ted heard Iris's voice whisper into his ear. "Beep. Beep. Beep."

Logic fought for attention in his brain. *How can your mouth be in two places at once?* he thought.

Iris continued. "Beep. Beep." But her voice became more rhythmic, more electronic, until all that remained were the wet caresses under the sheets.

TED OPENED HIS eyes to the clock radio on the bedside table. It read 6:00 a.m., flashing with each beep. He groaned as he reached out and silenced the alarm.

You have got to be kidding me, Ted thought, as he turned his head towards Iris's side of the bed. Crumpled sheets remained where she had been sleeping. Ted heard the shower shut off and the stall door open and close in the ensuite bathroom, yet the wet sensation on his backside remained.

Wet and *cold*.

Then he heard a jangling collar. Ted reached down with his right hand to find a cold nose attached to a furry snout. He pulled back the sheets to reveal a seven month-old golden retriever nuzzling and licking his thigh.

"Buster!" The dog refocused on Ted's face, layering wet, excited dog kisses on his cheek. "Okay, okay. I'm up."

Ted swung his legs off the bed and sat up. His erection still commanded full attention inside his boxer shorts.

I'm really up.

He looked down at the tent in his shorts and considered rubbing one out in the main bathroom, but an inquisitive head-tilt from Buster distracted him.

"Going to have to teach you about consent, buddy. My butt's off limits." Buster moved to rest his head between Ted's legs, which was a little too close to his deflating erection. He intercepted the dog's playful approach with a head scratch. "Above the waist is okay. Below… not so much." He wagged his finger back and forth and made a *tsk-tsk* sound.

Buster chuffed like he understood.

"Where's Mom?"

The dog navigated to the foot of the bed and scratched the door to the ensuite bathroom.

Ted followed Buster's path, gave the bathroom door a knock, and opened it. The ensuite bathroom was warm, steamy, and smelled like sweetened coconuts. Iris stood in front of the mirror with a large towel wrapped around her body, hand-drying her hair with a smaller chamois. Beside her on the counter sat her phone. She was lost in serious thought until she saw Ted at the door.

"Hey you," she said with a smile that faltered once she spied Buster panting next to Ted's feet.

Ted recalled fragments of his recent dream before they tumbled out of reach. "I just had a great dream about you."

Iris looked at the receding bulge in his boxers. "That's nice, hon."

Ted stepped up behind her and planted a line of kisses, starting just below her right ear and down to her shoulder. "Want to get busy? We got time."

Usually this was a turn-on for Iris, but she deflected. "I have depositions scheduled all day, so I need to get to the office early."

Buster trotted into the bathroom and began to lick Iris's feet and legs.

"Read my mind, buddy."

"No dogs. Out!" Iris shooed Buster out. "Go." She waved

her hands. Buster got the message loud and clear. He whined and made a hasty retreat back into the bedroom.

"He was just saying hello."

"I know," Iris said, "but I just got out of the shower. I don't want to smell like dog."

"Besides…you don't smell…like dog," Ted said, punctuating his words with more kisses. "What do you say?"

Iris could sense his hard-on through the towel. "Rain check?" Her phone chimed an incoming text alert. She turned and offered a quick kiss on Ted's forehead before grabbing her phone and leaving the bathroom. The accordion doors to the walk-in closet squeaked open and Iris began to pick out her clothes for the day.

Ted looked at the empty shower stall. He imagined his remaining arousal swirling the drain. A tile next to the hair trap had chipped off.

Got to fix that, he thought.

As Ted closed the bathroom door, he could hear the familiar clacking sound of a phone keyboard. Iris was texting a reply to someone. It was a sound he had begun to loathe, and one more reason to dislike cell phones. Technology got in the way too much these days.

Ted dropped his boxers and sat on the toilet. He never stood up to pee at home. Iris had drilled that habit into him early on in their relationship. But in an attempt to reassert his manhood, he stood up to pee in every other bathroom in the free world (but mostly in Portland.)

Peeing sitting down with a hard-on was particularly difficult. To pass the time, Ted grabbed a Wired Magazine from the back of the toilet and began flipping through it. Just as he was settling into an article, he heard Iris knock.

"The dog's hungry and I'm running late," she said through the bathroom door.

"His name is Buster."

"What?"

"Never mind. I'll take care of him." Ted tossed the magazine aside, flushed, and washed his hands.

TED'S CONDOMINIUM WAS appointed with modern furniture and appliances, but represented more of Iris's style than Ted's. Iris loved European high-end design and tended to favor form over function. Ted was the opposite. If it was comfortable, reliable, or easy to use, it got two thumbs up. Most of the time they were able to compromise, but Ted would never understand why a plastic chair had to cost almost two hundred dollars.

"It's the design that's important," Iris would say on their many trips to Contempo Imports, their current go-to store for "fine furnishings and state-of-the-art appliances."

Ted tucked his well-worn button-up shirt into his jeans. Buster whined at his feet. "I'm hungry too, buddy, but you're going to have to wait a bit."

The dog's nails clacked on the engineered hardwood floor as he scrambled to all-fours and led the way to the kitchen, just as he had every day for the past seven months. The aroma of fresh-brewed coffee permeated the space.

Iris looked sharp in the outfit she had picked for the day. She always looked sharp. Ted recalled falling head over heels five years ago, his first sight of her confident walk in a black-skirted business suit with a baby blue blouse, hem at a tasteful knee-level, and the shine of her straight, auburn hair.

Today Iris wore a dark gray skirted suit with a white blouse. Her hair was tied back with a narrow red ribbon. Iris preferred skirts over pant suits because she considered her legs an asset. She wanted to assert her confidence and individuality as a woman in the firm, especially since she was trying to make partner. Wearing a pant suit felt like being one of the guys.

Ted walked past the kitchen counter and watched Iris. He still felt horny as hell. The small, red ribbon in her hair didn't help.

"I love that outfit on you," Ted said.

Iris sat at the dinner table, eating a muffin between sips of coffee from her favorite Contigo travel mug. When her hands were free, she typed notes into her open laptop as fast as her fingers could manage. An incoming text chimed on her phone and Iris switched gears, answering the text without delay.

"Aw, you're sweet," she said without looking away from her phone. "It's one of my power suits. Oh, by the way, we're out of coffee."

Ted grabbed the French press that sat on the counter, emptied its contents into a mug and took a gulp. He was met with a mouthful of lukewarm grit and dumped the rest into the sink.

"Can you bring some home today?"

"Yeah, sure," Ted said as he worked grains of coffee out of his molars with his tongue. He walked over to Iris and kissed the back of her neck, smelling a mix of perfume and faint coconut. He got down on one knee.

Iris stopped cold and looked at him. "Ted...? What are you doing?" There was an odd hint of terror in her eyes.

Ted ran his hand down Iris's left leg, then back up, stopping at the hem of her skirt. "Someone finished the coffee. I need some kind of morning stimulation."

"Rain check, remember?" Iris's face relaxed and she presented her travel mug. "Want a sip?"

Ted accepted the casual rebuff. "Nah. I need sugar in mine. I'll wait until I get to the shop." He stood up, kissing the top of Iris's head on the way by.

Buster sauntered over and gave Iris's leg a lick.

"Not my nylons, Buster." Iris shooed the dog away. "I don't want hair on me."

Ted walked back to the kitchen to inventory the remaining coffee beans. When Iris said they were "out of coffee," that usually meant there wasn't enough beans for a full pot. "Come here, boy. Mommy's busy." Buster trotted back to Ted.

Iris clenched her teeth. "Don't call me that."

"Oh, come on. Work with me. You're Buster's mommy and he loves you, don't you, boy?"

Iris shot a look at Ted, her eyes narrowed. "I'm *not* his mommy." She closed her laptop and placed it in her attaché case. Ted remembered buying it for their first date anniversary. Iris was difficult to buy for, but the case was one thing he got right. She used it every day and it had become scuffed and worn in places.

Buster whined and nudged his food dish towards Ted with his snout.

Iris wiped muffin crumbs from her mouth with a napkin and slung her attaché and purse over her shoulder. She finished her text and dropped her phone into her purse. Then, as if on autopilot, she dug out a compact mirror and refreshed her lipstick.

Ted met her at the door, holding her travel mug. "You almost forgot this."

"I didn't forget it, but thanks."

Ted leaned in to kiss Iris, but she turned her head and presented her cheek.

"Lipstick."

"Right." Ted planted a light kiss on her cheek, again reminded of how terrific she smelled.

"I'm probably going to be late tonight." Iris opened the door and stepped into the hallway, walking towards the elevators.

"Maybe we can talk about that *rain check* later."

"Maybe," Iris said without looking back.

"The fine print says it expires soon."

Iris punched the elevator's call button and glanced back at Ted. "You're funny. Don't get drunk with the guys, especially Ray."

"Ray's just misunderstood."

"I understand him just fine. He's gross." The elevator *dinged* and the door slid open. Iris offered a small wave as she stepped inside.

Ted placed his hand on his heart. "Until tonight, my love." His words arrived too late. The elevator doors had already closed.

Buster whined again and looked at his empty food dish.

Ted sighed and closed the door. He kneeled beside the dog and gave him a scratch and a hug. "I know you're hungry. Just a little while longer."

✂

THE WAITING ROOM at Pets West Veterinarian Clinic was packed and heavy with warm dog breath.

"It's pretty funky in here this morning."

The receptionist gave Ted a warm smile. "It's always like this on a Monday." As Ted checked in, he made a mental note not to make an appointment on Monday again.

Buster sat on the floor next to Ted. The dog was on edge, as were all the other pets waiting their turn. Ted imagined that they all had an innate sense that something unpleasant was going to happen to them.

Ted reached down and gave Buster's head a scratch. "I know it's your big day, buddy. Mommy just forgot." Buster emitted a low whine.

Next to Ted and Buster sat a chihuahua with numerous bald patches breaking through its thin fur coat. Despite being held on its owner's lap, the little dog trembled so badly that Ted thought he could hear the dog's teeth chattering.

Neurotic, Ted thought, as he began to scan the room. Project Diagnosis was a game he played in waiting rooms to pass the time. Animals were more of a challenge.

Next to the chihuahua sat a bulldog, with drool mixed with what Ted hoped was food flowing off its tongue in rivulets. *Halitosis*.

The pug in the corner looked over-fed and struggled to breathe. That one was easy. *Asthma*.

The Doberman and the German Shepherd sat bolt upright next to their owners. They kept at least one eye on each other at all times and watched for any breach of waiting room protocol. *Aggression issues.*

A veterinarian assistant in her mid-twenties entered the waiting room carrying a clipboard. "Buster…and Ted?"

"That's us." Ted stood up, prompting Buster to stand as well.

The assistant extended her hand and smiled. "Hi Ted. I'm Cherise. I'll be cumming during our encounter."

Ted did a double-take as he shook Cherise's hand. It was warm and smooth. "Pardon me?"

"I said I'll be accompanying Buster during his procedure." Cherise looked at Ted with a careful eye. "Are you feeling okay?"

Ted nodded, a little perplexed. "I'm fine." He crouched to Buster's level and ruffled his fur. "You be good, buddy. Okay? Treats for you for sure after." He kissed Buster's head and stood up. Ted handed the leash to Cherise. "When can I pick him up?"

"Anytime after four." Cherise jotted down some notes on her clipboard. "I'm open for anything."

"What?"

Cherise paused and stared at Ted with her dark brown eyes. "Um, we're open until seven."

Am I losing my mind? I could have sworn I heard something else, Ted thought, his brain racing in all the wrong directions but all involving Cherise in various stages of undress.

"Are you *sure* you're okay?"

"Uh…I just need a coffee and some fresh air." Ted headed towards the clinic's entrance. "Give Buster an extra Milk Bone for me."

Once outside, Ted took a deep breath, shook his head, and tried to piece together the last ten minutes.

What's happening to me? he thought. The answers he sought would come later.

TED HAD ALWAYS wanted to own a coffee shop. Now he was living the dream. Buster's Beans Coffee Shop was small compared to many, but what made it unique was its heritage. The shop had been built around an old freight elevator from the early 1900s. The interior was long and narrow, framed by old red brick walls, and the ceiling twice as high as a typical coffee shop. There were a few round tables at the front and rear, and a couple outside when the weather was agreeable. In keeping with the building's original purpose, the front of the shop could be shuttered with a rolling corrugated steel door.

It was comfortable inside Buster's Beans and the variety of coffee, warmed pastries, and bagels served provided a delicious olfactory experience. The shop enjoyed brisk business almost year round. It was a prime location for walk-by traffic in the mixed commercial and residential East Portland neighborhood.

In the five years that Ted had owned and operated Buster's Beans, he had developed a loyal clientele. There was enough business now to reliably support two full time employees.

Danielle and Joe were both in their mid-twenties, but Danielle had seniority, having worked at Buster's Beans for three years, compared to Joe's two. Danielle's favorite color was purple and she incorporated it into everything in her life, from her jewelry and make-up, to her form-fitting t-shirts in summer and long sleeves underneath during winter. Everything needed a touch of purple. Her hair hung shoulder-length, black and straight with purple highlights, but it was unclear if black was her natural hair color. That was Danielle's secret. However, it was her smile that lit up the place. It was one of the reasons Ted had hired her.

Joe was two parts barista and one part starving artist. Tall and wiry, his dirty blond hair was cut short on the sides, with the top pulled back into a loose man-bun. He took immense pride in his sculpted beard and manscaping prowess. Joe's wardrobe included many varieties of short-sleeved button-up shirts that were always one size too small to emphasize what little musculature he had. The top two buttons remained unfastened to expose his neck and give his beard "room to breathe."

Ted entered the shop just as Danielle and Joe were finishing up with the morning rush. "Sorry. The vet clinic didn't open until eight-thirty."

"You're the boss." Joe pointed at Ted with both index fingers. "You answer to no one."

"Should've seen it a half hour ago." Danielle placed both hands into her hair and squeezed in faux frustration.

"Are you still going to call this place 'Buster's Beans'? I mean…" He motioned to his own crotch. "It's inaccurate, anatomically speaking."

"Real funny," Ted said.

"What else would you call it? 'Buster's Decaffeinated Beans'?" Danielle gave Joe a friendly shove. "Don't be so literal. Besides, you can't change the branding now."

"Yes, exactly." Ted grabbed an apron as he pointed at Danielle in agreement. "I knew I hired you for a reason."

"You mean you didn't hire her for her spectacular breasts?" Joe smirked.

"Pig. That's harassment. I've got seniority here and I could have you fired."

"I'd be fine with it, too," Ted said. "I don't condone harassment of any kind."

Danielle threw a wet rag at Joe, hitting him in the face. "Go clean the toilet with that rat's nest you call a beard."

"Touché, my lady." Joe extended one hand, placed the other on his heart and settled down to one knee. "Forgive me for bestowing your ample bosom with compliments."

"Thin ice, Joe. Enough." Ted nodded towards the last remaining customers preparing their coffees at the condiment station.

The front door swung open, ringing the bell attached to the door frame. Kunal and Ray, Ted's besties, sauntered in. Kunal removed his mirrored aviators and placed them in the front pocket of his light blue silk shirt. His pressed khakis terminated in a pair of black leather loafer slip-ons. Everything he wore complimented his olive-skinned complexion.

Kunal had made his fortune creating mobile phone apps. Six years ago his Gigologo app, once described as "one stop shopping for people wanting to connect with single men," had gone viral. Gigologo had taken off in the U.S., and he developed versions for the United Kingdom and Canada soon after. It didn't take long for buyers to start knocking on Kunal's door. In the end, he sold his company in exchange for stock and an undisclosed sum, reportedly mid-eight figures.

Even Ted and Ray didn't know how much he'd been paid. Since then Kunal had devoted himself to realizing his notion of a trendy, playboy lifestyle.

Ray on the other hand couldn't find style if it hit him in the face. He wore a bright green track suit with white pinstripes extending down the arms and legs. The waistband was too tight, which formed a muffin top, even with his diminutive Asian physique. On his feet were a pair of red Adidas sneakers with white trim. His only modern feature was his close-trimmed beard.

Ray owned a medium-sized television and appliance store in Northeast Portland called Tronikusu. The name was inspired by the Japanese word for electronics. He made a modest living and paid his employees well. Unfortunately he often spoke and acted before his brain could catch up.

Ted had chummed around with Kunal and Ray since meeting in business school, long before Iris was on the scene. They had watched Ted's relationship with Iris develop over the years, and Ted had taken extra measures to keep their friendship alive, a fact that always irritated Iris. She took pleasure in calling the trio "The Three Stooges" whenever the opportunity arose.

"I'm just joking," Iris would say, but Ted never quite believed her. He was well aware of her deep dislike for Ray. However, Iris wasn't as forthcoming about her feelings for Kunal. At bare minimum, she admired his fashion sense, but she had no respect for Kunal's playboy way of life.

Ted waved the two over.

"Hey, dude." Kunal high-fived Ted over the counter.

Ray followed, checking out two women adding cream and sugar to their coffees at the condiment station. He nodded at them, winked, pointed an index finger at one, then raised his right hand, fingers in a "V" sign and was about to stick his wiggling tongue between them.

Ted knew Ray's unpredictable, yet predictable nature and tried to intercede. "Ray!"

Ray dropped his hand to his side and shrugged at Ted, but the damage was done. The two women left with visible disgust on their faces.

Ted tried to diffuse the situation. "I'm sorry, ladies. He didn't mean it." He ran out after them.

Ray sucked in his ample gut and placed his hand on his hips. "So? What do you think?"

"About what? The leisure suit?" Joe shot a quick glance at Kunal, then back at Ray. "Does it glow in the dark?"

Danielle sighed. "The beard. It's always the beard."

"Correction," Kunal said. "The 'Star Trek' beard."

"Nothing beats *my* beard." Joe ran his hand over his face, compressing and stroking the shaped hair. Danielle shook her head and snickered.

"Here's a hint." Ray exhaled and his gut flowed out past his belt line. Then he sucked it in again. "Shields up! Red alert!" he said in his best William Riker impression, which still wasn't very good. He held his gut in for a few seconds longer before releasing a tidal wave of flab back over his waistband.

Joe shrugged.

Danielle's jaw dropped and her eyes widened. "Seriously, Joe? Even I know that one. William Riker, 'Star Trek: The Next Generation.' "

"Nailed it!" Ray held up his hand, wanting to high-five someone. He settled on Kunal.

"Have you washed your hands?"

"Yeah."

Kunal accepted Ray's awkward high-five, then wiped his hand on his khakis.

"Hey. I said I washed them."

"Sorry, dude." Kunal shrugged. "Habit." He dug into his pocket, pulled out a small bottle of Purell, and squeezed a drop into his hand. "Want some?"

Ray pushed Kunal's hand away, annoyed.

Joe shook his head. "I'm drowning in a sea of nerds."

Ted re-entered the shop and slapped Ray on the shoulder.

"Hey!" Ray flinched. "Why'd you do that for?"

"Why? You know why."

Ray stared back, clueless. He was a loyal friend but had no social compass.

"For being a vulgar pig." Kunal looked at his fingernails, spotted a hangnail, and dug out a nail clipper.

"That, and disrespecting my customers. Even after giving them two prepaid coffee cards, I'm not sure they'll be back." Ted glared at Ray. "You're a friend, but I don't allow behavior like that in my shop. I'll ban you."

Ray stared back, surprised. "You wouldn't."

"Try me."

The two of them locked gazes, then Ray laughed. "Nah…I would've been kicked out long ago."

Ted stepped back behind the counter. "Don't fuck with my business, Ray. You're on thin ice as it is." He looked at Kunal trimming his nails. "And you…what are you, twelve? Do that somewhere else."

"Sorry." Kunal pocketed the clipper.

Danielle watched the door, then looked to the seating at the rear of the shop. No customers in sight. She leaned over the counter. "Look at this." She stuck out her pierced tongue and wiggled it. "I got it for my boyfriend."

Ray shifted his eyes from Danielle's breasts settling on the counter to her tongue moving in her mouth. "That's *hot!* You think my wife would go for it?"

"Not a chance in hell, dude," Kunal said, shaking his head.

Joe eyed Danielle's piercing, restraining his fascination and drying cups from the dishwasher. "But do *you* like it?"

"Not really…at least not yet." Danielle captured the metal bead in her teeth, then let it go. "It's hard to get used to, but it…" She glanced around the shop again before continuing. "It drives my boyfriend wild when I…you know."

"Okay, too much information," Ted said.

But it was too late. Ray's pupils dilated like he was high on drugs. His eyes followed the little metal bead on Danielle's tongue bounce up and down as she flicked it.

Ted tapped Danielle's shoulder. "Stop. You'll give him an aneurysm."

"I think she's already blown his mind," Kunal said as he scanned the boldly titled "stimulant" board. He turned on his bedroom eyes and gazed at Danielle. "What's *good* today?"

"The Nicaragua Jinotega is *good*." Danielle said, returning Kunal's look and raising the corner of her mouth in a sly smile.

Kunal raised his eyebrows. "Not a chance, huh?"

"Nope." Danielle grabbed a cup and poured a Jinotega for Kunal. "I got a boyfriend, remember?" She wiggled her tongue at him.

"Ray?" Kunal said. "You want anything?"

"Give him a Green Eye." Joe tossed his drying towel over his shoulder. "He'd be up for two or three days straight."

Ted shook his head. "For Ray? No, that would kill him."

Joe laughed.

"I'm serious." Ted stared down Joe's laugh. "Ray needs his sleep to live."

"I bet I know what he wants." Kunal revealed a perfect toothy grin and flashed his eyebrows.

"No." Ted wagged his finger. "The bathroom is off limits." Ted looked at Ray. "Remember what happened last time?"

"He's kind of creeping me out." Danielle handed Kunal his coffee. "Should we call someone?"

"Yeah, his wife." Kunal said, laughing as he walked to the condiment station. Joe and Ted joined in the laughter.

"Give him a moment," Ted said.

"We don't have a moment. The mid-morning rush is going to start soon." Joe filled a mug with cold water and threw it in Ray's face, breaking his trance.

Ray blinked and wiped the water off. "Did I zone?"

"Yeah, you did." Ted looked at him. "You want anything to drink?"

Ray shook his head.

"What are you doing later?" Kunal said to Ted as he sipped his coffee. Then he gave Danielle a nod, accompanied by his bedroom eyes again. "It's *good*. The Jinotega." She returned a smile and wiped down her section of the counter top.

Ted shrugged. "No real plans. Got to pick up Buster at the vet. That's about it."

"We should hit a couple bars," Kunal said. "Can you get past 'the guard'?"

Ted didn't appreciate the sarcasm. "Of course, but—"

"Cool." Kunal draped his arm around Ray's sodden shoulders. "I'll pick you up." The two of them were halfway out the door when Kunal called back, "Thanks for the coffee, dude."

Ted sighed. An evening of drinking wasn't what he had in mind. He had a rain check to claim.

TED LEFT THE shop early to pick up Buster from the vet clinic. He had all the windows rolled down in the SUV, letting the warm air circulate. He loved Portland, especially during summer.

This is a perfect place to raise a family, Ted thought as he drove along Southwest Capitol Highway. Dotted with houses, greenery and intermittent sidewalks, the route was more like a typical city street than a highway. Ahead, he spotted Ella, the daughter of his next door neighbor, Sheridan Blake. Her signature bright pink baseball cap topped long blond hair in the style she'd sported for the past year.

This section of Southwest Capitol Highway had no sidewalk. Ella sauntered along the side of the road wearing flip-flops and a pool cover-up, her knapsack in one hand. Ted honked his horn and pulled over.

"Hey, Ella," Ted said through the open passenger window. "Can I give you a lift?"

Ella stopped and approached the SUV with care. Upon recognizing Ted, she gave him a sweet smile and rested her forearms on the open window. "You going home?"

Ted thumbed at blankets and pillows in the back seat. "I have to pick up Buster from the vet, first. Then it's home. Is that okay?"

"Yeah, sure." Ella opened the door, threw her knapsack into the footwell and climbed into the front passenger seat. Her pool cover-up loosened and fell open just enough for Ted to see she was wearing a red and white striped bikini underneath.

Ella had been ten years old when Ted bought his condominium unit six years ago. While not technically friends, Ted had remained friendly towards Ella and Sheridan. He respected Sheridan's ability to raise her daughter as a single mother, and helped them out with chores whenever he could. Ted had watched Ella grow up and thought of himself as an honorary uncle, although he had never shared that notion with anyone, not even Iris. And for as long as he had known her, Ella had been precocious and intelligent. Now sixteen, nothing had changed except for her physical appearance. Puberty had a way of doing that. Ella would break some hearts, if she hadn't done so already.

Ted averted his eyes back to the road ahead. "Buckle up."

"Already on it." Ella pulled the seatbelt across her chest and waist and clicked the buckle into place. She pulled closed the gap in her cover-up.

Ted merged into traffic. Bits and pieces of his morning dream kept floating around his head, drawing his thoughts to Ella's bikini. Not the teenage girl that wore them, but the colors red and white. He had to force the image of Iris in the same bikini out of his mind.

"Rain check," Ted said.

"What?" Ella gave Ted a sideways look.

Ted shook his head. "Sorry. Thinking out loud."

"Oh." Ella returned her eyes forward. "You're working too hard."

"You're probably right."

The two of them drove on in silence. Ted gave Ella a look and a smile, which she returned, but it felt awkward.

Ted tried to ease some of the tension. "It's turning out to be a nice summer so far, huh?"

Ella slipped off her flip-flops and placed her feet on the glove compartment door. Her cover-up began to slide down her thighs, but she stopped it and kept it in place with her hands. "It's not hot enough for me."

"You like it hot?" The words were out of Ted's mouth before he could stop them.

"Um…"

"Hot out. I meant hot *out*." Ted kicked himself mentally as he felt the burn of embarrassment spread across his cheeks.

"I guess so." Ella dropped her feet back to the footwell and smoothed the cover-up over her thighs.

"What are you up to this summer? Anything interesting?" Ted was desperate to return to the previous level of awkwardness.

"Not really. Just swimming." Ella adjusted her baseball cap. "They've got an outdoor pool at Wilson High."

Ted nodded. Unlike the SUV, the conversation was going nowhere and Ted decided to stop embarrassing himself. The two of them sat in silence until they arrived at Pets West.

Buster was still groggy from the anesthetic. Ted carried

him to the SUV and placed him in the back seat on top of several pillows.

"You did real good today, buddy." Ted tucked blankets around Buster. Ella watched Ted work from the front seat and her eyes softened. Ted held Buster's head in his hands. "You comfortable?"

Buster chuffed and laid his head to one side. The dog had a black and gray striped BiteNot collar around his neck to prevent him from licking the incision site.

"That's a good boy." Ted planted a quick kiss on Buster's head and returned to the driver's seat. He navigated out of the clinic's parking lot and began the journey home.

Ella looked back at Buster trying to snooze in the back seat. She returned her gaze forward, stopping on the way to study Ted's face in profile for a second. Her lips curled in a faint smile.

"So, any summer jobs lined up?"

"No." Ella fidgeted with her hands. She turned and looked back at Buster again. "So, what's wrong with Buster? Did he get hurt?"

"Nothing that dramatic," Ted said. "He just got neutered."

"Really?" Ella looked at Ted in surprise, then back at Buster. "Aww." She unbuckled her seatbelt, kneeled in the passenger seat, and worked her way towards Buster. The dog spied her approaching hand with a sleepy eye.

"Hey. Put your seatbelt back on."

"Poor little guy." Ella stroked Buster's groggy head and the dog closed its eyes again. "You can't make babies anymore."

Ella reached farther forward to get closer to Buster and run her fingers over the dog's fur. Her cover-up slid up her back, exposing her red and white bikini bottom.

Ted looked in the rear view mirror, and that's exactly what reflected back at him: a rear view of Ella in her bikini.

Objects in mirror are closer than they appear, Ted thought. *That's for damn sure.*

"You want to sink your face in my ass, don't you?"

Ted's eyes flicked forward. "What?"

"I said, do you think he's going to be mad at you?"

I'm going crazy, Ted thought. *First, the vet clinic, now this.* "Uh…I hope not." He looked over his shoulder. Ella's raised backside was impossible to miss.

"I think I'd be mad at—" Ella turned her head as she backed out from between the front seats and caught Ted looking at her behind.

Ted returned his eyes to the road, trying to look as if nothing happened, yet feeling the heat of self-consciousness rising on his neck.

Ella returned to the passenger seat, a smile creeping across her face. "Were you just checking me out?"

"No," Ted said without hesitation. "Get your seatbelt on."

"It'd be okay if you were."

"No, it wouldn't…and no I wasn't." Ted reached for the paper cup of coffee from the dash cup holder, brought it to his lips for a sip, only to discover the cup was empty. He fumbled and dropped it into the footwell.

Ella stared at Ted's face. She took pleasure in making him squirm. "Do you think I have a nice body?"

"What? Oh, Jesus." Beads of sweat began to dot Ted's hairline. "Uh, it's fine. Now *please*, put your seatbelt on."

Ella spotted Ted's phone sitting in a cubby in the dash and grabbed it. She worked the display with her nimble fingers.

"Hey, what are you doing with that? Put it back."

"This is an 8? Cool." Ella swiped the screen into camera mode and leaned back into Ted, her cover-up laying open and slack. She held the phone out from her body and framed the two of them in a selfie: Ted driving and looking very annoyed and Ella grinning and wearing practically nothing.

Click!

"Give me the phone!" Ted took his right hand off the steering wheel and reached out. Ella began to giggle. She swapped the phone into her left hand and hid it under her left thigh.

The SUV drifted onto the shoulder. Ted over-corrected, causing the vehicle to swerve and sway. Ella slipped off Ted's shoulder, the back of her head landing in his crotch.

Ted's eyes bugged out. He grabbed the steering wheel with two white-knuckled fists and slammed on the brakes. The SUV skidded to a stop.

Buster cracked one eyelid open, looked around, and closed it again with a huff.

Face damp with sweat, Ted looked down at Ella giggling in his lap, cover-up open, pink baseball cap knocked askew, without a care in the world. She raised the phone again and framed a photo. Ted reached out to stop her before she—

Click!

The selfie captured Ella laughing, head in Ted's crotch, with his arm reaching out over her sixteen year old biki-ni-clad body.

Ted was livid. "Seatbelt. *Now!*"

Ella righted herself, tucking in her cover-up and buckling herself into the passenger seat again.

Ted held out an open palm. "Phone."

"Can I take Buster's picture?"

Ted just stared at her. Ella stifled a giggle and returned the phone. He began to work the passcode when Buster whined from the back seat. He placed the phone back into the cubby in the dash and looked back at him.

"Sorry, buddy. We'll be home soon." Ted reached back and gave Buster's head a scratch, which helped to diffuse his anger. He looked at Ella. "When you're in this vehicle, you're my responsibility. We could have gotten into an accident. You could have been hurt or killed."

Ella sat, glued to her seat, and said nothing. The fun was definitely over.

"Not a peep." Ted checked his side mirror and pulled out into the road. "And no funny business."

Ella's luck had run out. She did as she was told and kept her eyes front and forward.

"I always knew you cared." She grinned to herself as the gears in her head began to spin.

Bikini

TED STEPPED OUT of the elevator to the fourth floor, followed by Ella in her pool cover-up and with her knapsack slung over one shoulder. Buster, still groggy, lay in Ted's arms.

They walked down the hallway to Ted's door in silence, except for the low hum of the building's air conditioning, the churn of the elevator returning to the first floor, and Ella's flip-flops slapping her heels.

Ted looked at Ella, surprised to realize that she was almost as tall as he was. "Hey, could you do me a favor and unlock my door?"

Ella looked at Ted, then down at the front pockets of his jeans. The denim fit him well, accentuating all the right parts. She reached for the closest pocket.

Ted whistled. "Up here." He jangled the ring of keys hooked onto the index finger of his left hand. "There's nothing in those pockets."

Ella took the keys, unlocked Ted's door and placed the key ring back on Ted's finger. "Thanks for the ride, Mr. Cooper. See you around."

"Yeah." Ted carried Buster into his suite and closed the

door, not with a slam but with enough force to indicate his annoyance.

He dropped his keys on the kitchen counter, then carried Buster to his dog bed next to the entry. The dog whined briefly but soon settled into the soft padding of the bed without fuss, laying his head and the BiteNot collar over his front paws.

Ted returned to the kitchen and rummaged through the cupboards until he found a can of dog food. He crouched down to Buster's level and held the can up.

"Hungry?"

Buster heaved a sigh and didn't move.

Ted looked at the glistening meat chunks depicted on the side of the can. "It's beef, chicken, heart, kidney and liver… in a rich tasty jelly that dogs love."

Normally Buster would wag his tail, whine and sometimes bark to show his eagerness, but the dog didn't budge.

"I'm with you on that one." Ted carried the can back to the kitchen and set it down on the counter. "Dogs love jelly?"

Someone knocked on the door. Buster's ears pricked up. Ted opened the door and found Ella standing exactly as he had left her. Now, she looked a little cold.

"Can I ask a favor?" Ella turned on her adorable switch and batted her eyelashes a few times.

Ted stood in the doorway, waiting, drumming his fingers on the door frame. He wasn't buying it. He had had enough of Ella for one day.

"Look, my mom would shit if she knew I walked home in my bikini." Ella dialed back her teenage flirting. "Can I use your bathroom to change?"

Ted considered her request, then stepped aside, letting her in. "Down the hall, first door on your right. Make it quick."

"Thanks." Ella hustled down the hallway and disappeared into the main bathroom and locked the door.

Ted returned to the kitchen. He dug out a can opener, removed the lid to the dog food and inverted the can. A congealed column of mystery meat fell into Buster's food dish with a wet *plop*. Some of the "rich tasty jelly" splashed onto Ted's hand.

A text chime sounded. Ted dug into his pocket and pulled out his phone.

"Bar hop 2nite, dood!" Kunal's text read.

"No thanks," Ted tapped in response, spreading some of the dog food jelly across the display by mistake. "Ugh."

He jammed the phone back into his pocket and rinsed his hands in the sink.

ELLA STOOD IN Ted's main bathroom and dropped her knapsack, taking in her surroundings. Everything was hard-edged, in black, gray or white, even the toilet. She had never seen a square toilet before. She lifted the lid and the seat inside looked just as sharp and hard as the outside.

That can't be comfortable, Ella thought.

All fixtures were modern brushed steel, but the sink was an anomaly. It was smooth, oval, and looked like a large egg with half of the shell sheared off at a slight angle. The sink was spotless, with a bottle of high-end hand soap next to it. The towels looked freshly laundered and there was a full supply of toilet tissue under the counter. It was obvious that a woman lived here. A neat freak. No guy (or even a teenage girl) would keep a bathroom this neat.

It was common knowledge that Iris lived with Ted. Ella had run into her in the hallway many times, but Iris kept to herself. Ella couldn't figure out if Iris didn't like her or teen-agers in general.

She slipped out of her thin cover-up, threw her baseball hat on the floor, and stepped in front of the floor to ceiling mirror next to the sink. She placed her hands on her hips, just above her bikini bottom, and struck a pose. She mussed up her hair and held another pose.

I look hot, Ella thought with a smile.

There was a terry cloth robe hanging on the back of the bathroom door. Ella ran her hand over its plush weave. She took the robe down and wrapped herself in it, soaking in its softness.

An impatient knock erupted from the other side of the door. "Almost done in there?" Ted said.

"Yup. I'll be out in a second."

Ella grabbed her knapsack and unzipped it. She wiggled out of her bikini bottoms, dropped them to the floor, and pulled on a dry pair of underwear and denim shorts. She was careful to rehang the robe on the door, then removed her bikini top, swapping it for a sports bra and a shirt from her knapsack.

She pulled on her baseball cap and grabbed her bikini off the floor. Her hand stopped and hovered over her knapsack.

What if…? Ella nibbled her lower lip as her brain began to work. A slight, sly smile worked its way across her face. *I already know he thinks I'm hot.*

Without hesitation, she took her bikini bottom and dropped it back on the floor, next to the hinges of the bathroom door, so that they wouldn't be seen when the door was open.

Ella threw her bikini top into her knapsack, slipped on her flip-flops and left the bathroom. There was still a remnant of a smile on her face when she met Ted waiting in the living room.

"Took you long enough. What were you doing in there?" Ella's possible responses rolled through Ted's head. "On second thought, never mind."

"I was just checking out your *square* toilet. They're supposed to be round."

"Yeah, that's Iris." Ted scanned the room. "In fact, everything you see, the furniture and appliances, is Iris."

Ella tilted her head and looked a question at Ted. "What's you?"

Such a simple question, but Ted had a hard time answering. He shrugged. "The French press is me, and so is Buster. I don't need much."

Upon hearing his name, Buster raised his head until he was convinced there was nothing of interest going on.

Ella crouched down next to Buster and caressed his head. "I'd take Buster over a square toilet any day." She stood and looked around. "I like the layout of your place better than ours."

"That's great, Ella, but I'm kind of busy, so…"

"Oh. Okay." Ella opened the door and stepped into the hallway. "Later."

She latched the door. Within a few steps, that sly smile returned to her lips as she walked towards her suite.

✂

TED HAD BROUGHT home two packages of coffee: Columbian for Iris and Jinotega for himself. Iris didn't drink anything else, but Ted liked to keep things interesting. Besides, it was his job to know coffee and all its varieties.

He opened the bag, inserted his nose and inhaled. Apart from drinking coffee, taking in its rich aroma before brewing and trying to isolate the individual scents was one of Ted's favorite rituals. The dark roast had a lightly fruity essence with stronger overtones of fresh butter and chocolate. He believed separating the scent components of coffee to be more difficult than that of wine.

He scooped several tablespoons of coarsely ground coffee into the French press and filled it half-way with boiling water. Ted keyed in the requisite four minutes on a digital timer, then brought his nose to the French press and took in its bloom.

This would go great with cannoli, Ted thought. He looked around the kitchen for anything that came close, but came up dry. It was a long shot.

After thirty seconds had passed, Ted gave the coffee a stir to break up the coffee ground crust and filled the press with the remaining water. He set the plunger and lid on top and waited for the timer to count down to zero.

He mulled the day over in his head, beginning with his intense dream. Pieces of it still clung to him like that red ribbon. And why was he mishearing what women were saying to him?

Am I sexually frustrated? Ted thought.

After five years of being together, Iris still pressed all of his buttons. From Ted's point of view, their sex life was still exciting and fulfilling. However, their encounters had been less frequent in recent months.

Is Iris losing interest in me? Ted didn't like questions like this because he feared the answers. He feared losing her.

The digital timer went off with a *beep-beep-beep*. Ted refocused on the French press and pressed the plunger all the way down. He poured himself a cup, leaving room for a shot of cream and a tablespoon of sugar.

Ted sat down next to where Buster lay snoozing and set his coffee mug on the floor. He stroked the dog's head.

"Quite the day we've had, eh buddy?"

Buster chuffed.

"Yeah, you got the short end of the stick." Ted sipped from his warm mug, swishing the coffee in his mouth to capture all the flavors. "Sorry about that."

Ted looked around his condo, at all the funky furniture and state-of-the-art appliances. "She's god-damned right," he said to himself, thinking of Ella's earlier comment. "What part of this *is* me?"

But despite Ted's thoughts, at that moment, drinking damn fine coffee and sitting next to his best little buddy was exactly where he wanted to be.

Three knocks on the door broke Ted out of his serene bubble. He set his coffee down and approached the door. He disregarded the peephole. He was sure it was Ella.

Ted flipped the deadbolt. "What is it now?" he said as he pulled open the door.

It wasn't Ella. It was the polar opposite of Ella. Kunal stood in the doorway, with Ray next to him.

Ray held up a six-pack with one can missing and belched. "We got tall boys!" He pushed past Ted, reeking of beer and something else sour, and set the remaining beers on the kitchen counter. "Can I use your bathroom? I got to piss like a racehorse."

"Is this a bad time?" Kunal raised an eyebrow and grinned.

Ted sighed and glared at him. "Honestly? Yes, but lucky for you Iris is out late tonight."

"You bailed on bar hopping, so we brought the bar to you."

"How thoughtful."

"No chicks, though." Kunal mimed two breasts with his hands and squeezed the air.

"I noticed." Ted picked up his mug of coffee from the floor. "Keep it down. Buster's had a rough day."

"Shit," Kunal, said. "It's like you got kids."

"It's part of the deal."

"You got to get out more…out of this…" Kunal looked around the condo. "…This IKEA catalog."

"I like it," Ted lied.

"I call bullshit, dude."

Ted shook his head. "You guys got to go."

"Nope. We're staying."

"Fine." Ted sighed. He was in no mood to argue. "But you got to be out of here before Iris gets home."

Kunal pried a beer from the six-pack's plastic rings. "Forget Iris, dude. Just for tonight at least."

"Look, I got to live with her. She doesn't like surprise visits."

"You mean surprise visits *from us*."

"I didn't say that."

"Whatever, dude. That's her problem." Kunal cracked

the beer and handed it to Ted. "You need a guys' night out. Babes, booze, live a little." Kunal grabbed another beer and broke its seal. "You got to relax, have some fun, be happy."

"I am happy," Ted said.

"Are you?" Kunal swigged a mouthful of beer.

Ted took in the hanging silence. It was too quiet. "Where's Ray?"

"He's probably busting a nut."

"Oh shit."

Kunal pulled out a chair from the dining table and sat. "He's been raving about Danielle's tongue piercing all freaking day."

"Did you find it hot?"

Kunal shrugged. "Not really. I've had chicks with tongue studs blow me and it doesn't feel any different. Danielle on the other hand is off the hook. I'd like to—"

"Enough." Ted drank his beer. "Plus, she's got a boyfriend."

"Killjoy. What are you, her father?"

"Hey, Kunal." Ray's voice echoed from the main bathroom. "Someone's been busy." He walked into the kitchen twirling Ella's red and white striped bikini bottom on his right index finger, a toothy, pervy grin spread across his face. Ted saw the bikini bottom and choked on his beer.

Kunal set his beer can on the table and snatched the bikini bottom off Ray's finger. He held them up by the waistband, accentuating their size.

"Whoa, dude. These are too small for Iris." Kunal looked at Ted over the waistband. "You holding out on us, Ted? Getting your 'barely legal' on or what?"

Ted approached Kunal with an open palm. "Hand them over."

"You dipping your wick in some strange, dude?"

"Are you crazy?"

"Already having fun with some hot little eighteen year old?"

"No. Give them here." Ted swiped his hand to grab the bikini bottom, but Kunal pulled it away just in time. Ray yanked the bottom from Kunal's hand and crumpled them into his face, sniffing them.

"Damn." Ray looked down at his crotch where his green track suit stood at attention. "I'm going to have to use your bathroom again."

Ted shot a look at Ray. "You didn't. Tell me you didn't."

Ray shrugged and offered a regretful grin.

"Jesus Christ, Ray! Why do you *do* that?"

"What can I say? I got uncontrollable urges."

"You cleaned up, right?"

Ray sniffed Ella's bikini bottom again. Ted lunged for the red striped fabric, but Ray switched hands to evade Ted's grasp, then tossed them to Kunal.

Keys sounded in the door.

Kunal saw terror flash in Ted's eyes and knew they had gone too far. He threw the bikini bottom to Ted and Ted threw them back to him.

Kunal spun around and concealed the bikini bottoms behind his back just as the door to the condo swung open. Ted and Kunal froze in their tracks and tried to look casual. They just ended up looking odd.

Iris paused in the doorway, looked at Kunal, then sent a disapproving look at Ted. Kunal noticed the exchange and filed it away.

"Hey, babe." Ted said with a sheepish smile. "You're early. How was your day?"

"I'm not that early." Iris dropped her attaché and purse on the dinner table. "Can't wait to get out of these shoes." Iris took note of the silence, the oddness. "It's not guys' night, is it?"

Kunal grabbed his beer with one hand, and held it up. "No, but it could be. Want to join us?" His other hand still clutched the bikini bottoms behind his back.

Iris looked at Kunal and rolled her eyes. "Uh, no."

"We were just celebrating Buster's…uh…ball busting." Ted punctuated his awkwardness with a swig from his beer.

"Oh, right." Iris kicked off her shoes. "How's he doing?"

"He's okay. Pretty out of it." Ted motioned toward the dog bed.

Iris looked at Buster snoozing with the BiteNot collar wrapped around his neck. Her eyes softened as she crouched next to him and scratched his head. Buster peeked up at her, sighed and closed his eyes again.

"Poor little guy." Iris stood and walked toward the bedroom, passing Ray coming out of the main bathroom.

"Hey, Iris."

"Ray." Iris felt a twinge of nausea creep up her throat as she passed him.

Ray followed Iris with his eyes, settling his gaze on her behind. If Ted had been in range, he would have smacked the back of Ray's head. Kunal moved toward the couch and brought the bikini bottom out from behind his back.

Iris's phone chimed in her purse. She doubled back toward the dining area, noticing Ray's wandering eyes. "My face is up here."

Kunal straightened up and turned to one side, stuffing

one hand and the bikini bottom into his pocket, unseen by Iris. He reached out and clinked his beer can with Ted while still sitting on the back of the couch, then took a swig. The gesture looked awkward at best.

"Ted?" Iris grabbed her purse off the dinner table and pulled out her phone. She paused at the kitchen counter, her eyes scanning the text message. "Did you remember the coffee?"

"Sure did. Columbian dark roast."

"Thanks, hon." Iris retreated back to the bedroom, passing Ray again. "Get a hobby, pervert," she said with disgust.

Ray didn't hear any of it. He'd been focused on her body the whole time. He shot Kunal a "thumbs up" as Iris closed the door to the bedroom.

Kunal pulled the bikini bottom out of his pocket and stuffed it under a couch cushion. "Shit, that was close."

Ted beckoned Kunal with his free hand. "Party's over guys."

"She hates us, doesn't she?" Ray said, joining Kunal at the couch.

Ted lied as he ushered his two friends to the door. "She doesn't hate you."

"Yeah, she does." Kunal looked back at Ted, annoyed. "You can do better, dude."

"Out." Ted grabbed the remaining beers and handed them to Ray.

"We're not finished here," Kunal said.

"Tonight, we are." Ted closed and dead bolted the door. He looked through the peep-hole in the door expecting Kunal and Ray to be lingering about, but the hallway was empty. Ted rested his forehead on the door and his thoughts drifted back to Iris…and his dream that hadn't yet evaporated completely.

Ted walked to the bedroom door, knocked and eased it open. "The guys are gone."

"Thanks for the update." Iris stood in the walk-in closet hanging up her skirt suit. Her purse and phone lay on the bed. As Ted approached her from behind, his eyes drifted over the curves of her body, clad in only a bra and panties.

Ray can't do this, but I can, Ted thought. He placed his hands on her warm shoulders and began to massage away the stress of her day. He felt her body trying to relax. Iris closed her eyes and leaned back into Ted's chest, but she was unable to let go.

"Sorry about the guys dropping by," Ted said between rubs. "It wasn't my idea."

Iris took a deep breath. "I can tolerate Kunal, but Ray… he's a sexist pig. He creeps me out."

"Many would agree. But, deep down, he's a good guy. Really. You should see him with his kids."

"That means he's had sex." Iris tensed up at the image. If Ted had been facing her, he would have seen an expression of complete revulsion. "Ugh. Change the subject."

"Okay. I have an idea." Ted began to pepper Iris's neck and shoulders with light kisses. He unhooked the clasp of her bra and slid it off. It landed in a silken heap at her feet. "Remember that rain check?"

Ted turned her around, took her face in his hands and kissed her mouth, moving her towards the bed until her calves touched the bedspread.

They both fell back onto the bed where Ted continued

his foreplay, moving his kisses down her neck and across her breasts. He knew where all Iris's erogenous zones were, but today they weren't lighting up.

"I'm late, Ted."

Ted continued to leave a trail of kisses down Iris's body, moving past her navel and towards the waistband of her panties. There was no little red bow on this pair.

"Late for what?" Ted began to tug at Iris's panties.

Iris placed her hands on Ted's cheeks and pulled him up to face her. "Ted."

He looked at Iris, now aware of the serious tone of her voice and expression. "What is it? What's wrong?"

"I'm late…as in I might be pregnant."

"You're late." Ted's entire world shifted. All of his arousal wilted like an ice cream cone on a hot day, leaving his boxers a moist, sticky mess. He rolled off Iris and lay beside her. "We've been careful. How is that possible?"

"I don't know." Iris felt a chill in the air and pulled the bedspread over her. "I just know my body."

Ted closed his eyes and sighed. "When did you find out?"

"Three weeks ago."

"Three weeks?" Ted propped himself up on his elbows. "What the hell, Iris!"

"Hey, you're part of this, too."

"Apparently not, if I'm finding out now."

"You know what I mean."

Ted sighed. "But I always use a condom. You know that."

"The only thing that's one hundred percent effective is—"

Ted shook his head and lay back down on the bed. "Don't start. We've been through this."

"But a vasectomy is quick and easy. It's perfect."

"Maybe for you. I don't want anything…sharp getting close to my junk." Ted pictured hundreds of scalpels flying towards his crotch from all directions.

"You know I've been off the pill for a while. And IUDs scare the shit out of me." Iris stared at the ceiling. "So, it's either major surgery for me or a simple vasectomy for you. What would you choose?"

All Ted could think about was silvery edges of sharpened surgical steel…cutting.

Iris rolled over and placed her mouth at his ear. "Wouldn't you like to *rawdog* me again? Like we used to when I was on the Pill?" she whispered, her hot breath floating past his ear. "It would feel *so good*." Iris licked Ted's earlobe.

The idea of sex without a condom compared to getting a vasectomy was like matter and anti-matter to Ted. The words couldn't exist in the same sentence and caused his thoughts to short-circuit.

"I choose condoms," he said finally.

Iris rolled onto her back and crossed her arms, fuming in frustration. "I've been late before, you know."

"You never told me that."

"You didn't need to know."

They both fell silent.

Ted turned to look at Iris's face. He traced her features, her high cheekbones, her slender nose, her delicate ear. He loved her even when they fought. "If I get a vasectomy, we can't have kids."

"I don't want kids." Iris spoke without hesitation.

In the five years Ted and Iris had been together, he couldn't remember talking about kids before. Or if they had, it was never in any depth. Ted had always assumed kids would be in the picture some day.

"Ever?"

"It's not in the plan."

"Wait. What plan? Your plan or our plan?"

Iris clammed up and Ted chose not to open that can of worms. Instead, he pictured Iris holding their baby. The image made him smile.

"You know, you'd make a great mom."

"Just stop it, okay?" Iris bolted from the bed, stomped down the hallway and into the main bathroom. The slamming door echoed through the condo.

"Shit!" Ted punched the bed. "Shit, shit, shit!"

It had only been a few seconds when Iris yelled out, "Ted!"

Alarmed, Ted sat up on the bed. "What?"

"TED!"

Ted ran to the main bathroom and burst inside. "What's wrong?"

Iris struggled to contain her anger. Words eluded her, so she pointed at the toilet and around the floor with a shaking index finger. Translucent globs of a stringy, sticky substance hung slackly from the toilet seat and down the angled sides of the toilet bowl as if in suspended animation. It could be only one thing: Ray's jizz.

"Oh shit." Ted closed his eyes and rubbed his forehead, preparing for the fallout.

Iris managed to break past her fury and speak. "Ray did this, didn't he?"

Ted didn't answer. He didn't have to. Ray had history and this mass of splooge was one of his calling cards.

Is his brain so sex-addled that he can't see the mess he leaves behind? Ted had thought on many occasions. The last time Ray's "cumsplosion" had burst forth, it was in the unisex bathroom at Buster's Beans. Ted was made aware of it after a customer complained. How many customers had navigated the mess and had politely gone about their business was anyone's guess. Ted shuddered at the memory.

"He's *disgusting*." Iris pointed at more glistening globs on the floor. "You're cleaning that *shit* up." She stormed out of the bathroom and back to the bedroom.

Iris had been gone for a only a few seconds when she returned and grabbed the terry cloth robe from the back of the bathroom door. "You need to find some new fucking friends."

Ted stood, taking in the scope of his cleanup task. The image of Ray masturbating to Ella's bikini bottom pushed its way to the front of Ted's mind. He grimaced and swallowed his nausea.

I got to get rid of those bikini bottoms, he thought. *What if his jizz was on them?* Thinking back, Ted couldn't remember if the bikini bottoms were damp or not when they were being thrown around.

Ted grabbed some toilet paper and began to wipe up the mess, only to discover Ray had hit the toilet paper as well, soddening one side of the roll. As cleanup progressed, Ella's bikini bottom became less and less a priority.

"Fucking Ray," he grumbled.

Cut

TED HAD TEMPORARILY moved Buster's dog bed from beside the front door to his side of the bed so he would have some company during the night.

Iris had opposed the idea. "The room will smell like dog," she had said.

The sedative had worn off but Buster was still subdued. It was obvious the dog needed a little extra love.

"It's only for a couple of nights. He deserves it."

Ted refused to back down and Iris went to bed in a huff.

Things will blow over by morning, Ted thought as he drifted off. He couldn't have been more wrong.

The alarm clock broadcast its familiar six o'clock *beep-beep-beep*, pulling Ted out of sleep. There was no sexy dream hangover this time. There was no dream at all that he could remember.

He silenced the alarm and looked down at Buster. He returned Ted's gaze, sitting in his dog bed, panting. Buster looked like he was smiling, even with his collar, and his brown eyes seemed a little clearer.

"Hey buddy. Sleep well?"

Buster continued panting and tilted his head to one side.

Ted rolled over to kiss Iris's shoulder but her side of the bed was empty and cold. His nose kicked in and the smell of coffee wafted into the bedroom. Then he heard the front door close and the deadbolt engage.

For the past five years, Ted had made it a habit to see Iris to the door each morning before she headed off to work. Often they'd kiss, even after nights when they had fought. This small ritual started the day off on the right foot.

But today, Iris had ducked out on him. Something was wrong. Ted jumped out of bed, wearing nothing but his ratty old boxer shorts, and ran to the door. Buster followed, wagging his tail.

"Sorry, buddy." Ted let himself out and blocked Buster from following him with his legs. "I'll be back in a bit," he said through the gap in the door.

Buster barked as if he understood and didn't like being excluded.

Ted latched the door and flew down the stairwell to the parkade. Iris had just opened the door to her sedan.

"Iris," Ted called as he ran toward her from the stairwell door. The concrete of the parkade felt cool and smooth on his bare feet.

She looked back at his approach, then threw her attaché and purse onto the passenger seat and got in. Ted arrived at her sedan and intercepted the driver side door from closing.

"What's going on?" Ted said between breaths.

Iris stared at the steering wheel and sighed. She turned to look at him. "I need some time."

Ted shook his head in confusion. He hadn't quite woken up yet. "What do you mean?"

"I need time away from you…and your *gross* friends."

"Wait. If this is about Ray cumming all over the bathroom, I'm going to talk to him about that."

"That's just part of it. Let go of the door."

Ted let go and stepped back. Iris pulled the driver-side door closed and started the sedan's engine.

"Iris. Come on." Ted said through the driver-side window. "Let's talk about this. Roll down the window?"

Iris backed out of the parking stall and drove towards the automatic gate. Ted jogged beside the sedan and rapped his knuckles on the window.

"I'll get the fucking vasectomy, okay?"

Iris struggled to keep her gaze forward, but the tear tracks on her cheeks betrayed her attempt at stoicism.

"Iris?" Ted tapped on the sedan's window.

The parkade gate opened and Iris accelerated out and into the street. Ted ran as far and as fast as he could in bare feet.

"Iris!" Ted cried out as he stopped to catch his breath. He massaged a stitch in his side as he watched the sedan disappear down the street. He then heard the automatic gate begin to close behind him. "Fuck!" He ran back to the parkade entrance only to find himself locked out.

Ted walked gingerly around to the front of the building and scanned the directory for "Blake." Ella and Sheridan were the only other people in the building that he was on friendly terms with. He entered the Blake's suite number into the intercom's keypad and waited. After a few minutes, Ted rang their suite again.

Whose ass will I have to kiss? Ted thought. *Please don't be Ella. Please don't be Ella.*

The intercom crackled. "Who is it?" It *was* Ella's voice, half-drunk with sleep and filtered through a cheap speaker.

"Hi, Ella," Ted said, stammering. "It's Ted. I locked myself out of the building. Could you let me in?"

"Mr. Cooper?"

"Yeah." Even unseen, Ted could feel the embarrassment in his cheeks. "Please let me in." He banged his forehead against the glass side panels beside the main entrance. Ted was just about to press Ella's intercom button again, when the lock on the door clicked open with a sustained electrical buzz.

He skipped the elevators, opting for the stairs since they exited closest to his condo. But just as he reached the fourth floor landing, he remembered why the elevators would have been a better option.

Ted stepped out into the hallway and looked past Ella's door towards his own. The coast was clear and he began to tiptoe. Then he remembered he was wearing the boxer shorts Iris had given him on their first date anniversary. On the front of the shorts was an illustration of a squirrel holding an armful of acorns. Across and just under the waistband were the words "Play with my nuts."

Abort! Abort! Ted thought. But it was too late.

Ella must have been listening for him, because she popped her head out of her door before Ted had a chance to duck back down the stairwell. She was wearing bright pink shorts with a loosely tied drawstring and a white Betty Boop tank top with the words "Can't touch this!" underneath. A high, sleep-frazzled ponytail sat atop her head.

Ted glared at her as he passed. She smiled and looked him up and down.

"Play with your nuts, huh?" Ella snickered.

The heat of her stare followed him to his door. He glanced back at Ella. "Not another word."

She raised a hand to stifle a giggle as she retreated into her condo.

"Uh…Ella?"

She stepped back into the hallway, an expectant look on her face.

"Thanks for letting me in."

"You owe me, Mr. Cooper." Ella disappeared inside her condo and closed her door. Ted thought he saw a grin on her face.

Buster greeted Ted inside, his tail wagging a mile a minute. Ted reached down and gave Buster's head a scratch.

"Hey buddy, got any beers? I'd give anything for a beer."

Buster barked and nosed his empty food dish.

"I'll get you breakfast in a second." Ted grabbed his phone from the kitchen counter. He called up text messaging, selected Kunal as the recipient, and tapped out "Bar hop tonite." Without hesitation, Ted hit "send."

To Kunal, a night of bar-hopping represented a challenge: hit on as many women as possible at as many bars as possible before getting wasted. Ted's definition was quite the opposite. To him it meant hopping to one bar and settling into a ripe stupor. Nights like that were cheaper but had a more limited selection of women. Depending on the time of day, sometimes there were no women customers at all, with exception of the waitresses. Kunal preferred variety over saving money.

Tonight, much to Kunal's annoyance, Ted decided to meet at Quinn's Cavern, a pub the guys had frequented a few times a month since they first met. The pub was located in a designated heritage building a few blocks northeast of Ted's condo, which meant the option of walking home was always available. The pub's owners had embraced their Irish background and favored authenticity instead of attempting to appeal to the hipster crowd and their affinity for furniture built from recycled building materials. The interior featured tables and booths made from darkly stained wood with brass accents. The comfortable and well worn seating was upholstered in genuine leather and each booth had its own set of jacket hooks.

Ted, Kunal, and Ray sat in a circular booth, well into their first pitcher of beer. Kunal topped up their mugs and signaled a waitress for another pitcher.

Ray looked at Kunal. "I thought you said the beer would fix everything?"

Kunal shrugged, gulped his beer, and watched the crowd.

Ted slouched in the booth and glared at Ray. "You're an idiot."

"I'm sorry," Ray said. "How many times do I have to say it?"

"You're an idiot with no impulse control." Ted slammed his hand on the table, then belched, as if one action caused the other. "I'd still have a girlfriend if it wasn't for you."

"That's so much bullshit." Ray shook his head.

"She found your…spunk…and went ballistic. It was the last straw."

"Dude, to be honest, there's been quite a few *last straws,*" Kunal said.

Ted pointed at Kunal but kept his eyes on Ray. "Shut up. This is between me and Jerk-off here."

"Jerk-off?" Ray furrowed his brow, crossed his arms, and grunted in annoyance.

Kunal leaned into the table. "Hey, you said Iris needed some time. That doesn't mean it's over. You should be thanking Ray for breaking you free for a while."

"Yeah," Ray said, bolstered by Kunal's words. "You should be thanking me."

"You're taking his side?" Ted looked at Kunal, his eyes widening. "Next time *you* clean up his mess."

Kunal nodded. "It's true. Ray does have a problem with discretion. I'm just pointing out the facts."

"I'm working on that," Ray said.

Ted gulped his beer. "Work harder, Jerk-off."

"Stop it with the jerk-off, *Jerk-off*."

"If the splooge sticks…"

"Hey." Kunal looked at Ted and Ray. "Enough jizz talk." He turned to Ted. "She's just late, dude. I've known chicks at the gym who were late but weren't preggers. You're not a daddy yet, so quit worrying about it."

"And I may never get to be one if she gets her way."

Kunal and Ray shot each other confused looks.

Ray responded first. "What are you talking about?"

A waitress approached their table with their second pitcher of beer balanced on a serving tray. She set it down on the table and collected the empty pitcher.

Kunal winked at her. "Thanks, Chloe."

Chloe batted her lashes and smiled. "Any time, Kunny Bunny. Call me." Kunal sent her a nod.

"*Kunny Bunny?*" Ted laughed.

"Dude, she can call me anything she wants." Kunal watched Chloe's behind move under her serving skirt. "She fucks like a mink."

Ray's jaw went slack, as if in preparation for his tongue to roll out of his mouth and drop on the table.

"You…and her?" Ted said.

"Yeah." A grin spread across Kunal's lips. "We've exchanged more than just phone numbers."

Ray groaned. "I need to go to the bathroom."

"Focus, Ray. Discretion and restraint." Kunal refilled Ted's mug with beer, then Ray's.

"But I need to piss."

"Not buying it, Ray…So, Ted, you were saying you won't get to be a dad?"

"Uh…" Ted looked at Kunal, surprised.

"Don't say I never listen."

Ted raised his beer and drank several swallows. "Iris wants me to get a vasectomy."

Ray cringed. His hands disappeared under the table and cupped his crotch in an involuntary protective gesture.

"Whoa." Kunal's eyes sparkled just a bit brighter. "Do you want one?"

Ted took no time to think about it. "No…at least I don't think so? But I don't want to lose her, either."

"You sure? Because vasectomies are fucking awesome. Rawdogging it, dude. It's pure pleasure."

"Iris already tried to convince me with the 'no condom' angle. I can't get past the scalpel." Ted brought his mug up to his lips. "Besides, how would you know?" He took a swig of beer.

Kunal had Ray's and Ted's full attention. He took a long drink from his beer, set his mug down and pointed down at his crotch.

Ray's eyes went wide. "No way!"

"When?" Ted said.

Kunal shrugged. "Couple years ago."

"And you didn't tell us?" Ted slumped back against the booth seating. "Bastard."

"I got to keep some secrets to myself." Kunal beamed. "It's completely liberating. Women love it."

"Except women who want kids," Ted said.

"I don't sleep with women who want kids, and even if I did, it wouldn't matter. I may be shooting blanks, but I'm shooting blanks *every* night." Kunal smiled. "You get me?"

Ted nodded.

"Does Iris want kids?" Kunal had a way of cutting through the bullshit, right to the important questions.

"No," Ted said.

"Do you?"

"I don't know."

"You better know. If you get one, do it for yourself." Kunal burped. "I sleep with different women a couple of times a week. Sometimes more." Kunal looked over at the bar. "I just might hook up with Chloe again tonight."

"And these women…they just believe you?"

"If they need proof, I ask them to feel up my balls. If that doesn't work, I have a hand-held stud detector that does the trick. You can get them at any hardware store."

Ted laughed. "You're taken seriously when you pull out a *stud detector?*"

"The women are fascinated, actually. I have a lab test as a backup, but I've never used it."

"What about STDs?" Ted said. "A vasectomy isn't going to prevent a nasty case of the clap."

"I choose women that celebrate good personal hygiene the same way I do."

"Huh." Ted sat back and folded his arms. "If anyone needs a vasectomy, it's Jizz-Master Stud, here." He hooked a thumb at Ray, whose face was now covered in sweat.

"Ray?" Kunal looked into Ray's eyes. His pupils were dilated, large and black. "You okay?"

"It's all this sexy talk. But discretion and restraint, right?"

Kunal nodded. "Right."

"I don't need a vasectomy," Ray said, back from his momentary lapse.

"Oh?" Kunal raised his eyebrows. "Why's that?"

"Low sperm count due to—"

"Excessive wanking?" Kunal laughed.

Ted shook his head. "Where'd you learn that? The Internet?"

Ray returned a sheepish look to his two friends. "Uh, I read it somewhere. Can't remember."

"You've been married for six years and you have four kids, with one on the way," Ted said.

Ray shrugged.

"You don't need a vasectomy because Vivian is always pregnant," Ted said. "You don't even need to do the math. I wouldn't be surprised if you have more sex than Kunal and me combined."

"Hey." Kunal choked on a mouthful of beer. "Speak for yourself."

"Let me ask you this." Ted cracked his knuckles, making Ray cringe. "What are you going to do when Vivian says no to more kids? Switch to condoms?"

Ray held his mug of beer with both hands, like it was a security blanket. "I don't know. I'll cross that bridge when I come to it."

"Cum *on* it, you mean." Kunal chuckled to himself.

Ray gave Kunal a sideways look. "Very funny. Speaking of kids, Angie, my oldest, is having her fifth birthday in a few weeks. You guys are invited."

"I'm there, dude." Kunal clinked mugs with Ray. "Congrats."

"Thanks." Ray glanced at Ted. "How about you?"

"I'll think about it."

"Come on, man. Angie adores you. She thinks you hung the moon."

Ted drank his beer, content to let Ray convince him to attend the party.

"There might be some single moms there." Ray flashed his eyebrows.

Kunal gave Ted a "thumbs up," but Ted remained silent.

Ray sighed. "I promise to never jerk-off at your place again." Silence settled over the table.

"Jerk-off?" The three of them turned to see Chloe standing at the front of the curved booth with a disgusted look on her face. "Um, like, I'll check back later."

Ted, Kunal, and Ray burst out laughing.

"Okay. I'll go." Ted held his gut. "Chloe's expression was gold."

"Alright!" Ray reached out and high-fived Ted. "Do you

think she heard me?" Ray flicked his eyes back and forth between Ted and Kunal.

"Of course she heard you."

"Do you care?" Kunal said.

"Well, yeah."

"Why? You're married. You don't have to impress anyone anymore, except Vivian."

"But now she probably thinks I'm a perv."

"Ray." Kunal tilted his face forward. "You *are* a perv." He finished his beer and refilled all three mugs. "So, what's it going to be, Ted? All the sex you want and no responsibility?"

"But it's permanent," Ted said.

"Permanent bliss, dude. Don't you find that appealing?"

Ted sipped his beer. "You know…it does sound pretty good."

"That's what I'm talking about." Kunal raised his mug and clinked it with Ted's and Ray's. "Here's to sex, rawdoggie-style."

They all drank and Ted's mind swirled with possibilities. His life was about to change for the better. That was the plan, anyway.

Now that Ted had decided to get a vasectomy, everything seemed a bit brighter. Even though he didn't know Iris's exact whereabouts and all his calls went to her voicemail, Ted felt at peace. The next chapter of his life was unfolding. He wiped down unoccupied tables at the front of the shop and greeted seated customers with a smile. He whistled Bobby McFerrin's "Don't Worry Be Happy" as he worked.

Buster sat in his usual spot next to the front entrance of the shop. He was still somewhat subdued as he recuperated from his surgery and snoozed for most of the day in his special coffee-bean-shaped dog bed. Buster received many sympathetic head scratches from customers, and despite the BiteNot collar around his neck, he wasn't suffering much.

Joe and Danielle were serving customers when Kunal burst in through the front door. There was a touch of panic on his face.

"Dude, I got to talk to you."

Ted folded his cleaning cloth and tucked it into his apron string. "What's wrong?"

Kunal looked around the shop, noting where all the customers were. "Not here." He led Ted into the back of the shop where there were several more vacant tables.

Joe and Danielle, always wanting to be involved in the day-to-day goings-on at Buster's Beans, especially the gossip, divided their attention between customers and Ted and Kunal.

Kunal chose a table in the back furthest from the front entrance and sat down. He waited for Ted to take a seat across from him.

"What's up?" Ted said. "Did Ray do something inappropriate again?"

"No." Kunal looked back at the counter to see Joe and Danielle keeping an eye on him. He leaned over the table and lowered his voice. "About last night. All the talk about..." Kunal looked around again and dropped his voice to a whisper. "About getting snipped, you know?"

"Yeah? What about it?"

"Vasectomy isn't for you, dude."

"How would you know?"

"I just do."

"You made a pretty convincing case for it yesterday."

Kunal shook his head. "I was drunk. Call it seller's remorse. You're a family guy." Kunal hooked a thumb over at Buster snoozing in the sun. "You've got a dog. You're halfway into family territory already."

Ted leaned back in his chair. "Look. I'll tell you what I am. I'm unhappy. My relationship with Iris is in the toilet. I'm sexually frustrated. I haven't had sex in over two months. And you're right, I need to cut loose. Or fix things with Iris. Either way, getting snipped will solve all that."

"Why not take after Ray and give yourself the odd handy?"

"I do, but it's not the same."

Kunal lowered his voice. "Get a Fleshlight."

"What? I don't need one of those."

"Don't knock them. They're great for building stamina."

"You speak from experience?"

Kunal leaned back and raised his palms, a subtle satisfied smile on his face. "Just saying."

"No, I've made up my mind."

"Okay." Kunal sighed and slumped his shoulders. Relief washed over his face. "I just wanted to make sure it wasn't the beer talking. It's a life-altering decision. For me, it was the right one."

"I'm so sure, I've already booked a consultation."

"Whoa, dude. You must really be frustrated."

"No shit."

"Well, you know what we got to do now, right?" A wide grin spread across Kunal's face.

Ted's curiosity was piqued. "What?"

"Got anything going on tonight?"

"No. Why?"

Kunal stood up and pulled out his phone. "I'll text you the deets." He dialed a number and began talking as he left the shop.

Danielle followed Kunal with her eyes until he left, then turned back to Ted. "Everything okay?"

Ted gave Danielle a thumbs up. "Just another day at the office." Except it wasn't, not by a long shot.

✄

KUNAL LIVED IN a modern condominium complex eight blocks away from Buster's Beans, off Southeast Ankeny Street. The five-story building was named The Penthouse, even though all the suites were functionally identical. The name suited Kunal's playboy lifestyle and Ted was convinced it had played a part in convincing Kunal to buy into the building.

Ted stood outside the main entry and buzzed up. His watch showed it was just after seven o'clock.

"Castration central." Ray's voice crackled over the intercom. "Do you have an appointment?"

"It's Ted. Let me in."

"Ah yes. Ted Cooper. Nut sack research."

"Ray…just open the door."

The front entrance unlocked with a *buzz-click* and Ted pulled the door open.

"Mr. Cooper, before entering the elevator, remember to kiss your balls goodbye." Ray began to laugh before the intercom cut out.

Ted entered the building but decided to take the stairs instead. Five flights of stairs left him slightly winded.

Kunal met Ted at the door to his suite and handed him a shot and a bottle of beer. "Dude, come on in. Sorry about Ray. He's a little excited."

"What's this?" Ted motioned at the shot.

"Tequila with a beer chaser," Kunal said. "You're going to need it."

"For what?"

"You'll see. Down the hatch." Kunal waited for Ted to toss back the tequila before directing Ted into his living room.

Kunal's choice of furnishings reminded Ted of Iris's style, with a few exceptions. Kunal lived a bachelor life and took pride in minimalism. Despite his impressive net worth, he owned just enough to exist on. However, the furniture, electronics, and appliances scattered through his suite were as high-end and state of the art as possible. "The best I can afford," Kunal would say. If he ever settled down with one woman, he would have to make some stylistic compromises.

Ted remembered asking how Kunal could live so simply. "I believe in freedom, in all forms," he had said. "I seek it out. The fewer possessions I have, the freer I feel." Ted never forgot that.

The living room featured a big screen television, a small coffee table and a couch. Kunal had connected his laptop to his television wirelessly.

"The patient has arrived." Ray swigged from his beer bottle. Apparent from his red cheeks and the way he swayed side to side, Ray was already two out of three sheets to the wind. He pointed at the supple leather couch. "Sit. Be comfortable. I hope you relish your beer as much as I."

Ted cocked his eyebrows and looked a question at Kunal.

"I don't know, dude. Probably some obscure Star Trek reference."

Ray belched. "Yup. Balok, bitches. The Corbomite Maneuver."

"Okay, then." Ted flopped onto the couch, flanked by Kunal and Ray. On the television screen was the front page of YouTube.

"Since you're going to get a vasectomy," Kunal began, "you need to know what to expect. Search for 'vasectomy.' "

"Seriously?" Ted drank from his beer. "This is something I can do on my own time."

"Why waste time when you can get the goods from someone who's already gone through the process?" Kunal smiled and clinked Ted's beer can. Ray tried, but missed due to drunken coordination. "That's what friends are for, right?"

Ted nodded at Kunal. "Fair point." He typed "vasectomy" into YouTube's search field. A list of results and thumbnail images flashed across the screen.

"Scroll down." Kunal wagged his index finger. "Look for 'no scalpel.' "

Ted worked his fingers over the laptop's track pad, scrolling the results. Listed were videos of men praising vasectomy, doctors explaining the procedure with fancy graphics and animation, and wives explaining getting pregnant afterward, but a great majority of the videos focused on close-ups of the procedure itself. It was the surgical show-all videos that gave Ted's stomach a flip.

"Stop. There. Click on that one."

Ted looked at the video thumbnail Kunal was pointing at. It showed a latex-gloved hand holding a pair of scissors and digging into what looked like a partially dried apricot. But he knew it wasn't an apricot. Ted didn't know it at the time, but he would never eat apricots again.

I'm watching nut sack surgery videos on YouTube...by choice, Ted thought and he felt his stomach lurch again. He clicked "play."

Ted and Ray craned their necks forward, then tilted their heads in unison as the doctor on the screen began the procedure. Kunal grinned and leaned back, taking in the reactions of his two friends.

Ray swigged from his beer and squinted at the television. "Jesus Christ, that's a big needle."

"It's anesthetic," said Kunal.

"Go full screen."

"What?" Ted groaned and backed away from the laptop. "I've already seen enough."

"No way, we're just getting started." Kunal reached over to the laptop and switched the video into full screen, filling the television with fifty-five inches of shaved scrotum.

Ray began to laugh and raised his beer. "Looks like my grandma's tits."

Kunal and Ted glanced at Ray with looks of confusion mixed with disgust.

Ray shrugged. "What? She's a free spirit."

"I worry about you sometimes, dude."

Ted watched the faceless doctor's hand work. "Do we have to watch this?"

"Aren't you curious?" Kunal said. "This is for your benefit."

"Yeah, but this is…in HD."

Ray leaned in close enough to tickle Ted's cheek with his beard. The hoppy odor of beer floated around Ray's head like a wreath. "Just think. This is the closest you're ever going to get to another man's cock."

"Ray," Ted pushed Ray back. "You're not helping."

They both returned their gaze to the video, fascinated and repulsed at the same time. It was like a car wreck. They didn't want to see what they were looking at, but at the same time, they were drawn to it like moths to a flame. They could not look away.

"What's he doing with that…thing?"

Ted set his beer down on the coffee table. "So when the doctor says 'no scalpel,' what he really means is he'll use something equally as sharp. And then he's…Ow! Damn!" Ted cringed, raised his knees and by instinct covered his crotch. The doctor in the video had produced a small opening in the scrotum, then wiped away a bead of bright red blood.

Kunal doubled over laughing.

Ted placed his hand over his eyes but continued watching through the gaps between his fingers. "This isn't funny. Jesus."

"Skip ahead, dude," Kunal said between guffaws. Ted scrubbed the video's time line. "Stop. There. This is the good part." Kunal began to laugh again.

Ray stood up and pointed at the screen. "What's that *thing* he's pulling out?"

Fighting tears of laughter, Kunal managed to describe what was happening in the video. "That's the tube jizz flows through, in your case, several times a day."

"No shit!" Ray stared at the video. "That's amazeballs."

Ted swallowed hard. "I don't feel so good." All color had drained from his face, leaving it waxy and ashen.

The doctor in the video placed small metal clamps on the tube and crimped them closed with a more precise set of pliers.

Kunal clapped his hands. "And those are the keys to the kingdom."

"Just like when my kids step on the water hose."

"Stop." Ted's vision dissolved into black and white, with stars dancing on top, and his skin turned cool and clammy. His eyes drifted upwards.

"You're going to miss the big finale, dude." Kunal nudged Ted. "And…snip! Done deal."

Ted looked down just as the doctor cut the tube with a distinctive *snick*.

"Amazing." Ray clapped his hands. "Bravo."

"One side done," Kunal said. "Now the other side."

Ted leapt to his feet and hustled to Kunal's bathroom. His eyes, brain and stomach had had enough stimulation for one day.

"Pussy!" Ray picked up Ted's beer and finished it off.

Kunal gave Ray's shoulder a shove. "Back off. Dude needs time to adjust. He'll thank me later."

Ted closed the bathroom door and splashed cold water on his face. He looked at himself in the mirror, pale and shaky.

I can do this, Ted thought. But the more he thought about

it, the more doubts he had. Questions swirled in his head. *What if Iris doesn't want me back, even after getting snipped? What if it's not about sex at all?* Iris had made her dislike of Kunal and Ray clear to Ted on many occasions during the past five years, but who he chose as friends was one issue he refused to budge on.

Could a vasectomy fix everything? The answer was "yes" if Ted were to believe Kunal's advice. There was only one way to find out.

Consultation

The parking lot at East Portland Medical Center was full when Ted arrived for his consultation. He pulled into the congested lot and began navigating the rows of parked vehicles.

"Shit." Ted looked at his watch. His appointment was in ten minutes and he was going to be late. He shook his head.

This is a sign, Ted thought. *I shouldn't have—*

His thoughts were interrupted as a zippy compact car pulled out of a parking stall in front of him and drove away. He blinked at the empty space, not quite believing his good fortune. A honk from the car behind roused him from his private victory and he pulled into the stall. Ted bought a parking ticket, placed it on his dash and headed to the front entrance, whistling as he walked and reveling in how life events can change on a dime.

East Portland Medical Center was a featureless four stories tall, built in the 1970s when drab earth-toned brick and rows of identical windows ruled the skyline. A fountain in front of the main entrance provided an appealing visual distraction from the monolith behind.

Ted consulted the building's directory and after a short elevator trip to the third floor found himself outside the office of Dr. Palmer and Dr. Neandross, specialists in urology and nephrology.

I can do this, Ted thought. *It's only a consultation.*

He opened the office door and stepped inside. The waiting room was full of people, both young and old, some with children and some without.

As Ted scanned the room, his eyes settled on a bespectacled receptionist, her wavy ginger hair falling just below her shoulders. She had half of her hair pulled back and woven into a loose braid. It was her smile that drew his attention the most as she greeted the next person in line. Captivated, Ted stepped into the queue.

In front of him stood a blond-haired mother holding a baby girl less than a year old. She searched through her purse with her free arm but was unable to find what she was looking for. The baby stared at Ted with her clear blue eyes and waved her arms with excitement.

In exasperation, the mother turned to Ted. "Could you please hold her for a moment?"

"I, uh…"

The mother handed the baby to Ted before he could object. He took the child, cradled her in his arms and their eyes locked. He found it surprising how intense a baby's gaze could be. The baby girl reached out and touched Ted's nose.

The line advanced and the mother found the papers she was looking for. She handed them to the receptionist.

"You're a natural," the mother said. "She normally screams at strangers, but she likes you. Can I take you home with me?"

"Sorry, I'm not housebroken yet." Ted and the mother shared a laugh.

"Oh, I can fix that."

As Ted passed the baby back, he noticed the mother's wedding ring. "Besides, I don't think your husband would approve."

"Oh yeah, him." The mother shared a playful smile and waved her free hand. "Thanks for reminding me."

"What's her name?"

"Jessica."

The receptionist handed the papers back to the mother. "Please have a seat, Mrs. Bryant."

Ted leaned in and waved. "Bye bye, Jessica. Nice to meet you."

The receptionist studied Ted's interaction with interest. "Good afternoon, sir," she said with a warm, inviting smile.

"Hi." Ted faced the receptionist, noticing the name tag on her blouse: Casey. "I'm here for my three o'clock appointment."

"So you are. Your name?"

"Ted Cooper."

Casey flipped through her appointment book. Ted watched her hands as they brushed over the pages. His eyes moved to her face and he noticed she had small silver Mickey Mouse earrings.

"Well, Mr. Cooper, I don't have you written down." Casey double checked her book once more. "Are you sure your appointment was for today?"

Ted felt embarrassment creeping up his face. "Pretty sure, but let me check." He pulled out his phone and tapped the display a few times. "Yup. Today at three. I got it right here."

"What did you need to see the doctor about?" Casey's vibrant green eyes locked with Ted's.

"I, uh…well, I need, uh…"

Casey stood up, leaned over the reception desk, and motioned to Ted with her index finger to move closer. He did as instructed, leaning close enough to catch a scent of hyacinth in her hair.

She positioned her mouth next to Ted's ear and whispered, "Soon I'll be fucking you."

"What?" Ted said, taken aback.

"You're here to see doctor two?" Casey repeated her whispered words. "The urologist?" She returned to her chair, regarding Ted with an expectant look.

All moisture had evaporated from Ted's mouth, making it difficult to speak. Instead, he nodded while his brain tried to sort fact from fantasy.

What the hell is going on? Ted thought. *Am I going crazy?* He was sure he had heard Casey come on to him, but that didn't make sense. Her reaction and the context suggested that he had misheard her. He recalled the unfortunate episode with Ella in his SUV and Cherise from Pets West. *Maybe I am going crazy.*

"There's two doctors' offices here." Casey pointed across the waiting room. "I work for doctor one. The doctor you want to see is on that side. You know, doctor two. We share the waiting room."

"Oh." Ted imagined his face was a hot shade of crimson. "Sorry."

"Don't worry about it." Casey flashed her lashes at him. "It happens a lot."

"Thanks. I feel a bit better." A pleasant energy passed between them, something that Ted hadn't felt since his early days with Iris.

TED WANDERED TOWARDS the opposite side of the office. Casey watched him go, smiling to herself until the next person in line broke her stare.

The second receptionist across the entryway and opposite Casey wore a pressed white uniform. She stood out from the other doctors and office assistants who dressed in a casual and comfortable style. Her name tag spelled out "Blanche" and her graying hair was pulled up into a tight and perfect bun. Not a hair out of place. She looked over the rims of her glasses at Ted and gave him a once over. A scowl passed over her lips as she grabbed her appointment book.

Ted closed his eyes and waited for her to say something inappropriate. *I'm not crazy. Please don't say anything crazy.*

"Your name?" Blanche grabbed a marker and waited.

"Ted Cooper."

Blanche found Ted on her list and crossed him off with a thick black permanent line, the kind that bled through to the other side of the paper.

"Take a seat." Blanche pushed the appointment book aside and busied herself collecting paperwork. "The doctor will see you in a moment."

Ted found an empty seat in the waiting area, one that allowed a direct sight-line to Casey. From the rack on the shared wall he grabbed a magazine without looking, but it wouldn't have mattered if he had. The only magazine the shared office subscribed to was Family Circle.

The magazine was camouflage anyway. Ted flipped it open and pretended to read as he watched Casey work. Whenever he sensed that she might look his way, he averted his eyes back to "The 20 Most Influential Moms of 2016."

A burly bearded man next to him with his Outdoor Life magazine open to "Cleaning Your Guns" shielded his face and leaned closer to Ted.

"Hey buddy," the man whispered. "Don't look at her. She's psycho."

"Who?"

"Nurse Ratched over there." He motioned with his eyes towards Blanche. "Trust me, from one brother to another."

"Thanks." Ted nodded and motioned at the man's magazine. "Where did you find that? All I see is Family Circle."

"Brought it from home."

"Smart move."

The man returned to his article.

"What are you in for, if you don't mind me asking?" Ted realized his question sounded like they were both in prison.

"You know…what every guy is in here for I'd imagine, including you." The man made a scissor motion with his index and middle finger. He scrunched his brows and motioned at Ted's Levi 501s. "But you're not wearing sweat pants."

Ted remembered Project Diagnosis and looked around the waiting room. All the guys were wearing loose fitting sweat pants and clutching little white paper bags. They all shared a look of panic.

"If you were getting snipped today, you'd be wearing sweat pants too."

"Just a consultation." Ted scanned the waiting room again. "What's with the paper bags?"

"Medical supplies," the man said. "Ointment, pain killers, medical grade titanium clips."

"Okay, then." Feeling his stomach roiling, Ted looked past his magazine to find Casey staring back at him. *Busted*, he thought. She offered a small wave and a smile. Ted waved back and returned his eyes to his magazine. As he did he noticed Blanche behind her desk glowering at Casey, then she shifted her disapproving look back to him. Ted took a hint and buried his face behind his magazine.

"By the way, the name's Jake." He presented his hand to Ted and both men shared a subtle but firm shake. "It's my second time on this merry-go-round."

"Jesus. Sorry to hear that."

Jake shrugged. "Nature works in mysterious ways and I got twin daughters to prove it. Can't complain though. They're the best thing to ever happen to me."

"Well, I don't want kids. I—" Before Ted could complete his sentence, Blanche's grating voice cut through the silence of the waiting room.

"Ted!" Blanche stood no more than six feet away but spoke as if she were addressing a crowd. "The doctor will see you now."

Ted dropped his Family Circle on his chair and stood up.

"Magazine rack, please." Blanche barked like a drill sergeant.

Jake leaned over and grabbed Ted's magazine. "I'll take care of it."

"Thanks, and good luck."

"You too, brother," Jake said as he placed Ted's magazine back on the rack.

✂

TED STEPPED FORWARD and cast a quick glance at Casey. She was in the middle of dealing with a patient, but again, Blanche noticed Ted's distraction.

"This way." Blanche directed Ted into a hallway behind the waiting room that led into several examination rooms. She stopped at one room and opened the door. "Stay away from her. She's a filthy trollop."

"What the…?" Ted asked. "Who?"

"You know who." Blanche pointed into the examination room. "Take a seat."

Ted did as he was told and Blanche closed the door with a slam. The room was clean and sparsely furnished, and didn't look much different than his own doctor's office. On one wall were two posters showing cut-away views of both the male and female urinary tract and reproductive organs. The examination table was lined with sterile paper.

Low volume music filtered through a desktop speaker system, powered by a docked MP3 player. It only took a few seconds for Ted to notice a theme. Bryan Adam's "Cuts like a Knife" faded out into a cover of "The First Cut is the Deepest" sung by Sheryl Crow.

Cat Stevens' original version is better, Ted thought.

The door to the examination room opened and the doctor entered in pressed khakis and a white button-up shirt. A stethoscope hung around his neck and he held a clipboard in one hand. His short cropped white hair bore a deep contrast to his deep brown tan. This was a man who either loved the outdoors or the tanning bed. Ted knew the answer almost immediately.

The doctor consulted the clipboard. "Ted…Cooper?"

"That's me."

The man extended his left hand. "Good to meet you, Ted. I'm Doctor Palmer. Doctor 'Hairy' Palmer."

Expecting professionalism, Dr. Palmer's joke caught Ted off guard.

"Get it? Hairy…palms?"

Ted nodded. "Uh, yeah. I get it."

"Oh good. I thought you were a little slow for a second there." Dr. Palmer chuckled as he scanned his clipboard. "Hairy palms. I love that joke." He cocked his ear to one side just as Sheryl Crow crooned about being cursed. "Ah, Sheryl Crow. You think she's hot?"

"Yeah, I guess."

"Come on. She's a babe." Ted was sure he heard Dr. Palmer sigh just before he added, "I'd sure like a taste of those muffins."

Is this guy for real? Ted thought. *And do I want his hands anywhere near my junk?*

"How do you like the music?" Dr. Palmer smiled, his bleached teeth shining like headlights in the fog. "It's a new addition to all the rooms."

"Music's fine, Doc," Ted said. "And I got the theme right away. I'm not one of those slow people."

"Yeah? Guess what's up next." Dr. Palmer flashed his eyebrows like a kid about to be told where the treasure is buried.

Ted gave his answer some thought. "I don't know. 'Mack the Knife?' "

"Oh, shit! That's a good one." Dr. Palmer scribbled the

title down on the top corner of the clipboard. "Don't have that one. I'll add it to the playlist. Guess again."

Ted shrugged. He felt annoyance start to burn in his gut.

"Okay, I'll tell you. 'Great Balls of Fire.' You know, by Jerry Lee Lewis. Isn't that a scream?"

"That wasn't the first thing that came to mind." Ted considered dropping the subject, but his aggravation got the better of him. "Wouldn't something more relaxing be better?"

"Bah." Dr. Palmer dismissed the suggestion. "Just having fun. Keeping it light…So, you want to get snipped, huh?"

Finally, Ted thought. "Yes."

"What do you do for a living, Ted?"

"I own a coffee shop."

"Huh." Dr. Palmer jotted notes on the clipboard. "Got kids?"

"No."

"Want kids? I guess if you're here you don't want kids, but I got to ask. Policy."

"There's no kids in my future."

"Oh…so you're a player." Dr. Palmer nodded his head in subtle approval as his lips curled into a sly grin. "A real swinging dick, huh?"

"Well, I—"

"You do understand this procedure is permanent?"

"Yeah, but there's a guy in the waiting room that's been through this once before."

"Jake? He's one in a million. The odds are so low that recanalization almost never happens."

Ted focused on Dr. Palmer's eyes. "Almost?"

"I have to say that, because it happens." Dr. Palmer sought

refuge in his clipboard. "But it's effectively a zero percent chance. Besides, Jake's a sex addict. He didn't wait after the first procedure." Dr. Palmer stopped writing. "You didn't hear that from me."

"Look, I just want peace of mind," Ted said.

"Or a piece of ass." Dr. Palmer's greasy grin was back. "Am I right?"

This guy is *for real*, Ted thought. *His work must be exceptional or he'd have his license revoked.*

Dr. Palmer laughed and nudged Ted's shoulder with his knuckle. "Am I right? Nothing like going balls deep in a nice juicy peach without having to worry. Know what I mean?"

Dr. Palmer pumped his hips back and forth, his hands held in front as he mimed. From the way he was moving, Ted assumed it was doggy style. He tore a sheet of paper from the clipboard and handed it to Ted.

"Take this to ol' Battle Axe out front." Dr. Palmer continued his pelvic air thrusts. "One more thing. You're going to have to shave your balls yourself. I don't do that. Close the door on your way out."

As Ted left the examination room, his new task of manscaping his privates competed with the image of Dr. Palmer dry humping the air. Both were equally unappealing.

AT THE RECEPTION desk, Blanche eyed Ted with a wary glance. "That didn't take long. Did you change your mind about living a life of sin?"

"No," Ted said in a hushed voice, aware that Casey could be within earshot.

"Well, I hope you don't get cancer…down there." Blanche flicked her eyes down to Ted's crotch.

"What?" Alarm bells rang in Ted's head. He lowered his voice again, almost whispering. "Dr. Palmer said nothing about cancer."

"It's God's punishment for abusing your body for pleasure."

"Wait." Ted gave Blanche a sideways look. "You're making this up. You're trying to scare me."

"I guess that's for me to know and you to find out." She pulled out her appointment book and flipped through the pages. "Thursday the 23rd is available."

Blanche's plan to cast doubt on Ted's decision was working ever so slightly. "Can I take a few days to decide?"

"No, you may not. The afternoon of Thursday the 23rd is your only choice." Blanche stared back at Ted, waiting for an answer.

"I guess it'll be the 23rd then."

Blanche scribbled Ted's name into the appointment book, then presented him with a pre-made scrip.

"Get these prescriptions filled promptly. And bring them with you to your appointment."

"Thanks." Ted crammed the scrip into his front pocket.

"And don't forget to shave." Blanche pointed a rigid index finger towards Ted's crotch.

Battle Axe is right, Ted thought, and he had had enough. He leaned down close to Blanche, almost nose to nose.

"Oh, you mean shave my *balls*?" He emphasized the word

"balls" in a low, throaty whisper. "Dr. Palmer mentioned that. I'll make sure my *balls* are soft and supple, just for you, *Blanche*."

Blanche shivered. "Ugh. Go, you heathen."

Ted was pleased that he had elicited such a response from her. He turned his head and saw that Jake had been watching the exchange. Ted winked at him and gave him an "A-Ok" sign followed by a "thumbs up."

Jake chuckled and returned a "thumbs up" of his own until he felt Blanche's stink eye upon him. He straightened up and resumed reading his issue of Outdoor Life.

"Thanks, Blanche," Ted said. "See you soon." He turned and left the office.

Casey smiled and waved at Ted as he passed. He waved back, pleased to be remembered. Her eyes followed his denim-clad backside as he walked toward the elevators.

Casey's phone rang, but she didn't answer until she could no longer see Ted. "Dr. Neandross's office," she said in a sing-song voice.

"You're a dirty little harlot." Blanche's voice filtered through the ear piece.

Casey turned and saw Blanche on her phone. Both women's eyes narrowed in a stare-down across the entryway of the office. "Sit and spin, bitch," Casey said.

At the elevators, Ted felt relaxation wash over him, despite what Blanche had said earlier. He was happy with his decision and looked forward to telling Kunal and Ray. He jammed his hands in his pockets and felt the scrip Blanche had just handed him.

First things first, get this prescription filled, thought Ted. His phone vibrated and chimed in his pocket. He extracted it and saw that a text from Kunal had arrived.

"Tall boys @ Pinehurst," the text message read.

The prescription could wait a day. He didn't know it then, but Ted's life was about to get a whole lot more interesting.

Coffee

P INEHURST P ARK WAS located a five minute drive north of the University of Portland. The park was well forested and provided ample shade on hot days. It contained one path that circumnavigated the entire park, plus numerous paths that branched throughout. Benches were placed at regular intervals all along the main path and each one had a brass memorial plaque with the name of a community member engraved on it. The paths were frequented all year round by walkers and joggers alike.

Ray was partial to a bench near the duck pond, not for the view but because the bench marked the halfway point of the main path. Joggers picked this spot near a water fountain to pause and take their pulse before continuing the rest of the way.

"Being halfway made the math easy," Ted had once told Ray. But Ray didn't care about the math. All he cared about was watching the joggers come and go, specifically the female joggers.

The three of them took a seat and Ray cracked the seals on three twenty-four-ounce cans of beer and presented one to Kunal and Ted each, wrapped in its requisite paper bag.

"Your tall boys, gentleman," said Ray.

Ted tapped away at his phone, oblivious to everything, including the beer in Ray's hand.

"Earth to Ted." Ray placed the beer on top of Ted's phone.

"Oh, thanks." Ted swallowed a mouthful of beer and set the can down next to the bench.

"You okay, dude?" With a casual glance, Kunal tried to read the screen of Ted's phone. "Anything you want to share with us?"

"I'm good." Ted punctuated his minimal response with a resounding belch.

"On that note, let the festivities begin." Ray drank from his beer and tried to outdo Ted's burp.

"Not even close." Kunal clinked the top of his can with Ray's and took a swig. "I still can't believe you replaced Riker. That beard rocked."

Ray's William Riker beard was gone and instead he sported large, bushy sideburns that spanned the entire length of his jaw.

"Got to keep things fresh for Viv. It's Neelix today."

"Who?"

"Neelix…from Voyager."

Kunal stared at him and shrugged. "I never watched Star Trek Voyager."

"You got to get educated," Ray said. "The only difference is mine is black. Neelix's beard was blond."

"If knowing more about Star Trek will get me more action, I'll consider it." Kunal spotted a woman jogging towards their bench. "Looks like our first contestant has arrived."

Ray positioned his free hand in front of his face to obscure the lower half of whatever he looked at. Kunal raised his brow in a mixture of confusion and curiosity.

"What are you doing?"

"Try it."

"Try what?"

"Just hold your hand up like this." Ray shot a quick glance back at Kunal to try and egg him on.

"No." Kunal laughed. "You look like an idiot."

"Come on. You're missing it." Ray returned his gaze to the jogger. "If you don't look at the legs, it's like they're all having cowgirl sex." He looked back at Kunal, his smile sliding into a leer. "It's awesome."

Kunal couldn't help but appreciate Ray's misguided enthusiasm. He watched Ray as another woman jogger approached their bench, bouncing in all the right places. Reluctant at first, Kunal raised his hand in front of his face, joining Ray in what must have seemed to the joggers to be a weird and creepy salute.

The second woman stopped and jogged in place as she noted the time and her pulse.

Ray was right. When Kunal obscured the jogger's legs from view, context was lost and it was easy to imagine a different scenario. The woman's torso moved up and down in a steady rhythm. Her face was flushed, pink and sweaty, and her ponytail bobbed side to side, up and down. It was oddly erotic.

"I see what you mean," Kunal said as he lowered his hand again.

"Damn. I want to motorboat those tits."

"Lower your voice and keep it in your pants, dude." Kunal drank from his beer. "Besides, you're all talk."

"No way. I'd do it."

"Bullshit," Kunal said. "Assuming she's into you, and that's highly debatable, you mean to say that you'd place your face between that woman's breasts, right now, even though you're married?"

"Well, I…," Ray stammered.

"Like I said. You're all talk." Kunal nudged Ray. "There's a time and place for talk like that and this ain't it."

"What?" Ray shoved Kunal back. "There's nothing wrong with window shopping."

"Except when you got to clean the window after." Kunal laughed at his joke. "Isn't that right, Ted?"

Ted didn't hear a thing. He was immersed in the zone, tapping away at his phone.

"Ted, you're missing the action." Kunal got no reaction from him. "Two can play that game." He grabbed Ted's phone and stood up.

"Hey!" Ted tried to reclaim his phone. "Give it back."

Kunal stood half a foot taller than Ted and it took no effort to keep the phone out of his reach. Kunal spun around so he could read the screen, deflecting Ted's attempts at retrieval.

"How to shave your sack?" Kunal read out, surprised.

The woman jogger gave the three guys a bewildered look and continued her run down the main path.

"Maybe you could say it *louder*?" Ted stopped trying to grab his phone back and held out his hand, palm up.

"Don't tempt me." Kunal gave Ted a warm smile and returned his phone. "Dude, we're your friends. It's nothing to be embarrassed about."

"Oh, really? You shave your…" Ted lowered his voice from

an excitable level to a more conversational tone and made sure there was no one within earshot. "You shave your sack?"

Kunal sat back down. "Actually I do and I'm not ashamed to say it." He spread his legs and held his hands palm up, presenting his crotch for praise. "Manscaping's in. Women love it."

"I don't know." Ted sat next to Kunal, shoving his manspreading out of the way. "I'd imagine having no hair on your junk makes you look like a middle-schooler. That's a turn on?"

"Just reporting my experience. A smooth sack, and shaft for that matter, just beg to be touched." Kunal closed his eyes and reclined on the bench, clasping his hands behind his head. "Get a little lube down there and…well it gets a thumbs up from me."

"What about you, Ray?" Ted asked.

"Nah. I'm into body hair." Ray raised his hand up to his face as another woman jogger passed by.

"Wow, Neelix. You're kidding!" Kunal slapped his knee and began to laugh.

Ray glowered at him. "Shut up."

Ted gave Ray a curious glance. "What's he doing with his hand?"

"Don't ask," Kunal whispered out of the side of his mouth. "Easy Ray. I'm just busting your balls."

Ted scrolled through search results on his phone. "What's your technique?"

"I have no technique," Kunal said. "I go to a salon and come out sexy smooth."

"I got to shave for my vasectomy, so I was thinking I'd try it out first."

"To be honest, I don't get shaved. I get waxed. But a shave is a good start. You won't regret it."

The gears in Ted's head began to turn. "So is it a man or a woman who does it?"

"It's mostly women because they do a better job."

Ray's ears pricked up. "Did someone say hand job?"

"No. No, Ray. There's no hand jobs," Kunal said. "These men and women are professional aestheticians, not prostitutes. If you got out of line, you'd probably get tased."

"But what if you get a hard-on?" Ted asked.

Kunal could see it was a legitimate concern. "It happens. We're all adults. I move my junk around when I'm told to, the wax is applied and the hair is pulled out."

Ted cringed. "Does it hurt?"

"Like a motherfucker." Kunal grinned. "The first time is the worst, but it does get better after repeated sessions. Shaving doesn't hurt at all."

Ted drank from his beer, quenching his suddenly dry throat. "I think shaving is more my speed."

"Want a salon recommendation?"

"I'll let you know." Ted drank more beer. "I might do it myself."

"Whatever, dude," Kunal said. "We're here to help."

Ray's eyes went wide and almost choked on his mouthful of beer. "I'm not going to help him *shave his balls!*"

A group of men and women joggers overheard Ray's comment and began to laugh as they passed.

"Shut up, *Neelix.*" Ted ignored the snickering crowd and began to formulate a plan.

Shaving my own sack, he thought. *How hard can it be?*

ONE TALL BOY at Pinehurst Park had led to a few more at Quinn's and Ted was comfortably buzzed. He shared a taxi with Kunal and Ray, and Ted's condo was last on the route home.

"Hey buddy." The taxi driver addressed Ted through the rear view mirror.

"Yeah?"

"I didn't mean to eavesdrop, I mean it's hard not to." The driver pronounced his "s" with a "sh" sound. "I know your friends think the Gillette Fusion 5 is the way to go, with its five blades and all, but you don't need anything more than the Mach 3. The flexball is a gimmick."

"Thanks for the info," Ted said.

The taxi rolled up to the front entrance of Ted's condo. The driver twisted in his seat and faced Ted.

"I mean who are you going to believe? Two guys who can't grow a beard to save their lives, or me?" The driver pointed at his handlebar mustache. His cheeks had already developed a substantial five o'clock shadow.

"Good point." Ted looked at the meter and dug out his wallet from his back pocket.

"Now, I don't shave my sack. Maybe I should. But if I did, it'd be with the Mach 3. There's a version with a trimmer attachment too. Now, that would be handy, right? I just don't like the idea of anything sharp down there. You know?"

"Duly noted." Ted handed the driver a stack of bills for his portion of the trip and stepped out of the car.

The driver looked at the bills. "Thanks for the tip, buddy."

"Don't mention it." Ted gave the driver a quick wave.

"Good luck with the shaving and…all that." The driver waved an arm around and pointed at Ted's crotch. "I hope your lady likes it."

"Me, too." Ted closed the taxi door and headed for the front entrance of his building, looking forward to the cool quiet the lobby would provide.

He punched the elevator call button and waited. Images of razors and trimmers swirled in his head. The elevator doors opened and Ted stepped in, still swimming in a nice beer buzz. He pressed the button for the fourth floor.

At one point during the elevator's rise, Ted was convinced the elevator had tilted to one side. His confusion evaporated when the doors opened to the familiar Aztec-patterned carpet. Black, brown, red and orange in repeating rows of triangles and diamonds. Iris had never liked it and had said if she had a choice, she'd replace it with a solid dark gray.

Boring, thought Ted.

Ted closed his eyes and rested his forehead on his door as he dug into his pockets for his keys. He found them by feel, pulled them out and tried to unlock the door the same way but had to open his eyes to align the key just right. The deadbolt slid into the door and he pushed it open.

The door closed on its own and he was about to re-lock it when he spotted Iris sitting on the floor beside the dog bed. Buster rested his head on Iris's lap as she stroked his fur in long, gentle movements.

Ted found her behavior curious. She had never shown much affection towards Buster since he had joined the family.

"Iris…" In a beer haze, Ted almost lost his words. "This is

a nice surprise." He hadn't intended to use the word "nice" but his brain had added it in at the last minute.

Iris didn't answer. Instead, she continued to give Buster loves and the dog wasn't going to budge. He knew a good thing when he had it.

"What is it?" Ted sat next to Iris. "What's wrong?"

In her free hand Iris handed him a pregnancy test. The result window was a single blue line, a clearly negative result.

"Apparently, nothing's wrong."

"But we don't want kids, right? Shouldn't this be good news?"

"It should." Iris wiped her eyes with a quick twist of her wrist. "I guess part of me liked the idea of getting pregnant. Then reality set in…the morning sickness, sleepless nights, engorged breasts."

Ted leaned into Iris, resting his head on her shoulder and sneaking a peak down her blouse at the same time. "I like the breasts part."

Iris laughed. "You're drunk." She wafted Ted's beer breath away from her nose. "Still, I wasn't expecting reality to sting so much."

"Have you changed your mind?" It was a loaded question and Ted knew it. *What if she changes her mind?*

"No," Iris said without hesitation.

"That's good, because I've booked a vasectomy for next week."

Iris looked at Ted directly for the first time since he'd arrived home, but it was an expression of surprise.

"It'll help us get back on track." Ted kissed her cheek. "Soon all our worries will be a thing of the past."

He caressed her cheek with the back of his hand, then turned her head towards his for a kiss on the lips.

Iris turned away. "I got to go." She began to collect her things.

"Why?" Ted tried to make sense out of what was going on.

"I need more time."

"How much more?"

"Ted." Iris grabbed her attaché and purse from the dinner table. "Please don't make this harder than it already is."

"What?" Even if Ted had had a clear head, he still would have been confused. "What am I doing?"

Iris's phone chimed in her purse.

"I'm glad your phone works." Ted said, annoyed. "I've been trying to talk to you since you left."

Iris shook her head. She didn't want to fight. "I'll call you later."

Ted and Buster watched Iris step to the door and leave. The door closed with a *thud*, leaving them both in silence. Buster began to softly whine.

"It'll be okay, buddy." Ted scratched Buster's head and they both sat in the quiet, which seemed more intense now that Iris had left. "Hey are you hungry?"

Buster's ears pricked up.

"How about some mac and cheese?"

Buster raised his head and began to pant.

"I'll take that as a yes." Ted stood up, walked to the kitchen and began collecting the necessary utensils and ingredients.

Less than twenty minutes later, Ted was back sitting next to Buster, eating macaroni and cheese dinner right out of the pot.

He shared ample spoonfuls with Buster. "You like that, huh?"

Buster responded by gobbling up the pasta with complete abandon. As soon as it reached his mouth, it vanished.

Ted looked around his apartment as he scooped some of the congealing macaroni into his mouth. Only Iris's style screamed back at him. "You think she's coming back?"

Buster licked his chops, waiting for another bite, his eyes watching the spoon in Ted's hand. He uttered a low whine.

"Yeah, I hope so too." His decision to get snipped felt even more right. Ted scooped one more bite for himself, then held the half empty pot in front of Buster's nose. "Chew it up really well, buddy. You know what happens when you don't."

Buster tilted his head as if to look a question at Ted.

"Don't play dumb with me, pooch." Ted smiled at the dog and set the pot in front of him.

Buster hopped out of his dog bed to get better access to the pot and wolfed the rest of the macaroni dinner.

THE NEXT MORNING, Ted woke to find Buster curled up beside him on the bed. Normally off limits, he wasn't going to shoo him away now. Ted hopped into the shower and washed what was left of his beer-induced stupor down the drain.

Clean, washed, and dressed in comfortable denim, Ted felt good despite the incident with Iris the previous night. He grabbed his phone and called, but got Iris's voicemail again.

Too soon, Ted thought. *Either that or she really doesn't want to talk to me.* He hung up, leaving no message.

He fed Buster and made himself a pot of coffee. From the cupboard, Ted dug out a coffee mug he rarely used. Iris hated it. The cup was brown and shaped like a pile of poop, with the words "Coffee makes me poop" written on the side in playful block letters. Ray had given it to him when he had opened Buster's Beans. The cup was odd, but it also reflected Ted's sense of humor.

As he sipped his coffee his eyes scanned the kitchen, the only area of the apartment Ted felt completely at home in, despite the few high-end appliances littering the counter that Iris had chosen.

His eyes settled on the coupon that had been stapled to the back of the scrip Blanche had given him yesterday.

"30% OFF AT WALGREENS," it yelled from the fridge in bold black letters. But the coupon had a condition: *Offer valid only at East Portland Medical Center location.*

As a business owner, Ted made a habit to pay attention to good deals. Taking advantage of said deals was a different matter. Some weren't worth the time or effort to attain and for others, the quality wasn't quite up to Ted's standards. This was different. Other than the special titanium clips, the rest of the scrip was basic pharmacy stock. Plus a Walgreens located in a medical building would more likely have the specialty items.

How convenient, Ted thought. *One stop shopping.*

Ted dropped Buster off at the shop and continued on to the pharmacy. Parking was easier today. He made his way to the back of the Walgreens and stood in line to drop off his prescription. On his way, Ted had passed the shelves of condoms. The thought of not having to worry about them anymore caused a grin to cross his face. He tried calling Iris, but was shuffled to voicemail again. Ted contemplated sending her a text, but dismissed the thought as quickly as it came.

The line for drop-offs wasn't long and he figured he'd be back at the shop well before ten o'clock in the morning. At that moment, the friendly receptionist from yesterday emerged from one of the aisles carrying a shopping basket. Her hair was unbraided today and fell loosely around her shoulders. Ted spotted her first, then perhaps she felt his stare. They locked gaze and smiled in unison.

As she approached him, Ted realized that he had forgotten her name.

"Hi," she said. "It's…Ted, right?"

Of course you remembered my name, Ted thought as he felt his face break out in a flush. "And you are…from the doctor's office upstairs." Ted stammered and searched his brain without success. "Sorry. I forgot your name."

Casey dug into her pocket and pulled out her magnetic name tag. She placed it on the left side of her flower-patterned top.

"Casey! Right." They both shared a nervous laugh. "Funny meeting you here, in the building where you work. Me in the drug store. What are the odds?" Ted heard himself screaming in his head to *stop talking*.

"Pretty good actually." Casey glanced at the scrip in Ted's hand. "I hope you don't come here often."

Ted noticed the shift in her eyes and hid the scrip in his hand "No, I'm just here for a prescription…for my feet. I have this thing…" *Stop talking!*

Casey watched Ted's meltdown and smiled. "Well, I hope you have insurance so you don't have to *foot* the bill."

"Oh, I do, but this is a small expense."

An elderly woman standing in line behind Ted snickered. He cast her a confused glance, then back to Casey, who was also smiling coyly.

"The deductible would be…" The joke dawned on Ted and he tried to laugh it off. "Wait. I get it…No, I will *foot* the bill."

"You sure know how to *toe the line*." Casey winked. The woman in the line smiled to herself and nodded with approval. "It was good to see you again, Ted." She flashed her lashes twice and continued to the next aisle. "Bye."

"Um…Bye." Ted watched her go. But was it goodbye? Did it have to be? His life with Iris had been good for a while, but now it felt different. Iris had said he needed some new friends. What about a friend who's also a woman? *That's probably not what Iris meant, but what the hell*, he thought.

Ted found he liked Casey. Everything he had seen so far he had liked. She turned him into a nervous ball of restrained energy and she sure had him beat on the witty repartee.

If I don't do this, I'll always wonder what could have been. Ted seized the moment. "Casey?"

She turned to face him, quick, as if she had been waiting for him to say something else and was sure it would happen. Her hair followed in a fiery arc.

"Yes?"

The people waiting in line ahead and behind Ted began to watch and listen more closely, either fascinated or entertained by his interaction with Casey. It wasn't anywhere close to

Hollywood romantic comedy-worthy dialog, but it was still an amusing way to pass the time.

"I know I barely know you, but…" Ted paused to choose just the right words. He looked around and found many curious and expectant eyes watching him, waiting. "Do you want to get coffee sometime?"

The crowd heaved a collective *sigh* but Ted couldn't tell if it represented satisfaction or disappointment.

Casey considered the offer. Answering too quickly or slowly would send the wrong message. She aimed for somewhere in between. "Yes. Okay."

"What day and time works for you?"

This time Casey didn't wait to respond. "How about tomorrow? One o'clock?"

Ted paused and rolled details around in his head.

"Too soon?"

"Nope." Ted shook his head. "That's great, in fact. Give me your hand."

Casey, as well as the onlookers, looked confused by Ted's request until he pulled out a ballpoint pen from the breast pocket of his denim shirt.

"Don't you have a phone?" Casey asked.

"I do but I barely use it." Ted beckoned for Casey's hand. It was his turn to drive the conversation.

Casey presented her hand and Ted turned it palm up. He took in the softness of her hands as he wrote his name, phone number and the address of Buster's Beans onto her outstretched palm. "This is more fun, don't you think?"

"It tickles."

"It does? Oh, sorry."

"Don't be." Casey's cheeks flushed a gentle rose. "I don't mind." She watched Ted concentrate as he scribed the details onto her hand and smiled.

"There." Ted let go of Casey's hand. It was perfect timing too since he had noticed that both of their hands were getting a little sweaty. "I'll see you tomorrow."

"Yup. One o'clock." Casey turned to continue shopping in the next aisle.

"Bye." Ted waved.

"Bye." Casey disappeared from view. Unseen to Ted, she dug out her phone and took a picture of her hand.

Ted felt a tap on his shoulder. It was the elderly woman standing in line behind him.

"You started weak but finished strong," the woman said. "I like strong finishers." She let her eyes wander from Ted's face to his crotch and back. "If you get stood up, call me. Give me your hand."

Ted presented his hand to the woman.

"Pen?"

Ted gave her his pen. The woman wrote her name and phone number on his palm and handed it back.

The woman leaned close to Ted and whispered, "I'm recently divorced, if you know what I mean." She clicked her tongue and winked.

Ted offered a slow nod as he placed his pen back in his pocket. "Okay. Thanks…" He looked at his palm. "Thanks, Gladys."

Ted put the last few minutes behind him and focused on his date tomorrow with Casey. There were still a few people ahead of him, but he didn't care. He rocked back and forth on his feet and found himself filling with giddy excitement.

After dropping off his prescription, Ted had fifteen minutes to kill. He strolled to the Men's Grooming aisle and browsed the shaving supplies. There were at least a dozen different shaving creams and gels, and so many razors and shavers it made his head spin. He wasn't usually picky. He used an electric razor for his face, but his nether region demanded the best. There were razors with one blade, razors with five blades and everything in between. He didn't like the idea of five surgically sharp blades down south, and the razors with one blade looked like a kid's toy.

Ted recalled his bizarrely specific conversation with yesterday's taxi driver. *Mach 3 with trimmer attachment.* He picked up one of the packages.

"Engineered for a closer shave without all the redness," he said to himself, shaking his head. "Redness bad."

"A smooth face is best for oral sex," a voice announced behind him. Ted turned to find Gladys leering at him. She winked and carried on up the aisle. "You got my number, honey."

"Yes…I sure do." Ted looked at his palm and saw Gladys's number already beginning to smear.

In the end, the taxi driver's advice won out. Ted threw the razor into his plastic shopping basket, accompanied by his favorite shaving gel.

The easy part was over.

THE LUNCHTIME RUSH had just tapered off. Buster dozed in his dog bed near the store's front door. Bright sunshine slashed across the floor of the shop in diagonal lines. The south-facing storefront meant that the shop benefited from sunlight all day. It also made it quite hot in summer but that brought in customers looking for iced coffees and specialty juices.

Danielle and Joe worked the front counter while Ted wiped down tables. They watched him work with interest. Ted paid more attention to one particular table, making sure the glass surface was spotless. He placed a "Reserved" tent card in the center of it.

An elderly woman entered the shop. Buster cracked a lazy eye as her feet and cane moved toward the front counter, then went back to snoozing.

Joe leaned towards Danielle but spoke loud enough for Ted to hear. "He's sure making a big deal about this."

"She…Casey doesn't know I own the place," Ted said as he wiped past and present dust from the two chairs at the reserved table. "I wanted to surprise her."

"Why?" asked Joe.

"I thought it would be fun." Ted paused his harried cleaning and looked at Joe and Danielle. "I just haven't done this kind of thing for a while."

Joe and Danielle shared a glance. "It's a date," they said in unison.

"It's *not* a date! It's just coffee between friends."

Joe began his cross-examination. "How long have you known her?"

"A day or so."

"What's her last name?"

Ted balked for a moment, knowing he had no answer. He

threw his rag over the front counter to try and divert the conversation.

The elderly woman ordered a coffee, then watched as Joe prepared it, all the while listening to the ongoing conversation between Ted, Joe and Danielle.

"Dani," Ted said. "Could you get me an Americano with a shot of cinnamon syrup, please?"

"He's avoiding the question." Danielle prepared the espresso, tamping down the ground coffee into the portafilter.

Joe nodded. "I know."

"I'm not avoiding the question."

"Okay." Danielle locked the portafilter into the espresso machine and started the flow of hot water into a cup perched below. "So, her last name is…?"

"I don't know," Ted said.

"You know…" Joe finished up the elderly woman's coffee order. "This is just like hooking up at a bar, but *without* the sex."

"Correction. With an expectation of sex *later*." Danielle handed the espresso cup to Ted.

"I'm not expecting—" Ted noticed the elderly lady listening intently and lowered his voice. "I'm not expecting sex."

"Don't stop on my account." The elderly woman took her coffee and handed Joe a five dollar bill. "Keep the change, son. Consider it admission."

Joe chuckled. "Thanks, ma'am."

Danielle cocked her head to one side. "Does Iris know about this?"

The elderly woman flashed her eyebrows in surprise. "Who's Iris?"

"His girlfriend," Joe said.

The elderly woman gasped.

"*Ex*-girlfriend," Ted added quickly.

"When did this happen?" Danielle asked.

"A couple days ago? It feels so much longer. It doesn't matter."

"It does matter," Danielle said. "If you're not officially broken up with Iris, you're skating on thin ice."

"It's a trap!" Joe said in his best Admiral Akbar impression. The quip fell on deaf ears.

"So is it official?"

Ted sent a sideways look at Danielle. "All my calls go to voicemail. And my texts go through but she never responds."

"It's only been a couple of days." Danielle rearranged the baked goods in the display cabinet. "Sounds like you want it to be over."

Ted shrugged. "Maybe I do."

"It's a date," Danielle said to Joe.

"Yup."

"It's not!" Ted said.

"She's meeting you here, so I assume you invited her, and not the other way around?" Joe wiped behind the counter. "I mean, what are the odds that she'd pick this place?"

Ted sighed. "Yeah, so what?"

The elderly woman sipped her coffee at the counter and took it all in.

Joe hung his dish towel over his shoulder and placed his hands on the counter. "Okay. Let me recap. You've invited a woman for coffee that you've known for one day. You don't know her last name and your girlfriend doesn't know anything about her."

"*Ex*-girlfriend." Ted stares back.

"*Unconfirmed* ex-girlfriend."

"No. Don't do that." Ted pointed at Joe. "Iris lives on her phone, but she clearly isn't interested in talking to me. This is *just* coffee and I'm not going to feel guilty about it."

The elderly woman looked from Ted to Joe and Danielle and back. "It's a date."

"It's *definitely* a date," Danielle said. "But one fraught with danger."

Ted scoffed.

"Don't say I didn't warn you."

Joe spotted Casey walking outside the shop, looking up for signage. "Is that her?"

Ted looked over his shoulder and felt his stomach do a back flip. "Shit!" He ran to the reserved table and sat down in one of the chairs.

"Ted!" Joe pointed at him.

"What?"

"Your apron!"

Ted realized his error and began to take off his apron. His progress snagged on a knot in the drawstrings and he managed to throw the apron to Joe just as Casey entered the shop. He sat down.

Casey spotted Ted and he waved her over. Joe, Danielle and the elderly woman watched Ted stand to greet her. They shared a quick hug and Ted caught a light scent of hyacinth in her hair again. He pulled out Casey's chair and seated her before sitting himself.

"Reserved?" Casey said. "For us?"

"I made sure of it."

The elderly woman turned to Joe and Danielle. "I give him full points for being a gentleman." She took a sip from her coffee. "And as much as I'd like to stay and watch, I have my afternoon errands to run." She waved goodbye and headed for the exit.

"Thank you. See you again soon." Danielle said as she and Joe settled into watching Ted and Casey's first date.

"You can bet on it." The elderly woman passed Ted and Casey's table. "He's a keeper, dear," she said to Casey.

"Oh, um, thank you." Casey nodded to the elderly woman.

Ted felt the blush of embarrassment flood his cheeks.

"Ted…" Casey cast a curious glance across the table. "Are you sweating?"

"It's just a little hot."

"Oh." Casey looked around the shop. When her eyes passed the front counter, Joe and Danielle made themselves look busy. "This is a nice place."

"Yeah, it's my usual haunt." Ted spotted Joe and Danielle at the counter, both cupping their faces in their hands, elbows on the counter as if they were watching the cutest thing ever. "I've been coming here for years."

Danielle brought Ted's shot of espresso to the table and gave him a knowing glance and a wink before returning to the counter.

"What would you like?" Ted asked.

Casey puckered her lips and thought for a moment. Ted took the time to notice how conservative her make-up was. A light rose lipstick not much different than her natural color, light pink blush and just enough eye shadow to give her eyes alluring definition behind her glasses. It was a good, natural look.

"I don't know," Casey said finally.

"Come on. Let's take a look." Ted offered his hand, which Casey took. He thought he detected her cheeks flush with a warmer red, but he couldn't be sure.

Casey looked up at the chalk-written menu on the wall and began to sort through her choices. Joe caught Ted's eye and gave him a discreet thumbs up and mouthed "It's a date."

"It all looks so yummy." Casey faced Ted, her vibrant green eyes locking with his. "I can't decide. What do you recommend?"

For a moment, Ted was unable to move. Casey's eyes and her easy smile held him in a willing trance. *I could easily get lost in those eyes,* he thought.

Joe cleared his throat and Ted snapped back into reality. He walked around to the back of the counter, picked his apron from the wall and put it on.

"You look like a mochaccino girl to me." Ted began creating Casey's coffee.

Casey watched Ted work, both fascinated and a little confused. He moved with quick and effortless precision, like his arms knew what to do without being told: tamping the ground coffee and extracting espresso, mixing in chocolate syrup, and pouring steamed milk with a side-to-side motion to fill the cup and leave an intricate design on top. In this cup, Ted topped the mochaccino with a white heart shape.

Casey looked at Joe and Danielle, who were both standing off to one side watching their exchange.

Danielle shrugged and hooked a thumb in Ted's direction. "We work here. He owns the place."

Casey's eyes lit up. "Really?"

"Guilty as charged, my lady." Ted offered a playful grin.

"I should have guessed." Casey sniffed the air as if to confirm her suspicions. "You smelled like coffee yesterday. Like really strong coffee."

"Yesterday?" Danielle whispered out of the side of her mouth at Joe.

"He usually reeks of coffee," Joe said. "It could be worse, though. I knew a guy who reeked of garlic—"

Danielle elbowed Joe in the ribs. "You know anything about yesterday?"

Joe shrugged and rubbed his side.

Ted had already left his post behind the counter and was on his way back to their reserved table. He presented Casey with her mochaccino. She saw the white heart of steamed milk floating on the surface and blushed. Ted was sure of it this time.

"Thank you," she said.

Ted took off his apron, tossed it behind the counter for the second time, and sat back down across from Casey.

Joe caught the ball of fabric and hung it up again. "Smooth move, Casanova," he said to himself.

There was a moment of silence between them as Ted and Casey faced each other. Some might say it was awkward, but the two of them were so wrapped up in each other they didn't notice.

"That's a lovely dress," Ted said.

"You like it?" Casey's eyes lit up again as she talked and Ted found himself getting lost again.

"I love it."

"Thank you. I call it 'Summer Blossoms.' I made it myself."

Ted flashed his eyebrows in admiration. "You made that?"

"Mmm-hmm. Dressmaking, it's a hobby of mine." Casey caught an overflowing drip of mochaccino with her thumb and licked it. Even this small drop made her taste buds explode. "All my sisters sew, too."

"How many sisters do you have?"

"Two sisters, two brothers. How about you?"

"Just me." Ted sipped his espresso.

"Really?" Casey found herself studying Ted's face, his neck, the casual way his broad shoulders and full chest filled his denim shirt, almost derailing her train of thought. "I can't imagine growing up as an only child. Wasn't it lonely?"

"Not really. Plus there's perks. I didn't have to share my toys." Ted watched Casey run her index finger around the top edge of her coffee cup. "You should really give it a taste. It's pretty good."

"But it's art. I don't want to disturb it."

"I'd gladly make you another." Ted grinned.

Casey went to her purse and grabbed her phone. She framed up the coffee cup in the display. *Click*. "Take a picture, right? It lasts longer."

She dropped the phone back in her purse and took her first sip of her mochaccino, leaving a thin line of steamed milk and coffee foam across her upper lip. Casey closed her eyes, licked her lips and concluded with a contented sigh. "This is *so good*."

"Glad you like it." Ted envisioned leaning across the table and kissing her, tasting her lips mixed with mocha. "A little coffee, a little chocolate, a little magic."

"I like magic." Casey smiled and glanced around the shop. "So, who's Buster?"

Buster's ear's pricked up at the sound of his name, but his eyes remained shut. The dog was in stealth mode.

"Buster was the name of my dog when I was a kid. I guess that's another reason why I didn't mind being an only child. I had Buster." Memories of walking Buster Number One as a teenager and summers of playing fetch flashed through Ted's mind. "But he's also my new partner in this little venture. Let me see if he's up. Buster?"

Ted whistled. Buster cracked his eyes, then climbed out of his dog bed and wearily trotted over. Ted gave his head an ample scratch.

"Oh, a Golden," Casey said. "They're such gentle dogs."

"Buster keeps the customers in line, don't you boy?"

The dog chuffed as if in agreement.

Casey reached over and ruffled Buster's fur and ears. The dog wagged his tail enthusiastically and returned the affection by licking her face. She took it all in stride and didn't seem to mind. Ted was struck by the contrast between Casey and Iris, who would have leapt up to go wash her face and taken a lint brush to her clothes.

"Hello Buster. You're a good dog, oh yes." Casey nuzzled Buster's head. "How old is he?"

"Seven months. He lost his *beans* the other day." Ted used air-quotes to emphasize the word. "But he's almost back to normal."

"That's what the collar is for?" Casey continued stroking Buster's head and his tail swished back and forth. The dog was in heaven.

"Yeah. More comfortable than those lampshade ones." Ted watched Casey and Buster. "Looks like someone's found his new best friend. I hope—"

A bad smell floated by Ted's nose, something equivalent to a mixture of rotten eggs, spoiled cabbage and something else. It was a smell he had encountered before and it could mean only one thing.

"Uh, Joe?"

Joe looked up from the arts section of The Oregonian. "What's up, Boss?"

"Please take Buster out back. I think he needs some *fresh air.*"

The smell spread like wildfire and hit Casey's nose in seconds. "Oh, that's just nasty!" She placed her hand over her nose and mouth.

Ted stood and ran to the front entrance, locking it and flipping a "back in 15 minutes" sign in the window.

"I'm so sorry, Casey." Ted returned to his seat, noticing that her eyes were watering. Then he realized his eyes were weeping in much the same way. Ted kneeled down close to Buster. "You didn't chew your mac and cheese, did you buddy?"

Joe guided Buster out the back of the shop. Casey and Ted looked at each other's red, watery eyes, tears streaming down their faces. Casey's light mascara had started to run and it looked like they were breaking up instead of getting to know each other.

Casey was first to burst out laughing. "You're blaming Buster...*for that?*"

"What? Well, yeah!" Ted said. "That wasn't me. Really it wasn't."

"I believe you." Casey laughed her words out. "But promise me, whatever you do, don't feed him chili." She squeezed her nostrils together with one hand and waved the air with her other. "Whew!"

Ted joined in the laughter. "Deal. Maybe I should cut out the mac and cheese, too."

Casey nodded, laughing too hysterically to speak. She pulled a tissue from her purse to blot her eyes.

After Buster's miasma blew over, Ted and Casey continued their date. Their conversation flowed easily, like they had known each other for years. Afterward, they both stood on the sidewalk outside the shop. They exchanged phone numbers, caught in a loop of goodbyes.

Danielle and Joe craned their necks to see what was going on. Joe grabbed a rag and began wiping down tables close to the front windows, hoping for a better view.

"I had a great time, Casey."

"Me too, stink bomb and all. I can't say I've ever been hit on like that before."

"About that…"

"Don't worry about it." Casey turned serious and looked at Ted over the rims of her glasses. "Although I'm still not convinced it was Buster."

"Seriously," Ted said. "I wouldn't lie about that."

Casey swayed her shoulders back and forth and gave Ted a playful poke on his shoulder. "I'm joking." She giggled, leaned forward and planted a light kiss on Ted's cheek.

Again, Ted caught the light smell of her hair and the fresh scent of her skin. The softness of her kiss would remain on his cheeks for days. Ted wouldn't have been surprised if his beard stubble refused to grow where her lips had been.

"We should do this again. Call me, okay?"

Ted nodded. He felt feather light. "Okay."

Inside the shop, Joe and Danielle watched Ted watching Casey walk away. "He's a goner," Joe said.

"Yup." Danielle nodded in agreement. "Totally smitten."

"Have dinner with me?" Ted called out. "Let me redeem myself. I promise to leave Buster at home."

Casey turned and placed her pinkie finger and thumb to her face, mimicking a telephone. "Call me!"

Ted watched Casey walk down the sidewalk until she turned the corner and was out of view. He stepped to the shop entrance and noticed Joe and Danielle staring at him, both with wide smiles.

He stared back, then said through the glass, "Okay. You're right. It was a date." He entered the shop. "What did you think?"

Joe and Danielle answered his question with their grins.

"Call her," Danielle said. "If you don't, I'll kick your ass."

"I will." Ted paused, the glow of the coffee date still surrounding his head like a halo. "In fact, I think I'll call her now."

"Don't you think that's—"

Before Joe could say another word, Danielle thumped him in the shoulder. "Shut up. This is romantic." She looked at him. "You should be taking notes."

Ted grabbed his phone from his pocket and dialed Casey. Joe and Danielle were not surprised when Ted gave them an excited "thumbs up." Casey had accepted. If anyone had watched the two of them interacting in the shop this afternoon, they would have seen the instant attraction.

"Dinner." Ted beamed. "Tonight."

"Tonight!" Joe nodded, impressed. "You better leave early, boss. Make sure everything is perfect."

"Good idea. You'll be okay?"

Danielle shot him a look that said, "Are you kidding?"

Ted hooked Buster's leash into his collar and headed out the door, waving at Danielle and Joe as he went.

"Have fun," Danielle said, waving back, but Ted neither heard nor saw her gesture. He was on cloud nine. He floated to his SUV, with Buster sauntering along beside him. He had already picked out his clothes in his head. But first, he had a very important task ahead of him that couldn't wait.

He grabbed his phone and sent a flare to the guys, "My place, 30 minutes, Operation Clean the Carpet."

It'll be a surprise, Ted thought. *And if the evening goes right…* Ted smiled as he began his short drive home.

Shorn

TED STOOD IN his bathroom, freshly showered with a towel around his waist. In front of him lay his tools for the task ahead: shaving gel, razor with a built-in trimmer attachment, scissors (just in case), aftershave and extra towels. Behind him, reflected in the mirror, was his "cheering section" of Kunal and Ray. The two meant well, but Ted figured they were more interested in living vicariously through the experience.

Kunal held Ted's phone in his hand and scrolled through search results on how to shave a scrotum. Ray looked over Kunal's shoulder.

"Find anything yet?" Ted leaned toward the mirror to look at his face. His cheeks, chin and upper lip were peppered with stubble.

"Check out *that* one." Ray pointed to one of the results.

"How to shave your ass hair?" Kunal looked at Ray. "Seriously dude? Learn your anatomy."

"I know anatomy, but it said it had pictures."

Ted looked at Ray's reflection. "I'm not shaving my ass."

"I found one with multiple steps *and* pictures." Kunal scrolled through the web page. "It's rated pretty high. You want the overview?"

"Go."

"It says to trim your hair to a quarter inch or less first." Kunal read a bit further. "Avoid trimming the underside of your cock. Nicks there are painful."

"No shit," Ted said. "And don't call it my *cock*."

Ray laughed. "What else are we going to call it?"

"I don't know. Call it by its proper name. When you call it my *cock*, it feels like I'm in some weird porno."

Ray and Kunal looked at each other and shrugged.

"Whatever you say, dude." Kunal read further. "You can sit on the floor, the toilet, or stand, but they recommend lying on your back." He looked at the limited floor space covered in gray and white tile. "You might be able to do that but it'd be a tight squeeze."

"What's next?" asked Ted. His patience was wearing thin and he just wanted to get on with this bizarre task.

"Then it's like shaving your face." Kunal said, "Lather up and go to town, but use as little pressure as possible and make sure the skin is pulled tight. Follow with some aftershave."

"What if he gets a hard-on?" Ray was legitimately interested.

"They actually mention this." Kunal scrolled to the relevant section of the web page. "It says here that it can help keep the skin tight."

"Awesome." Ray pumped his fist. "Want me to find you some porn videos?"

Ted shook his head. "I'm good."

Ray looked up at Kunal. "What do they do when you pop wood at the spa?"

"They work around it... but remember, I wax," Kunal

said. "Shaving is something completely different and I have to say, you got balls, dude. I'd never intentionally bring anything sharp near my twig and berries."

"Thanks for the vote of confidence." Ted picked up the razor/trimmer combo. "I think I got it."

Ray and Kunal stared at the towel obscuring Ted's crotch.

"You guys can go now." Ted waved his hands at them.

"I'll leave your phone, just in case you need it." Kunal placed Ted's phone on the bathroom counter next to the sink.

Ray and Kunal shuffled out of the bathroom. "Good luck," Kunal said just before he latched the door closed.

"Thanks."

Now that Ted was alone, he dropped his towel. *I look pretty good,* he thought. His pubic area seemed more densely populated with hair than he remembered from his shower.

He grabbed the trimmer end of the razor and turned it on. It buzzed and vibrated in his hand.

"Here goes nothing." Ted shaved a swath through the hair above his penis. It left a white corridor across his abdomen. Ted couldn't help but think of mowing the lawn when he was a kid.

The tuft of shaved hair floated down to the tiled floor and began to spread, carried on the air currents.

"Damn." Ted crouched to collect the bits of hair and managed to throw most of them into the waste basket. Many short strands of hair remained stuck to his fingers no matter how hard he tried to shake them off. He positioned the basket between his legs and continued with the trimmer.

In a few minutes, most of the long, curly hair was gone, neatly deposited in the waste basket. Ted ran his hand across his newly stubbled crotch. It was weird to feel prickly stubble between his legs.

Ted popped the top off the shaving cream, squirted an ample portion into his palm and scooped some of it into his other hand. He was about to apply it when a knock sounded behind him.

"You okay in there? Need someone to polish your wood?" Ray guffawed behind the door.

"Thanks for caring, Ray." The distraction caused Ted to doubt the next step. With his hands occupied with shaving gel, he used his knuckles to key in his phone passcode, but even taking great care, Ted managed to smear the display with gel. Bits and strands of pubic hair still stuck to his hands transferred to the display. He tried to wipe the hairs off with the back of his hand but ended up making the mess worse. "Ugh."

Ted read and scrolled. When he was ready to continue, he lifted his right leg onto the counter, with his right foot in the sink in order to expose his sack. His thigh cramped like a sharp spear had been thrust through his muscles.

"Shit!" He had no choice but to lower his leg again.

He sat down on the edge of the closed toilet. This was a good position but his body cast a shadow on his work area. He turned his body sideways, which was a good compromise.

He applied the shaving gel to his sack and partially up the shaft of his penis. The stimulation caused tell-tale feelings of an impending erection, so he backed off. Rock hard was the last thing he wanted to be right now.

Ted grabbed the razor and glided it across his abdomen as a trial run, much like he had begun with the trimmer. He ran his fingertip along the smooth track of skin that was left behind. No stubble to be found.

Ted smiled. *This is going to be easier than I thought.*

RAY AND KUNAL sat on the couch, playing *Doom* on Ted's xBox. Ray had the chainsaw and was making short work of any demon he encountered. The game's heavy metal hellscape, the floor, walls and ceiling, were covered in blood.

"Do you think *Doom* was worth waiting ten years for?" Ray said as he bisected a demon in a shower of bloody flesh and skin.

"A year ago I'd have said no, but this is *awesome*." Kunal presented his hand and Ray handed the controller to him. "Let me show you how it's done."

Kunal guided Doomguy through a maze of catwalks and tunnels, slaying demons with a vast selection of weapons.

"What the hell is taking him so long?" Ray looked at his watch. "He's been in there for...over twenty minutes. Do you think I should knock again?"

"Give it a rest, dude." Kunal carved a demon in two with his chainsaw. On the screen, bloody gore flew everywhere. "He'll be done when he's done."

Ray looked back at the hallway leading to the bathroom. "The suspense is killing me."

"If it's anything like getting waxed, it takes time to get it right." Kunal pumped the buttons on the xBox controller. "You should try it some time and surprise Vivian."

"You think she'd like it?"

Kunal paused the game and shot a tilted look at Ray. "Not to get too personal, but do you go down on her?"

"Uh, yeah."

"Do you like a mouthful of pubes?"

Ray grimaced. "No."

"Who does, really?" Kunal shrugged. "If she doesn't like it, your hair will grow back."

Kunal could see the gears moving in Ray's head as he considered "going bare down there."

A loud shriek echoed through the condo. Alarmed, Buster poked his head up from his dog bed, alert and ready for action.

Ray's eyes bugged out. "What the hell was that?"

"I'm more concerned about why." Kunal dropped the xBox controller and bolted toward the hallway, Ray and Buster following close behind.

Kunal knocked on the bathroom door. "Dude? You alright in there?"

"What if he sliced his dick open and he's bleeding out?"

Kunal backhanded Ray's shoulder and lowered his voice. "Jesus, Ray. Don't say shit like that."

They both placed their ears to the door to try to gain clues. "Ted? Dude?"

Ray's eyes darted as his brain tried to decipher what he was hearing. "Do you hear heavy breathing?"

"Yeah." Kunal grabbed the door handle and knocked again gently. "Ted? We're coming in. Make yourself decent." He opened the door until Ted's leg blocked its swinging arc.

Ted lay on the floor flat on his back, a towel stained red in a few places collected over his crotch. Crimson drops and bloodied tissues lay scattered around him.

"Whoa." With Ted bleeding and sprawled out in front of Kunal, he couldn't help but be reminded of the gory mess they were making on the xBox in the other room. Ted's situation was tame by comparison, but what made it worse was that it was *real*. "What the hell, dude?"

"Is he dead?"

Kunal hit Ray again and glared at him.

Ted opened his eyes and shifted his gaze between Kunal and Ray. He began to shake his head almost imperceptibly. "Aftershave? Is that web site FUCKING SERIOUS?" Ted's eyes slid shut again. "No respect..."

Kunal looked around the bathroom, at a momentary loss for words. Buster poked his head between Kunal's legs. He bent down and grabbed his collar.

"It's not as bad as it looks," Ted said, his breathing normalizing.

"I don't know. It looks pretty bad."

Ray stepped out from behind Kunal. "What happened?"

"Everything was going great until I nicked the skin in a couple places." Ted propped himself up on his elbows and scanned the bathroom. "I made quite a mess."

"Do you need to go to the hospital?"

"No," Ted said. "The bleeding's stopped, thank God. But it feels pretty raw down there. The aftershave didn't help. It might have made it worse." Ted collected the bloodied tissues and tossed them in the waste basket. "Thanks guys, I'll take it from here."

"Okay." Kunal began to close the door, pausing half way. "If you need anything..."

Ted gave a thumbs up.

Kunal brought Buster back to his dog bed, then joined Ray in the living room. *Doom* on the xBox was freeze-framed on a blood-soaked parapet.

Kunal grimaced. "Let's play something else."

Ray flipped through Ted's limited selection of games. "Grand Theft Auto?"

"Not enough time," Kunal said.

"The Walking Dead?"

"God, no."

"Limbo?" Ray held up the game and scrunched his brows. The art on the cover was dark, moody and full of shadows.

"Great game, but no."

Ray flipped through the games in rapid succession. "He doesn't even have Super Mario."

"That's Nintendo."

"Oh yeah." Ray pulled out *Need for Speed*. "How about this?"

"Perfect." Kunal picked up a controller.

As Ray loaded the game, Ted poked his head out from the hallway. He had a towel around his waist, stained red in patches. "Disaster averted. I'm going to get dressed."

"Thanks for the update, Scroaty McScrotumson," Kunal called back.

But disaster had not been averted and Ted was unknowingly heading toward it at full speed.

A SHORT WHILE LATER, Ted joined Kunal and Ray back at his sofa. He wore black dress pants, socks to match and a deep blue button-up shirt. Iris had once said the color reminded her of a cloudless Colorado summer sky. Plus it was a power color, Iris had added. Ted just liked blue and the fabric felt good on his skin.

What didn't feel good was in the front of his underwear. His newly shaved pubic region itched more than it was sore. It itched like crazy. Ted had tried a sprinkle of talcum powder and even a small amount of calamine lotion, all without long-lasting success.

Kunal and Ray continued to play *Need for Speed* and raced their high-performance cars through a digital city that looked a lot like Los Angeles. Ted sat next to them, not paying much attention. Instead, he tugged at the crotch of his pants, trying to relieve the burning itch in his underwear. There was a heat to the itch too, like someone was holding his nuts to a hot iron.

Kunal cast a quick glance at Ted. Discomfort was written all over his face. "How do you feel?"

Ted looked at his silver Seiko Monster, a gift from Iris two birthdays ago. She had said it was "affordable luxury." All he cared about was if it could keep accurate time.

"Apart from it feeling like a colony of ants have moved into my underwear and my date starting in less than an hour, I feel great," Ted said. "Perfect."

"Do you think Iris will like your new 'buzz cut?' " Kunal asked, almost as an afterthought.

Ted stood and went to grab his sports coat, scratching madly at his crotch as soon as he was out of sight line of the guys.

"Wait, *are* you back together with Iris?"

Ted remained tight-lipped as he rummaged through the hall closet.

"Holy shit." Kunal set his controller down, crashing his car, and nudged Ray with his elbow. "It's not Iris, is it?"

"What?" Ted evaded the questions with ease. The feeling of fire ants crawling over his balls overrode most of his rational thought.

Kunal twisted his body on the sofa to watch Ted preening in front of the mirror off the hallway. "Your date isn't with Iris, is it?"

Ted looked at Kunal's reflection in the mirror. The jig was up and he didn't have the mental energy to concoct a story. "No."

Ray's eyes went vacant for a moment and his pupils expanded. He set his controller down too and turned toward Ted, a lascivious grin already on his face. "Is it bikini-girl?"

"Look," Ted said. "It's just someone I met at the doctor's office. I'm not going to put my life on hold just because Iris won't talk to me. At least I've made an effort."

"Dude!" Kunal smiled and nodded, clearly impressed. "I didn't think you had it in you."

"The night's not over yet." Ted shifted his hips to try and alleviate the itching.

"I miss those bikini bottoms." Ray set his chin in his left hand and slipped into a dreamy gaze, not looking at anything in particular. "Do you still have them?"

"No, Ray. We're not going there again." Ted smoothed out his sports coat. "And I got to go, so you guys need to go too."

Kunal hopped off the couch. "Come on, Ray. We got a date with *Grand Theft Auto* and tequila shots at my place."

Ray followed. "Hooker edition?"

Kunal shook his head and hooked a thumb back at Ray. "Mister One-track-mind, here."

Ted gave Buster's head a scratch and locked his door.

"Good luck." Kunal patted Ted on the back as all three walked toward the elevator. "We want deets later."

"*All* the deets," Ray said.

During the elevator ride down to the parkade, Ted could feel beads of sweat break out along his hairline. The itch in his crotch was excruciating. It took every fiber of his being not to scratch.

If a thirty-second elevator ride is like this, how the hell am I going to survive tonight? Ted pushed the thought out of his mind.

He waved goodbye to Kunal and Ray in the main lobby, then carried on down to the parkade. He slid behind the wheel of his SUV. Nothing was going to stop his date with Casey, but the future had other plans.

Dinner

THE DRIVE TO pick up Casey found Ted rubbing the front of his pants at every opportunity. Red lights were most difficult. Drivers who stopped next to him at an intersection, either on the right or left side of his SUV, might think he was doing something obscene. Ted paused his attempts at relief until the lights turned green again.

It was a twenty-five minute drive north to Casey's apartment building in Portsmouth. It was a simple-looking building, not memorable in any way except for horizontal lines of brick of a slightly lighter color, randomly distributed over the building's four stories.

Ted parked on a side street and walked back to the building's entrance. In front of him in a panel built into the wall were rows of buzzers for each apartment.

Shit, Ted thought. *I still don't know Casey's last name.* He pulled out his phone and texted his arrival instead. *Technology saves the day.*

Ted's phone chimed. "Be right down. xo," the phone's display read. He smiled and looked at the single red rose in his other hand, one he had purchased from a roadside stand along the way. He had carefully snapped off all the thorns.

Ted slipped his phone back into his pocket and took an opportunity to discreetly scratch his balls.

Ted had been facing the street when Casey unlatched the lock on the front entrance and stepped out into the evening sunshine. He spun around and was captivated by the gorgeous and graceful woman that stood before him.

I'm the luckiest son of a bitch on the planet, Ted thought.

Casey had her fiery hair half tied back in a braid, much like how her hair was when he first met her, but the braid was woven tight and neat. Her makeup was understated and fresh. Small silver hoops hung from her ears, a tiny silver Mickey Mouse hanging from one hoop and Minnie Mouse clutching the other. A white form-fitting baby-doll t-shirt, a pleated khaki skirt with the hem riding a couple of inches above her knees and a pair of impeccably clean white runners completed her ensemble. A small black leather purse with a string strap hung over her shoulder. Comfortable and classy, Casey looked ready for anything.

"Is that for me?" Casey motioned toward the rose in Ted's hand.

Ted stood wordless, his brain temporarily forgetting the rose, his unsoothable itch, and even why he was there.

Casey looked into his eyes. "Earth to Ted."

"Oh! Uh, yes." Ted handed the rose to Casey.

"That's very sweet of you." Casey held the rose under her nose, closed her eyes and took in the flower's delicate fragrance. "Thank you."

Ted scrunched his brows. "Your glasses."

"You noticed." Casey smiled sweetly. "I wear contacts too. On special occasions."

"With or without glasses, you look beautiful, Casey."

"You don't look half bad yourself, mister." Casey grinned and flashed her lashes at Ted, even as a light flush rose in her cheeks.

Ted held out his arm. "Shall we?"

"We shall." Casey hooked her arm with Ted's and together they walked to his SUV.

During the walk back, Ted's nether regions woke up. The itch was back with a vengeance.

I can ignore it, he thought.

Ted opened the passenger door of the SUV and helped Casey in. As he walked behind the vehicle to the driver's side, he slowed his steps and rubbed himself fiercely. For any onlooker, he must have looked like he was trying to tame an unexpected erection. Ted hopped into the driver's seat and closed the door.

"Where are we going?" Casey asked.

"Do you like Italian?"

"I like anything," she said. "And I'm starving."

Ted started the SUV. "I know a place I think you'll like."

Traffic was surprisingly light this evening. They had been driving for less than fifteen minutes before Ted rolled up to the curb in front of The Garlic Rose Bistro.

"Ever been here?"

Casey shook her head as she looked out the windshield at the front of the restaurant. The sun was dipping its way to the horizon. The sky began to take on a warm glow, tinting the restaurant's front windows in orange light.

"You'll love it. The calamari is to die for." Ted stepped out of the SUV and ran to the other side to open Casey's door for her.

She took Ted's hand and stepped out onto the street. Sweet smells of garlic, baked bread, tomatoes, basil, and cheese flooded Casey's nose. "It smells so good."

"It tastes even better." Ted plugged the parking meter and offered his arm again, which Casey took again.

The inside of the bistro was packed with people enjoying good food and conversation. The air was warmer, thicker, and carried the same scents as outside, only stronger. A waiter directed Ted and Casey to their reserved table by the front window, offering views of the busy street life. He left two menus on the table.

Ted seated Casey first, then himself. "This is one of my favorite spots. It's good to be back."

Casey looked around. "It's cozy. I might even say it's romantic. When was the last time you were here?"

Ted shook his head. "I can't remember. Maybe a year?"

"Why so long?" Casey studied Ted with her vibrant green eyes. She detected a hint of discomfort in his body language.

"You know, life gets busy." Under the table, Ted grabbed at his crotch. Nothing could quench the itching fire between his legs, so he decided to try and ignore it. He forced a smile, picked up his menu, and looked around the restaurant. "But I'm back now, with a lovely woman, too. Life couldn't be better."

Casey reached across the table and touched Ted's hand lightly. "You're sweet."

The waiter presented himself again. "May I get you some drinks to start? We have a house Chianti that goes well with most everything on our menu."

"Club soda for me." Casey looked at Ted, surprised. "Boring, I know. But I'm designated driver and all."

The waiter turned his attention to Casey. "And for you, miss?"

"The Chianti sounds nice, but I'll have a Coke." She smiled at Ted. "I guess we're the boring table."

"Not at all," said the waiter. "I'll be back in a couple of minutes to take your order."

Ted scanned the menu. "Any appetizers leaping out at you?"

"You're the expert. What's good?"

"Can't go wrong with calamari and aioli."

Casey crinkled her brow. "Remind me what aioli is?"

"It's a garlic dipping sauce," Ted said. "Garlic and olive oil blended together."

Casey nodded. "As long as we're both eating it, I'm game."

"Both? What do you…" Ted watched Casey tilt her head and send him a playful grin. "Oh."

"That's a lovely shade of red on your cheeks."

Ted laughed. "It goes with the tomato sauce of my main course."

"Oh!" Casey cast her eyes back to her menu. "What are you having?"

Ted pointed out his choice on Casey's menu. "Melanzane al forno. My favorite. Roasted eggplant, mushrooms, and cheese in a creamy tomato sauce."

"That sounds good, but I'll get something different so we can taste test." Casey looked over the menu, the tip of her tongue poking ever so slightly from the side of her mouth and resting on her pink lips. Ted found the gesture both endearing and alluring, as he was finding everything about Casey. It was a welcome distraction from the inferno in his underwear.

"Okay. I think I know what I'm going to have." Casey showed the menu to Ted. "The linguine con frutti di mare. I'm sticking with a seafood theme."

"And garlic."

"You're definitely going to have a bite."

"As you wish."

When their orders arrived, they ate slowly, their fun conversation helping to distract Ted from his discomfort. The calamari was fresh and delicious, as were both of their entrées.

Ted cut up his meal and ate it using only a fork. He kept his free hand below table level and resting near his crotch, ready to quench his need for a scratch at moment's notice. Casey held Ted to his word and they shared bites of each other's meals. By the end of the main course, both were steeped in the essence of garlic.

As TIME PASSED, Ted found it easier to ignore the hellfire in his underwear, but he still had to shift uneasily in his seat from time to time. Casey didn't seem to notice, or so Ted thought.

Mid-way through sharing cannoli for dessert, their conversation unexpectedly turned south, below the belt line.

"So I'm sitting there at work one day, greeting patients, and there was this guy…" Casey leaned in across the table and hushed her voice, looking side to side for potential eavesdroppers. "This guy just whipped it out and started masturbating. Right there in the waiting room. Can you believe it?"

Casey picked up a cannoli and bit into it, jettisoning

drops of creamed ricotta cheese out the other end and onto her plate.

The visual triggered an image of Ted's most recent episode with Ray. A small shiver of repulsion zipped up the back of his neck. "Actually, I can."

"Oops." Casey began to giggle. She scooped up the runaway sweetened cheese filling with a spoon and presented it to Ted.

He shook his head and tapped his stomach. "No thanks. I'm full. So what happened next, dare I ask?"

"Security took him away, but we had to steam clean the carpet."

"It's always good to leave your mark on the world."

They both laughed. Ted squirmed a little in his chair.

"Are you okay? You seem…fidgety."

"I'm fine." Ted's sack screamed otherwise. "I'm just a little nervous, I guess."

Casey smiled and reached across the table to touch Ted's hand. A brief touch. "You're a sweet guy. Do you want to go?"

"Yes please. And I've got this." Ted raised his hand and signaled the waiter. "Check please."

After paying, Ted and Casey collected their belongings and walked to the front entrance.

Ted hooked his thumb towards a short hallway nearby. "I need to visit the men's room. I'll be right back."

"I'll be here." Casey dug a compact out of her purse and began to refresh her makeup in the floor-to-ceiling mirror next to the entrance.

The bathroom offered one stall and one urinal. Ted tried the stall first, finding it occupied. He settled for the urinal.

He unzipped his pants and plunged his hand into his underwear to scratch. The relief was glorious.

"Oh yeah. That's the stuff." Ted continued to scratch, breathing heavily. From behind, an onlooker would have thought Ted was pleasuring himself.

The stall toilet flushed and a large bearded man emerged, headed for the row of sinks. He weighed at least three hundred pounds. Dense, black chest hair sprouted just below his collar bones and grew thicker as it flowed down under the "V" of his button-up shirt. He gave a curious glance at Ted standing at the urinal as he began to wash up.

Ted zipped himself up and moved in front of the adjoining sink. He casually met the large man's gaze.

"Razor burn."

The large man nodded in understanding. It was like an unspoken guy code.

"Been there, bro. Common mistake. Aloe vera is good for that."

"Thanks."

The large man turned off the tap and turned to Ted. "The first time I shaved my balls, I didn't trim first. Big mistake."

"Oh?" Ted wasn't prepared for an in-depth discussion on the nuances of manscaping.

"That's what you did, right?"

"Uh, yeah. I guess so."

"And now you itch somethin' fierce. Am I right?"

Ted nodded as he rinsed his hands and headed for the paper towel.

"Damn, I remember that itch. Christ on a cracker! It was

like I was covered with creepy crawlies." The man directed his eyes toward Ted's crotch. "That what you're feeling?"

"Pretty much."

"I'm a regular pro at it now. Silky smooth," the large man said. "Want to see?" The man began to tug at his belt.

"Nope." Ted made a line to the exit. "That's okay, man. I'll take your word for it."

"Hey, remember. Aloe's your friend," the man called out from inside the men's room.

Ted waved him off and rejoined Casey. He pushed open the front door of the Garlic Rose for both of them, and followed Casey out into the warm summer air.

"What was that all about?"

Ted shook his head. "I don't know. Some guy rambling about something. Let's go."

TED ESCORTED CASEY into the passenger seat of the SUV. As soon as Ted sat down behind the steering wheel, he felt the itch begin to rise again. He started the engine and pulled out into the street. "What would you like to do next?"

"I don't know. What do you want to do?"

Ted shrugged. "We could go for a walk along the Willamette, or catch a movie."

Casey's eyes went wide with enthusiasm. She straightened her posture and turned to face Ted. "I got an idea."

"I'm all ears."

She tilted her head slightly. "You up for some excitement?"

Ted cast her quick glance. "What did you have in mind?"

A devilish grin crept across Casey's lips. "You'll see."

Ted stopped at a traffic light. "What have I gotten myself into?" He looked at Casey, smiled, and leaned toward her but hesitated as thoughts of Iris competed for attention. Ted brushed his guilt aside and followed through, moving to plant a kiss on Casey's cheek.

At the last moment, Casey turned to face Ted and their lips locked. The softness of her lips on his did not go unnoticed. They felt softer than Iris's ever had.

It was a good first kiss, one both would remember.

The stop light turned green. A honk from the car behind brought them both out of their blissful moment.

"To be continued," Ted said.

"Now don't get a girl's hopes up." Casey winked, then directed her attention ahead. "After two blocks, make a right turn."

"Where are we going?"

"Are you having a good time?"

"The best." It was true. Despite the pervasive itch in his nether region, Ted couldn't remember the last time he had enjoyed himself like this. "But where—"

"Oh, you'll see." Casey vibrated with anticipation. "I haven't done this for years!"

Casey directed Ted through a seemingly random series of left and right turns. He tried to guess the final destination, but was thwarted every time Casey added a new direction.

One final turn revealed the answer: Jay Jay's Crystal Palace. Ted looked up at the building's sign, the words "Jay Jay's" blinking in alternating red cursive neon lettering. "Crystal Palace" followed in capital letters, lit by cycling marquee lights. The entrance was protected by an overhanging roof lined with flashing rainbow neon and both steps and a ramp led up to the double doors. The parking lot to one side of the building was packed.

"This is it!" Casey said. "The best roller skating rink in Portland."

A flash of panic shot through Ted. "I can't roller skate."

"Don't worry. I'll teach you." Casey's reassurance did little to ease Ted's mind as he turned into the parking lot to search for a spot.

"We would have been better off parking on the street."

"Ye of little faith," Casey said as she scanned the lot for open spots. "There! See, I told you we'd find one."

The vacant parking space was about as far from the front entrance as possible, sandwiched between a large 4x4 truck and a Caddy straight from the 1970s. It was a tight fit for the SUV, with barely enough room to open the doors. With a little squirming, Ted and Casey wriggled out of their seats and met at the back bumper. Ted took an opportunity to plunge his hands into his pockets and give himself a quick scratch.

Casey appraised Ted, from his black Brogues up to a grin that seemed just a little forced. But it wasn't enough to cause alarm bells to go off. The Crystal Palace beckoned.

"Come on." Casey held out her hand. "Let's go roller skating." Ted wrapped his hand around hers, soft and warm, and together they entered the vibrant electric oddity known to apparently everyone except him as "Jay Jay's."

"How did I not know about this place?"

"I guess you've led a sheltered life." Casey shifted her hand so their fingers meshed. It felt more intimate and Ted noticed. It felt right. "I've lived here my entire life, remember. My sisters and I used to come here every week when we were teenagers."

Casey paid their admission, including skate rentals, and they both stepped inside.

"It hasn't changed a bit." Casey took in her surroundings. "In fact, it's better than I remember."

The interior of Jay Jay's was just as vibrant and over the top as its exterior. The dark carpet was patterned with a combination of rainbow colored squiggles and small triangles over a black background.

To the left of the entrance was a wall of shelves housing the rental roller skates, all white and divided by gender and size. Next to that was a row of vintage upright video games. On the opposite side of the concourse Jay Jay's concession was doing brisk business selling everything from burgers, hot dogs and nachos, to milkshakes and ice cream sundaes. Seating, upholstered with the same style of fabric as the carpet, filled the center of the concourse.

Ted followed Casey to a bank of lockers where they stored their shoes and her purse. He pocketed the key.

"Let's go get our skates!" Casey ran ahead. Even though Ted felt apprehensive, Casey's enthusiasm began to rub off. He even felt a little less itchy. She beckoned with her hand. "Find your size."

On the floor in front of the roller skate rentals was a gray rug with red and blue foot shapes for men, women, and kids embroidered into it. Casey and Ted stepped onto the rug and found their sizes. The clerk handed them their roller skates and they sat down in the main concourse to put them on.

"This brings back so many good memories." Casey looked around the concourse and out onto the rink where groups of roller skaters were tracing a counter-clockwise path around the rink.

Ted tightened his laces. "What made you think of this place?"

"I don't know." Casey cast her eyes up and the tip of her tongue poked out of the side of her mouth, just like back at the Garlic Rose. "I haven't gone on a date for a long time and I guess this reminded me of being a teenager again."

"September" by Earth, Wind & Fire had just finished playing. A deejay seated in a booth in the corner of the rink queued up some Whitney Houston, a skating favorite. Cheers rose up from the rink.

"I want somebody to dance with." Casey smiled and stood, holding out both hands. "That somebody is you."

Ted looked up at her, dumbfounded by his luck, and stood, wobbling on his skates. Casey grabbed his shoulder and steadied him. "Who ever thought of putting wheels on shoes must have been nuts."

"They were a genius!" Casey guided Ted to the rink entrance. Multicolored lights illuminated the walls on the long sides of the rink and a slowly spinning mirror ball projected floating rainbow dots across the rink's hardwood floor. "I can't believe you've never gone roller skating."

"It was never on my radar."

"What about ice skating?"

Ted nodded. "Now *that* I've done, but it's been years."

"Good. Roller skating is a lot like that." Casey and Ted stood at the transition from carpet to hardwood. "Ready?"

"As I'll ever be."

The rink was buzzing with people, young and old. The lights on the walls and clustered around the mirror ball pulsed and changed color with the beat of the music.

Casey backed out onto the rink surface. Ted clung to the gate, waiting for a good time to join the throngs of circulating people. The perfect moment never seemed to come. There was always a skater who zoomed by at the last moment, rattling his nerves.

"There's no rush." Casey spun around and rolled over to him with an ease he wished he had. "Everyone starts at the bottom. Steady yourself on me."

Ted held his arms out and held onto Casey's shoulder with one hand.

"Put your feet in a 'V' shape," Casey said. Ted looked down at his feet and oriented them as instructed. "Now don't look at your feet again. Keep your eyes on me."

"Okay, that's easy." Ted grinned and winked at her. "Got that mastered already."

Casey returned his smile sweetly with one of her own. In the flashing colored lights, he couldn't tell if she was blushing or not. If the situation was reversed, he'd be sporting shades of scarlet, and that was good enough for him.

"Okay, now push to the side a little bit with one foot, then the other."

Ted pushed with his right foot, wobbled, and lost his balance for a moment. Casey grabbed him and he steadied himself. He tried again, this time maintaining his balance during the small push forward. Ted pushed with the other foot and moved forward a bit more. As he gained confidence and his skating legs, he was able to increase his speed a little.

Casey skated backwards ahead of Ted so she could face him. "That's all there is to it. It gets even more fun when you move to the beat of the music."

The deejay jumped a couple of decades ahead and began playing "Can't Stop The Feeling" by Justin Timberlake. Ted tried to match the rhythm of the music, but he wasn't moving his legs quite fast enough yet.

Casey let go of Ted's hands. "Bet you can't catch me!" She turned her body around and skated forward, but not so fast or far that Ted couldn't catch up. He increased his stride and picked up his pace, rejoining Casey in no time. She grabbed his hand and entwined her fingers with his.

"You're doing great! Want to go faster?"

"Normally I'd say yes, but…"

Casey pushed off and increased her speed. Ted tried to keep up but couldn't move his feet fast enough. Instead he opted to keep his feet together and roll in tow. He watched her legs work and her skirt ripple in her wake.

Soon, they were both flying around the rink, Casey smiling, laughing and swaying her hips to the beat of the music. Ted tried his best to look cool, even though he was terrified.

Casey looked over her shoulder. "Ready? One…"

"Ready for wh—"

They approached the curved end of the rink, their speed increasing, their arms stretched out and feeling the force of the turn.

"Two…"

She's going to slingshot me, Ted thought in horror. "Wait!"

"Three!" Casey let go of Ted's hand and catapulted him down the length of the rink. By a stroke of luck he didn't hit anyone, but Ted's luck ran out when he not only forgot to turn but didn't know *how* to turn.

Ted hit the side boards at the opposite end of the rink and flipped right over top and into the concourse.

"Oh, shit!" Casey put her hand to her mouth and giggled to herself. She skated to the boards where Ted had left the rink and looked down at him. He rubbed his head and grinned.

"Important question," he said. "How do I stop?"

"Give me your hand and I'll show you."

Ted gave her a wary look.

"I promise I won't catapult you." Casey grinned. "*This* time."

"Okay." He reached for her hand and Casey pulled him up.

"But that was fun, right?"

"Everything up to the impact."

Ted and Casey made their way back to the entrance to the rink and joined the other skaters. Ted moved slowly, but he took comfort in at least moving.

"There are lots of ways to stop, but the easiest for you is going to be the plow. It goes like this. Move your feet apart, wider than your shoulders." She demonstrated the motions as people flew by left and right. "Then angle your toes in. Your feet are going to want to come together, but keep them apart." Casey slowed to a stop and Ted bumped into her from behind.

"Oops. Sorry."

"You try." Casey turned and skated backward several feet. Ted worked his legs and began to move toward her a little faster. He pointed his toes in and felt the friction. He slowed, but didn't stop completely, this time meeting Casey face to face.

Ted reached out and Casey caught him. They both rolled toward each other until the space between their bodies melted away.

I want to kiss you again so badly, Ted thought, as his arms steadied himself on Casey's shoulders and then down to her waist. He smiled, his eyes warm as he locked gazes with her sparkling green eyes, and decided to wait.

"Looks like you got it."

"I think I do."

The next hour passed effortlessly. Casey showed Ted a few other ways to stop and they took turns pushing each other while squatting. Ted usually fell over but he didn't care. He was having too good a time. They both were.

"I think I'm ready for my first solo mission, Captain." Ted gave Casey a friendly salute.

The deejay cued up "Dancing Queen" by ABBA. The hem of Casey's skirt flipped around as she began to sway her hips and shoulders to the music.

"You mean queen, right?"

"Yes. That's right." Ted took an unbalanced bow. "I am ready, your Grace."

"I'm the dancing queen so I'll stay right here and watch."

"As you wish."

Ted pushed off and with every stride his speed increased. His confidence hadn't quite caught up, but being a little scared boosted his enjoyment. Soon he was at the opposite end of the rink and moving at a nice clip.

He looked over this shoulder and gave Casey a wave. She waved back, first calmly, then urgently.

She cupped her hands around her mouth. "Look out!" The sounds of ABBA and all the other skaters around him drowned her out.

"What?" Before Ted could react, he plowed into the back of an older woman, knocking her off her feet. They both fell to the floor, the older woman on top of him, cushioning her fall.

Casey pushed off and skated toward them both.

"Are you okay?" Ted got to his feet as quick as he could manage and offered his hand. "I'm terribly sorry, ma'am. It's my first time."

Whatever annoyance or anger the older woman had felt towards Ted dissipated when she laid her eyes on him. "I'll be okay, honey."

As Casey approached, she could see the older woman checking Ted out, head to toe and back. She smiled. The old woman had good taste in men.

"I'll be more careful next time, I promise."

The older woman waved him off. "I'll be fine." She saw Casey skate up next to Ted and sent her a knowing nod. "Save a dance for me, Casanova."

"Uh, okay."

Casey planted a kiss on Ted's cheek. "You make friends everywhere you go, don't you?" She grabbed his hand. "Let's skate, *Casanova*. And keep your eyes forward."

The pair rejoined the rest of the skaters and circled the rink. Every time they passed the concession, Ted caught the mingling smells of fast food and sweet confection. It didn't take long for his growling stomach to win out.

✂

TED AND CASEY sat at a table talking, both enjoying milk-shakes and sharing a large order of French fries. Michael Jackson's "Rock With You" played in the background.

Up until this point, Ted had almost forgotten about his southern discomfort. Now that roller skating was on pause for the moment, the itch began to wake up.

"Wait." Ted cocked his head. "Speleology?"

"It's the study of caves, the final frontier…on Earth that is." Casey took a sip of her milkshake. "Ever since I visited Carlsbad Caverns as a kid, I've been hooked. I'll finish my degree next year."

"The thought of millions of tons of rock over my head in an enclosed space kind of creeps me out."

"It does take a special kind of person. But the things I've seen…" Casey paused, as if she was having difficulty putting her thoughts to words. "It's so beautiful. It's like being on another planet."

Ted smiled, clearly impressed, and drank from his milkshake.

"What?"

"Dressmaker, roller girl, intrepid cave explorer. You ever stop being amazing?"

Casey took a French fry and crunched it. "I guess you're going to have to find out."

Ted studied Casey with easy eyes. "Want to get out of here?"

She nodded. "Read my mind." She took another couple of fries and one last sip of her milkshake.

They retrieved their belongings, put their shoes on and

returned their skates to the rental desk. On their way to the parking lot, Casey reached for Ted's hand and leaned into his shoulder.

Ted liked the direction things were going with Casey and wanted to take things beyond just being friends. But as much as he resisted it, Iris strayed back into his thoughts as he approached his SUV. Perhaps it was his guilt trying to fight its way to the surface. Spending time with Casey felt entirely different from the way his first few dates with Iris had felt. Iris ignoring his calls made his next decision so much easier.

Ted pulled out his keys and unlocked the doors of the SUV with the remote. He was about to open the passenger door for Casey when he took her face gently in his hands and kissed her for the second time. His pulled her close as his hands moved down her back and hers moved up his. Time stopped in the parking lot of Jay Jay's Crystal Palace.

"What took you so long?" Casey looked up at him with clear, emerald eyes.

"I'm a little rusty."

"Let's fix that."

They both hopped into the SUV.

TED AND CASEY stood in the elevator of his condominium building, ascending to the fourth floor. She held the rose he had given her earlier.

The itch was getting bad again and he tried to jostle things by just moving his hips. He had to be subtle because Casey was leaning in close.

"You know, I just realized we never talked about where we were going," Ted said. "I just assumed. We can go—"

Casey kissed him, then said, "It's okay. Your place is fine. But thanks for asking."

The elevator doors slid open to the fourth floor and the two of them strolled hand in hand down the corridor. Ted pulled out his keys and unlocked the door to his unit.

Ted spoke in hushed tones. "Buster's probably sleeping."

Casey saw Buster lying in his dog bed next to the door, one eye surveying their entrance. "Buster…the dog that stole my heart." She crouched and gave him a gentle head scratch. "He's so sweet."

Ted kicked off his shoes and threw his sports coat onto the dinner table. "My feet still feel like they've got roller skates on." He walked to the refrigerator and opened it. "Want a drink? Wine? Coffee?"

Casey stood and caught sight of Ted briefly rearranging his pants. "No, thanks." She slipped off her runners, dropped her purse next to them, and padded in bare feet up behind him, pressing her body into his broad back. She reached around with her arms and ran her hands across his chest, unbuttoning the top two buttons.

She pulled Ted around to face her and kissed him deeply. They both sensed each other's excitement through their clothes and shuffled their way over to the couch.

Ted ran one hand down Casey's back to her hips, where it took a detour to give himself a quick scratch.

Casey opened her eyes. Her light red lipstick was now evenly spread across both her face and Ted's. The sight made her happy, but she had other things on her mind.

"What's going on down there?" she asked with an inquis-itive grin.

"Down where?"

"Down where…" Casey gave Ted a sideways look, stepped back and pointed down. "Down there."

"Oh that." Ted had no words.

"You've been squirming all night. Don't think I haven't noticed."

"Well…"

"Just be honest with me."

Ted felt the heat of passion being replaced with the warmth of embarrassment. "Truth is, I've never shaved before…down there." He managed half a smile. "Let's just say my hand isn't as steady as I thought it would be."

Casey flashed her eyebrows and her eyes widened. "You shaved tonight? For me?"

"Apparently it's the 'in' thing for a guy to shave for a lady."

"Really? That's very sweet." Casey placed one hand on Ted's chest, feeling the divide between his pectoral muscles. "Presumptuous, but sweet." She turned and headed for the door.

"No, wait." Ted had visions of the date derailing into disaster. "I didn't mean it like that. I just wanted to be…"

Casey grabbed her purse and dug into it, retrieving a small squeeze tube.

"…to be prepared." Ted looked at the tube. "What's that?"

"Hand lotion. It's got aloe vera in it."

Aloe vera. Ted had a short-lived flashback of the large man at the Garlic Rose. A shiver ran up his back.

Casey loosened Ted's belt and unzipped his pants without taking her eyes off his. She squirted some lotion into her palm.

"This is going to be a little cold at first, so try and relax." Casey reached down into Ted's underwear and slid her hand under his balls. The coolness of the lotion was actually a relief as she worked it in.

Casey raised her eyebrows in surprise. "You did a nice job. Feels like a raw chicken breast."

"You sure know how to woo a guy."

"You don't work next to a urologist without picking up a few tips." They both laughed.

Casey pressed her body against Ted's as they moved back toward the couch.

"I am so turned on right now," Ted said.

"I noticed."

Ted kissed Casey hard and eased her down onto the couch. She kissed him back, bracing herself with her free arm until it slipped between a gap in the cushions.

Her hand ran through a piece of fabric that didn't feel like part of the couch. She pulled her hand from the gap. Ella's red and white striped bikini bottom hung from her thumb.

Casey removed her hand from Ted's underwear and sat up, her posture stiffening. She held the bikini bottom in front of Ted.

"I assume these aren't yours?"

Oh shit, Ted thought. He saw their perfect evening, both past and future, begin to disintegrate. "No, but I can explain."

Casey's playful, sexy demeanor disappeared, replaced with one of dead seriousness. "Do you have a girlfriend?"

"No…," Ted stammered. "Uh, I mean…kind of."

"You *kind of* have a girlfriend?" Color rose in Casey's cheeks, the color of anger instead of passion.

Ted's mind raced. He couldn't screw this up. "We're taking a break from each other."

Casey sat up. "What the hell does *that* mean?"

"It means we're probably going to break up."

"Probably?" Casey tossed the bikini bottom aside and wiped her hand off on the couch. "You mean you don't know?"

"No. We're going to break up. Definitely." The hole Ted was digging for himself kept getting deeper.

"Unbelievable!" Casey muttered to herself as she shook her head. "Why do I always pick the unavailable men?"

"I'm available! Really I am."

Casey stood up. "I think I better be going."

"No, don't go." Ted stood up to face her but she avoided his attempt at eye contact. "Casey, please stay."

"This has kind of killed the mood, don't you think?" She slipped on her runners and picked up her purse.

"We can just talk."

Casey looked at him, giving Ted the eye contact he was so desperate for. She could see Ted's words were genuine.

"I enjoy your company, Casey."

She sighed. "I do too, Ted. I really do. But the number one thing I can't stand in a guy is dishonesty."

"This is the first time it's come up," Ted said. "And I didn't lie."

"We went out together. We had a great dinner and the roller skating was the best time I've had with a man for a very long time." Casey paused to collect her thoughts. "But you did it all knowing that you weren't officially single."

"You're right," Ted said without hesitation. "How can I make this right?"

Casey shook her head almost imperceptibly. "I don't know if you can. But I'd suggest returning those *panties* to their rightful owner."

"They're bikini bottoms, not panties. And they belong to my next door neighbor…I mean her daughter." Ted's world opened up and began to swallow him whole. "Wait. She, uh…I was picking up Buster and…"

Casey watched Ted flounder, a man drowning in his own words. She almost felt a little sorry for him.

"She just changed into her clothes here. Honest. I mean she's *sixteen!*"

"Ted. Stop."

"What?"

"Stop talking." Casey gave him a longing once over. The evening could have played out so much differently. She looked down at Buster, sleeping through all the commotion.

Ted took one step forward, then stopped, defeated. His pants fell to his ankles in a heap.

"Look," Casey said. "I like you, Ted. And I'll give you the benefit of the doubt regarding your relationship status. But I can't be here right now."

"Okay," Ted nodded.

Casey opened the door and stepped into the corridor, then turned back toward him. "Call me later…but *only* if you're one hundred percent single. That's the only second chance you're going to get."

"I won't screw it up." Ted's pants impeded his shuffle toward the door. "I swear I won't."

Casey didn't answer. Instead, she walked to the elevator.

When the doors opened, she offered a small wave without a smile, stepped inside and disappeared.

"SHIT!" Ted slammed his door and engaged the deadbolt. He slid down the door to sit next to Buster and gave the dog's head a stroke. "You think I'm going to see her again, buddy?"

Buster closed his eyes and slept.

"I seem to ask you that question a lot." Ted let out a cleansing breath, and for the first time that evening, he noticed that he wasn't distracted by a burning itch below. "So aloe *does* work."

TED WAS UP early the next morning. He had hardly slept the night before, obsessing over how the evening had self-destructed. The last time he had seen Ella's bikini bottom was the day Ray exploded in his bathroom. It was the day before Iris walked out and told him to get new friends.

Who leaves their bikini bottom behind anyway? Ted thought. *A precocious and manipulative teenager, that's who.*

He filled Buster's bowl with kibble, took a quick shower, dressed and made coffee. It didn't take a lot of effort to determine that it must have been Kunal who had stuffed them between the cushions. Ray would have pocketed them, then done something disgusting to them.

Ted stood in front of the kitchen counter, sipping hot coffee. The bikini bottom was laid flat on the melamine surface. He set his mug down and picked up the bikini bottom, raising it up in front of him at arm's length. He examined it, noting its size.

"Jesus Christ, what was I thinking?" Ted imagined how bad it must have looked to Casey when she found them. He took another gulp of coffee, grabbed the bikini bottom and headed into the corridor, stopping at Ella's unit.

He knocked firmly, not caring if he woke anyone up. After a moment of silence, Ted knocked again.

"Okay…" an annoyed voice said through the door. "Hold up a sec."

That's got to be Ella, Ted thought, and wasn't surprised to see her pull open the door.

The surprise was on Ella's face instead. She had her hair pulled up with a bright pink jaw clip, and wore denim shorts and a loosely fitting t-shirt with the words "cute but psycho" written on it.

"Hey Ted…" Ella looked back into her apartment to see whether her mother was within earshot. "I mean Mr. Cooper. Why do you love early mornings so much?"

Ted said nothing. Instead he held up her bikini bottom.

Ella's eyes widened as she plucked them from Ted's hand. "You found them! I've been looking for them everywhere, for like, forever."

"Sure you have." Ted was fed up and Ella was a quick study.

"You didn't do anything pervy with them, did you?"

"You're welcome."

A voice called out from within the apartment. "Who's at the door?"

"It's just Mr. Cooper, Mom," Ella called back. "You know, from 408." She stuffed the bikini bottom into a front pocket.

Sheridan appeared beside Ella wearing a plush white bathrobe, the two sides forming a plunging neckline. She wasn't wearing much underneath as far as Ted could tell.

Sheridan was a tanning bed addict and even though she was around the same age as Ted, her skin appeared dry and wrinkled and was almost the same color as her brunette hair. The sash around her waist was tied loosely and Ted hoped it didn't fall open. He didn't want the situation to become any more awkward than it already was.

Sheridan squinted, working at her memory. "Ted, right?"

"Yeah."

She shrugged. "Ella's mentioned you before. The one with the dog."

"That'd be Buster."

"Mm-hm."

Embarrassed, Ella hid her face with one hand. "We've only lived next to him for, like, six years, Mom."

"Hey. Watch the attitude." It was clear that Sheridan wasn't into small talk. "What's up?"

Just returning your daughter's bikini bottom. "I, uh…" Ted's thoughts tripped up his words.

"Mr. Cooper just offered me a job at his coffee shop," Ella said.

Ted shot a quick glare at Ella. A devious smile spread across her lips and she patted her front jeans pocket just enough to draw Ted's eye. She mouthed the words "you owe me."

"Really?" Sheridan expressed genuine surprise.

"Uh, yeah." Ted avoided looking at Ella. His anger would have seeped through. "I'm anticipating a busy summer."

"That's great." Sheridan glanced at Ella. "I've been trying

to get her off her ass for weeks." She faced Ted again. "So when does she start?"

"I haven't done my staff scheduling yet. I'll let you know."

"Looking forward to it." Sheridan walked back into the apartment.

"No problem." Ted said as he walked back to his unit.

"Thanks, Mr. Cooper. I'm really excited about the job."

Ted opened his door part way. "I bet you are."

"How much will I get paid?" Ella asked across the corridor.

Ted glared at her. "Don't push your luck."

Ella crinkled her nose and smiled. It was a taunt and they both knew it. "Okay. Bye!" she said and closed her door.

I should have thrown the fucking thing away, thought Ted. Half of a bathing suit had nearly destroyed his personal life. He shook off his anger and began his day, a day that would be memorable for a much different reason than a red and white-striped bikini bottom.

Snipped

Ted stood in the bathroom and observed himself in the mirror. Beside his phone, in a white paper bag on the counter, was his "vasectomy preparation kit." An instruction sheet was stapled to it. He could hear Blanche's voice clear as day reminding him to bring it to his appointment.

He emptied the contents of the bag on the counter, revealing a tube of Polysporin, a pill container, some gauze, and a hermetically sealed plastic package with a compartment no bigger than his pinkie nail that contained six titanium clips.

He removed the sheet from the bag. The first instruction stated to shave around the procedure area.

Nailed that one…not, Ted thought. The good news was the itch was gone today, thanks to Casey's aloe vera lotion.

He read the second instruction: "Valium 10mg. Take one hour before procedure."

Ted picked up his phone and dialed Kunal. He answered on the second ring.

"Dude," Kunal said. "How's it hanging?"

"Fine." With his other hand, Ted picked up the Valium. "But it's about to get a whole lot better. Let's get this party started."

"All right! You won't be sorry." Ted could sense Kunal's smile through the phone. "Be there in fifteen."

Ted hung up and considered texting Iris one more time. Instead, he jammed his phone in his front pocket. He popped the top on the container of Valium and shook out the contents. He had expected one tablet to fall out, but three light blue tablets rolled into his palm instead.

Without thinking, he tossed all three into his mouth and washed them down with a glass of water. He returned the rest of his supplies to the bag and cinched the top with his fist. He carried the bag to the couch and sat down.

Less than twelve hours ago, Casey was on this couch, her hand on my...

Ted closed his eyes and drifted off, replaying the better memories of the past night.

A knock on the door brought both him and Buster out of their respective slumbers. Ted tried to focus his eyes, but everything swam in front of him like he was looking through rippling water. He slid off the couch and crawled toward the door.

"Dude?" Kunal knocked again. "You in there?"

Ted reached up and twisted the deadbolt. He sat on the floor and began to laugh.

Kunal and Ray stepped into Ted's condo. Buster perked up and chuffed at them.

"Oh shit." Kunal shot a concerned look at Ray and knelt in front of Ted. He gave his shoulders a shake, but got little response. He slapped Ted's face lightly. "Ted, you in there?"

Ted shot forward a thumbs up. "You got it, partner. Giddy up!"

Kunal opened the bag and took out the empty Valium container. "Dude, how much did you take?"

Ted stared at his extended thumb, moving it forward and back, trying to track it. "Buster wants a walk."

Kunal read the label on the pill container, then turned to Ray. "Looks like he took all three. Shit." He dropped the plastic container back into the white bag. "This might be more work than we thought. Help me get him up."

"He better not touch the beard." Ray sported a new Fu Manchu style mustache, the ends hanging two inches below his chin. "This cost me a fortune."

"If something happens, I'll buy you a new one," Kunal said, annoyed. "Now give me a hand."

Together, they slipped their arms under Ted's and raised him to his feet, but Ted wouldn't (or couldn't) lock his knees.

"Come on, Ted, dude. Straighten your legs." But Kunal's words went in one of Ted's ears and out the other. Exasperated, Kunal said, "We're going to have to drag him."

"Don't forget…take Buster for a walk." Ted turned to look at Ray and tried to tug on the ends of Ray's mustache.

"Sure thing," Ray said, his face playing keep-away from Ted's pinching fingers.

All three were almost out the door when Ted pointed at the paper bag on the floor. "My sack!"

Ray laughed at Ted's choice of words.

"Dude, come on! Grab it so we can go."

Ray ducked inside and plucked Ted's prep kit off the floor. "Did you lock the door?"

Ray stared at Kunal, his face a blank. "No. I don't have keys."

"Try his pockets."

Ray searched one of Ted's pockets and came up empty. He tried the opposite pocket and pulled out a mass of keys on a ring.

Ray sifted through the keys one at a time. "Shit, which one is it?"

Ted's head slumped forward as he looked down at his crotch. "Oh Casey, I love you."

"Casey?"

"Forget it. He's only going to be gone a couple of hours." Kunal checked his watch. "We're going to be late."

Ray pocketed Ted's keys and helped Kunal drag a completely relaxed and groggy Ted to the elevators. In all the commotion, no one noticed the door to unit 407 open just a crack, Ella taking in the entire operation.

✂

As Kunal wove his sedan in and out of traffic, Ted rambled nonsense in the back seat.

Ray sat in the front passenger seat and looked back at Ted. "He's completely trashed. It's like he's never been on Valium before."

"I remember taking it when I got snipped," Kunal said. "Knocked me on my ass but I don't think I was that bad."

Ted made a gun with his index finger and thumb and pointed it at Ray, clicking his thumb. "Gotcha, partner," he said, but it came out sounding like "pardoner."

Ted's head and eyes slipped down and he ended up staring at his crotch. He tugged at the waistband of his pants. "My boys need to be free."

"Shit." Kunal eyed Ted working his pants down off his hips. "Stop him."

Ray climbed between the front seats, exposing his butt crack to Kunal. He was wearing a red thong.

"Jesus. Can't unsee *that*."

Ray rolled into the backseat beside Ted. "What?"

"Nothing. Just deal with the strippergram. I don't think I can handle Ted high *and* nude."

"Okay, buddy," Ray said. "Pants back up. No need exposing yourself to the wrong people."

"But my boys." Ted spoke with heavy eyelids. "They want to feel the wind in their hair."

"You'll have plenty of time for that in a couple hours." Ray yanked Ted's pants back up. Ted protested vocally but didn't put up much of a fight.

Kunal turned into the parkade of the medical center, trolling for a free space. He wanted a space as close to the building as possible, but the lot was packed. With every slow, trundling pass, he moved farther from the entrance. He settled on a space near the back of the lot and hustled out of the sedan.

Kunal opened the passenger door and Ted flopped out on his back like a rag doll, a mad grin on his face.

Ted gazed at the sky. "I love clouds."

"That's great, dude. On your feet." Kunal grabbed Ted under his arms and slid him off the back seat. He grunted under Ted's relaxed weight.

Ray hooked his arms underneath to help. "Maybe I should try Valium."

"It would probably do you some good," Kunal said. "But it's addictive shit. I hear coming off it is worse than heroin."

"Viv would never go for it anyway."

The two guys pulled Ted out of the sedan and propped him up as Kunal engaged the door locks.

Ted twisted his head to look at Ray, then Kunal. "I love you guys. Have I told you that?"

"All the way here." Kunal rolled his eyes at Ray and they both laughed. "Now shut the fuck up."

"I mean it. I love you guys."

"We love you, too," Ray said.

"You ready?"

Ray grabbed one of Ted's arms and nodded. They half-dragged half-walked him through the parking lot toward the front entrance of East Portland Medical Center.

The three of them passed a young mother pushing her baby in a stroller. Ted leaned toward her before Kunal corrected his stance.

"I love you too!" The mother shared an awkward smile and hurried past. Ted's head lolled back. "And clouds. I love clouds. Look at that one…doggies. Buster! I need to take Buster for a walk."

"We got it covered, dude," Kunal said as he and Ray ushered a limp Ted through the front entrance.

"I love you, man."

KUNAL AND RAY escorted Ted into the shared office of Dr. Palmer and Dr. Neandross. A thick, red tape line on the carpet now divided the waiting room in half. A chair that straddled the line bore its own red dividing line across the cushion and seat back.

Blanche sat at the reception desk cutting sheets of paper into quarter pieces with a huge pair of scissors.

Ted leaned toward her. "Blanche, baby! Did you miss me?" He looked at the red tape on the carpet. "Love what you've done with the place." He turned to Kunal. "What'd I tell you? A totally smoking hot G-MILF."

Ray's ears perked up. "G-MILF?"

"Grandmother I'd like to—"

Kunal pulled Ted aside and spoke with hushed tones, but was clearly annoyed. "Dude, you need to be quiet."

"Name?" Blanche sat with her appointment book open, tapping her thick black pen on the paper.

"Ted Cooper," Kunal said. "I mean him…he's Ted Cooper."

Blanche found Ted's name and crossed him off with extreme prejudice.

Ray spotted Casey talking on the phone on the other side of the office. He tapped Kunal's shoulder. "Speaking of smoking hot, who's that?" He dropped Ted's arm and made a beeline for her.

Blanche cocked her head to the side, her rigid features expressionless. "Take a seat. Please."

"I shaved my sack just for you, Blanche."

Blanche stood and planted her hands on her desk, her arms straight and elbows locked. She hissed words through her teeth. "You will *sit down* and respect the other patients by keeping your mouth *shut*."

"Dude, let's go." Kunal directed Ted toward the chairs in the waiting area.

"I love you, Blanche."

Blanche sent daggers at Ted. "Not another word, you *heathen!*"

Kunal sat Ted down and spotted Ray across the office, staring at Casey over her desk.

"Snip, snip!" Ted whispered.

"Shut up, dude." Kunal looked at Blanche where she had resumed cutting paper into squares. "Did you see those scissors? Now don't move."

Ray leaned over Casey's desk like it was a bar counter. He flashed his eyebrows, smiled and puckered his lips, making smooching noises. His Fu Manchu mustache followed his awkward and inappropriate overtures. Casey refocused her attention to the caller on the phone.

Kunal approached Ray from behind and lowered his voice. "What the *hell* are you doing?"

Ray smiled dreamily. "Working my mojo."

"This isn't the time or place." Kunal grabbed the back of Ray's collar and pulled him back to the seats in the waiting area. Casey watched them go, then spotted Ted as the two guys parted and sat on either side of him. Ted sat repeatedly unbuttoning and buttoning his shirt.

"Working your mojo?" Kunal shook his head. "Spare me."

"What?" Ray glanced past Ted, settling on Kunal. "I'm overflowing with mojo."

"Dude, that mustache is a mojo killer," Kunal said. "And why am I always the one to remind you that you're married?"

"Ted?"

Ted looked up to see Casey standing in front of him. A warm smile filled his face. "Casey!"

Blanche's ears pricked up. She saw Casey's foot had crossed over the red tape into her half of the waiting room.

"What are you doing here?" Casey asked.

"You're so beautiful, Casey."

Ted began to slide off his chair but Kunal pulled him back. "It's his, you know…" He lowered his voice to a whisper. "His prostate."

Casey's eyes flicked from Kunal, to Ted's crotch, to Ted and back to Kunal. "It's not serious, is it?"

"Nah. Routine checkup. The doc prescribed a little Valium beforehand." He extended his hand. "I'm Kunal by the way."

Casey shook Kunal's hand firmly.

"You've already met Ray." Kunal studied her in a respectful way. Once someone got a taste of Ray's often disrespectful advances, it was easy to appear gentlemanly. "So you're Casey. Ted was talking about you and your date all the way here."

Casey blushed. "Oh God. What part?"

"All of it." Kunal chuckled. "Isn't that right, Ray?"

Ray flashed his eyebrows, grinned and made kissy-faces at Casey. He extended his hand, which Casey shook just as firmly as she did with Kunal, even though Ray presented as a little odd. If she had known what Ray did with those hands, she may have reconsidered.

"Nice grip," Ray said, winking, but not releasing her hand.

"Um, thanks." Casey's initial assessment of Ray being a little odd moved into wing-nut territory. "You can let go of my hand now."

"Overflowing with mojo, huh?" Kunal snorted to himself.

"Ted?" Dr. Palmer stood in the waiting room with a clipboard in his left hand. His right arm hung in a sling, with his wrist braced and wrapped.

Ted shot his right arm straight up as if he wanted to be picked to answer a question in grade school. "That's me!"

But even under the haze of Valium, he did register Dr. Palmer's injury and an inkling of alarm shot through the back of his mind.

If he can't use one arm, how is he going to…

Kunal stood and helped Ted to his feet. "Nice to finally place the face, Casey." They guided Ted across the waiting area to Dr. Palmer.

Ted looked back over his shoulder at Casey, the Valium still in full effect. "Casey! I love you. Please give me another chance."

Embarrassed, she looked around the waiting area. All the patients from both sides of the red dividing line were watching her every move. Those that were reading had dropped their books and magazines to take in the show.

Casey shrugged and offered a forced smile. She turned to make her way back to her desk, but was intercepted by Blanche, her leathery fingers wrapping around one of Casey's arms.

Blanche pulled her close. "You better pray for mercy on judgment day, you irreverent tramp." The smell of cigarette ash, strong mint, and something else floated out of Blanche's mouth as she spoke.

Casey felt her stomach lurch. "Is that…vodka on your breath? I'll bet Dr. Palmer would like to hear about that."

Startled, Blanche took a step back but held firm to Casey's arm. "You wouldn't dare."

Casey leaned in close. "Don't push your luck, bitch. You're the reason God invented the middle finger. Now, get your hands off me." She yanked her arm out of Blanche's grasp. "The Altoids do nothing, by the way."

Ted steadied himself on Dr. Palmer's left shoulder.

"Hey, Ted. Looks like you're feeling no pain already." The doctor looked over the notes on his clipboard. "They should call it vali-yummy, huh? You ready?"

Ted gave a "thumbs up" sign, then placed his thumb in his mouth.

"You got a fan club." Dr. Palmer looked at Kunal and Ray. "You all here to watch? I charge twenty bucks a head."

"What?" Kunal almost choked on his words.

Ted took his thumb out of his mouth, inverted it to a "thumbs down", and blew a raspberry.

Dr. Palmer laughed at Kunal's reaction. "I'm just bustin' your balls."

Ray pointed at the doctor's arm. "What's with the sling?"

"Too much gay clown porn," Dr. Palmer said.

Kunal and Ray shared an awkward glance. Even Ted furrowed his brow and looked at the doctor.

"I'm kidding! There were no clowns involved."

Kunal took a tentative step forward. "Ted, maybe we should—"

Dr. Palmer waved his clipboard. "No, seriously, I'm just saving my right arm for my golf swing. It won't affect the procedure, I promise." He nodded at Ray. "Hey, nice 'stache."

"Thanks." Ray elbowed Kunal. "See?"

"Dude, that's not a compliment."

"Shall we get started, Ted?" Dr. Palmer said. "I promise to be gentle."

"Okee dokee." Ted waved at Kunal and Ray. "See you guys later."

"Good luck," Kunal said.

Ted responded with another "thumbs up" as Dr. Palmer escorted Ted down the inner hallway to one of the examination rooms and closed the door.

Ted expected to see the room set up like an operating theatre, with the operating table covered with blue fabric and multiple overhead lights. Apparently he'd been watching too much television. Instead, the room looked almost identical to the room where he and Dr. Palmer had first spoken. On one side of the room sat a small metal examination table covered with a sheet of sanitary paper. Cabinets with rubber gloves, cotton swabs and other medical supplies were mounted on the opposite wall above a small but functional sink. In addition to the overhead fluorescent lights, there was one overhead light supported by a flexible arm, similar to what you'd see in a dentist's office. The walls were covered with the same posters showing cut-away illustrations of the urinary system, for both men and women. There was absolutely nothing memorable about the room, except for Dr. Palmer. But there was still something missing. The music.

"Drop your pants and underwear, but you can leave your shoes on." The doctor patted the examination table as he rolled a tray alongside with surgical tools laid out in an orderly fashion. "You get extra points if you're going commando." He took Ted's white bag and removed the titanium clips, placing them next to his other tools.

Ted loosened his belt buckle. "Gee, Doc. Aren't you going to buy me dinner first?"

"I don't know. Do you swing both ways?"

An awkward silence followed, which made disrobing even weirder. Dr. Palmer stepped to the sink to wash his hands as Ted dropped his pants and underwear, both bunched in a heap at his ankles. He planted his butt on the examination table, the paper crinkling against his skin, and swung his legs up. He cupped his hands over his crotch.

"Okay, now lie back." Dr. Palmer pulled rubber gloves onto his hands. "How are you feeling? Enjoying the Valium?"

"It was trippy, but I think it's wearing off a little." Ted laid back onto the examination table, keeping his hands over his genitals.

"You're going to have to move your hands to your side, or I can't give you a hand job…I mean I can't do my job." Dr. Palmer winked at him.

Ted hesitated, then let his arms fall to his sides, baring his manhood in all its shorn glory. This would make two people handling his private parts in the past twenty-four hours, but he couldn't bring himself to call it a personal best.

I hope Casey gives me another chance, Ted thought. "Where's the nurses?"

"Don't need them," Dr. Palmer said. "They don't call me 'Lone Wolf' for nothing. But if I did have nurses, they'd be sexy as hell with tits out to here." He extended his hands in front of his chest, like he was holding two imaginary melons. "You'd probably get a raging hard-on and that's a complication I don't want."

Ted passed the time by counting imperfections in the ceiling tiles. "You have a rich fantasy life, don't you Doc?"

"Keeps me sane."

Ted looked around the room and spotted the desktop music system. "Hey, where's the music?"

"Oh! Thanks for reminding me." Dr. Palmer turned to the

phone docked in the desktop speaker system. "Play ballsy music," he commanded.

The phone chirped and launched into the playlist. "Like a Surgeon" by Weird Al Yankovic floated out of the speakers.

"I have to ask if people want to listen to music now."

"You get complaints?"

Dr. Palmer shrugged. "People have no sense of humor."

"Maybe that's because you play Weird Al."

"It's a joke. Just trying to lighten the mood." The doctor swabbed Ted's sack and surrounding area with antiseptic and laid a stack of sterile gauze pads on his abdomen, just below his belly button.

"What's that for?"

"The gauze? For later."

"Later?"

"You're going to bleed." Dr. Palmer picked up a syringe of local anesthetic and began injecting it around the incision sites. Ted felt his crotch grow heavy and cool, like he was carrying dead weight between his legs.

"Bleed? How much?"

"Just a little bit."

"How much is 'a little bit?'"

"Hard to say." Dr. Palmer set the syringe back on his tray of tools and picked up what looked like a specialized pair of scissors. "Judging by the hack job you did shaving down here, I'd bet you're not the squeamish type."

Dr. Palmer palpated the skin and found his first incision point. He took the scissors and made the first cut with an audible *snip.*

"You feel that?" he said. "I'm in."

Ted's world faded to black.

"Ted? You with me?"

No response.

"I guess he was squeamish after all."

TED OPENED HIS eyes to Blanche placing pressure on his sack. His mind was clearer now and it raced in directions he didn't want it to go. Now three people had touched his nether regions in the span of a day. It was a record he hoped not to break ever again.

"Um, hello," Ted said. "I must have fainted."

Blanche stared at him with steely eyes and said nothing.

"Do you do this often?"

"The doctor had another procedure," she said.

"Did everything go okay?"

"Yes."

Blanche's fingers had long, purple manicured nails. They looked like claws, ready to rend and tear away the gauze and into Ted's functionally useless balls. Those nails were too close for comfort.

The music caught Ted's attention: "Got You By The Balls" by AC/DC. He smiled and said, "Appropriate choice of music, don't you think?"

"Rock and roll music is the devil's work."

"Oh, come on, Blanche. Relax. You'd like the lyrics." Ted nodded his head to the beat. "Have I kissed my balls goodbye, Blanche?"

She looked away and shivered with revulsion.

Getting under Blanche's skin was Ted's new favorite game. He cleared his throat and said, "Did you look?"

"What?" Blanche's eyes widened and her old, pallid skin flushed a light pink.

"You looked, didn't you."

Blanche huffed and diverted her gaze. "Lust is a deadly sin, and all sinners go to hell."

"Give it a rest."

"You must confess your sins and plead for forgiveness."

Ted propped himself up on his elbows. "Okay, we're done here." He tried to move but Blanche wouldn't let go of the gauze surrounding his sack. "Hey, are you going let go any time soon?"

Blanche reached for the tray of tools with her free hand, making sounds of unseen metal against metal between Ted's legs.

"What are you doing?" From Ted's vantage point, he couldn't see anything. "What is that?"

Blanche raised a hemostat up, handles first. To Ted, they looked like a large pair of scissors.

Ted panicked. "No no no. Okay, okay. I'll confess. Don't cut my balls off."

Blanche presented the hemostat to Ted, the removed pieces of his vas deferens clamped in its jaws. He nearly fainted again.

"It's standard procedure to provide proof of the vasectomy." For the first time since Ted awoke, Blanche smiled. *Grinned.* And there was a touch of evil in that grin.

"I wonder what Dr. Palmer would say about your *procedure.*"

Blanche's eyes narrowed and her face grew cold and hard. She removed her hand from the pile of gauze on Ted's crotch and threw the hemostat on the tool tray. She washed her hands and dried them off, all the while glaring at Ted.

"Get dressed and meet me out front." She opened the door, paused, then looked back over her shoulder. The creepy grin was gone, replaced with her now familiar scowl. "And make it quick."

Ted pulled on his underwear gingerly, then pulled his pants over top.

I should have worn sweatpants, Ted thought as he fumbled his way to the door.

✄

TED SHUFFLED OUT of the examination room towards the reception desk. His crotch felt three times larger than it appeared to be, like he had stuffed a softball into his underwear. He rounded the corner into the waiting room and spotted Casey at her desk on the far side of the office. Ted straightened his back and tried to look like he had just come from a routine checkup. His faithful friends stood up to greet him.

"Everything go okay, dude?" Kunal stepped forward to help him but Ted raised his hand, indicating he was okay.

"Yeah, I'm a free man," Ted said.

"You're a sinner." Blanche needled her eyes at him. "And sinners must repent...but..."

Blanche pulled out a piece of paper with a printed list of dos and don'ts. It was clear that she found it all distasteful.

"You can shower in two days," she continued. "No heavy

lifting, golf…" Blanche cleared her throat. "No vigorous *sex*…or *masturbation* for two weeks."

Ray leaned toward Kunal. "Is that *vigorous* masturbation or just regular?" Kunal elbowed him in response.

"Alternate between thirty minutes with an ice pack and five minutes squeezing your scrotum." Blanche strummed her purple fingernails on the desk.

"Did she show you?" Ray's eyes were alight with interest.

The image of Blanche's clawed hand on his crotch was still fresh in Ted's mind. He pushed it back amid a full body shiver. "More than you know."

Ray looked confused. "What does that mean?"

"Will you *shut up*?" Kunal said into Ray's ear.

"Here's a prescription for some pain medication…even though you don't deserve it." She placed the scrip on the desk and a small plastic lidded container next to it. "This is a specimen cup for your *semen* analysis in three months." Blanche shuddered with disgust. "Continue using condoms until then." She swallowed hard, like she was trying to suppress the urge to vomit. "Disgusting."

Blanche pushed the scrip and container across the desk towards Ted, trying not to touch it, as if it was tainted with disease.

"Thanks." Ted pocketed both items and leaned over the reception counter to get closer to Blanche. She rolled back in her chair slightly. "Why do you work here? You seem to hate your job and everyone here."

Blanch recoiled. "May God have mercy on your soul."

"Look. I may need to confess, but you know what you need, Blanche?" Ted paused for a moment but not long enough for her to respond. "A good *lay*. That's what you need."

Blanche's eyes went wide with mortification. Kunal and Ray shared a look of surprise and admiration.

"That's my boy," Kunal said to himself.

Casey spotted the three guys leaving and called over her desk. "Is Ted okay?"

Kunal stepped aside to address Casey as Ted and Ray continued down the hallway. "Ted's fine, but a little out of it. We're going to take him home."

"Oh. Okay." Casey tried to look down the hallway, but Ted and Ray had already moved out of her sight line.

"How do you know Ted, if you don't mind me asking?"

"We went on a date last night."

Kunal chuckled. "So you're the mystery woman! I had my suspicions after learning your name."

"What?"

"He wouldn't tell us who he was with last night." Kunal leaned a bit closer. "Usually he tells us everything."

"Well, it doesn't matter now because I found out he has a girlfriend." Casey looked a question at him. "He has a girlfriend…right?"

A warm, broad smile spread across Kunal's face. "You like Ted, don't you."

Casey stopped herself for a moment, as if considering the consequences of the words she wanted to say. "Yes, but don't tell him that, okay? I don't want to be the *other woman*."

"Oh, you're definitely not the *other woman*."

Casey furrowed her brow. "What are you talking about?"

"Sorry, did I say that out loud?" Kunal winked at her. "Look, I got to get going. I'll let Ted know you said hello." He turned to leave.

"Wait," Casey said. Kunal stopped and turned back. "Tell Ted I'll call him later."

Kunal nodded. "I'll do that. Nice to meet you." He headed down the hallway and out of sight.

Casey resumed work mode. Her smile dissolved when she spotted Blanche sending her an "evil eye" across the office. She rolled her chair over to her phone and dialed.

Blanche's phone rang. Casey turned in her chair to watch her answer. "Dr. Palmer's office. Blanche speaking."

"Thank you for middle fingers, God," Casey said.

Confused for a second, Blanche looked back at Casey to see her raise her middle finger, thrusting the gesture forward for added emphasis.

Blanche slammed the phone back on its cradle with anger and disgust. She turned her back to Casey and busied herself with the filing cabinet behind her chair.

Kunal joined Ted and Ray waiting at the elevator.

"What took you so long?" Ted cupped his crotch with his hands.

"I was talking to Casey."

"Oh Jesus. That's all I need right now."

"Take it easy," Kunal said. "Everything's good."

"What do you mean, *good?*" Ted gave Kunal a sideways look.

"Good as in she'll call you later."

"Oh." Ted blinked. "Okay. Thanks."

"No problem, dude. What are friends for?" Kunal patted Ted on the back.

"I'm hungry," Ray said, his Fu Manchu mustache fluttering with each breathy word. "Hungry and thirsty."

"No. Drugs first," Ted said. "I need drugs and fast."

Pulled Over

"Shit! I thought Walgreens was supposed to be open all day?" Ted stood in the lobby of East Portland Medical Center clutching his balls with both hands. The center's pharmacy was closed for the day. Ted looked at his watch. "It's not even five o'clock."

"Sucks to be you," Ray said.

"No worries. We'll hit another Walgreens." Kunal jangled his car keys. "Our chariot awaits."

The three made their way to Kunal's sedan, with Ted shuffling behind, barely keeping up. They piled in and Ted stretched out on his back across the entire length of the sedan's back seat.

"Let's hit Quinn's to celebrate!" Kunal said as he navigated to the exit of the parking lot.

"I'm down for that." Ray twirled the tail ends of his mustache. "How about you, Ted?"

"You forget about Walgreens already?" Ted closed his eyes and tried to block the pain. "Drugs first."

"Yeah, but what about after?"

"Sure. Whatever." Ted groaned and shoved his hands down his pants and into the front of his underwear.

Kunal drove as Ray faced the back seat. "You squeezing your sack, just like Blanche said?"

Ted took deep breaths and attempted to relax. "Bonus points for Captain Obvious."

"I hope people don't see you back there." Ray surveyed the traffic around the sedan. "Looks like you're jacking off."

"The only thing I give a shit about right now is drugs."

Kunal shot Ray a look. "Ease up on him, dude."

"What's it feel like?"

Ted cracked open his eyes and cast a tired look at Ray. "Imagine putting your balls in a vice…for an entire day."

"Oh." Ray contemplated the image. "So, it's not too bad, then?"

Ted shook his head. "What planet are you from?"

Kunal looked at Ted through the rear view mirror. "Vulcan. You know that," he said, smiling.

"You think so?" Ray said.

"No question." Kunal pulled into a Walgreens parking lot and killed the engine. "Give me the scrip."

Ted pulled one hand out from his underwear and fished the prescription out of his pocket.

Kunal grabbed it and hopped out of the sedan. "Back in a flash."

But a flash turned into five minutes, then twenty-five.

"What the hell's taking so long?" Ted rolled to one side and moaned.

"I can look in his glove compartment," Ray said in an attempt to be helpful. "Maybe he's got some Advil or something."

He punched the release on the compartment door and an avalanche of assorted items scattered across Ray's lap.

"Holy shit. Look at all this stuff." He began digging through it. "Dozens of condoms. I wonder how old they are? Gum…breath spray." Ray picked up a bottle of Astroglide. "Lube! Now it's getting interesting." He threw the pile of condoms back into the glove compartment, revealing a substantial vibrator on his lap.

"Pay dirt!" Ray picked up the sex toy and held it up for Ted to see. It was about a foot long, semi-transparent blue, and had a variable speed control on the handle. The sides were studded with evenly spaced bumps. Ray turned it on and cranked the speed to the maximum setting. The internals of the vibrator began whirring. "Shit, this is awesome."

Ted cracked his eyelids. "Put it away. You don't know where it's been."

"I have a pretty good idea." The gears in Ray's brain began turning.

"It's probably not sanitary."

"I don't know, man. There's a bottle of hand sanitizer here too."

"Just put it away." Ted closed his eyes again. "And *please* use the sanitizer. He's going to be back any moment."

As if Ted's words held magic, Kunal strolled out of Walgreens' exit doors, swinging a little paper bag by his side.

Ray scrambled to cram the rest of the items back into the glove compartment. The vibrator was the last to go in and he slammed the door closed.

Ray heaved a sigh of relief. "That was close."

"It's still on," Ted said.

"What is?"

"The vibrator. I can hear it."

Ray paused to listen and could hear the vibrations resonate across the dash of the sedan. "Shit!" He popped the compartment door again, partially stemming the flood of condoms and located the vibrator. He turned it off and shoved it back in, picking up as many stray condoms as he could. Just as Kunal rounded the front bumper of the car parked beside them, Ray locked the glove compartment. Three condoms didn't make it back into storage. He grabbed them and jammed them in his back pocket just as Kunal opened the driver's side door and sat.

"Sorry about the wait," Kunal said. "The cashier was smoking hot."

Ted took a deep breath as he tried to relax. "I'm glad you got your priorities straight. Now toss me the goods."

Kunal reached behind the driver's seat and dropped the bag next to Ted.

"What did she look like?" Ray asked.

"Dark hair, dark eyes." Kunal paused to admire the image in his mind. "Like I said, smoking hot. We friended each other on Facebook." He looked at Ray, his brow furrowed in confusion. "Dude, why are you sweating?"

"It's hot in the car."

"It is?" Kunal looked around the interior, at Ted, then back at Ray. "The windows are down."

"I don't know. I'm just hot."

Kunal shrugged, started the sedan's engine, and pulled out of the parking lot. Ted worked the pill bottle open and popped two into his mouth, swallowing them dry. He closed the bottle and carefully pushed it into his front pocket. "How much do I owe you?"

"Forget it. Consider it a contribution to your recovery." Kunal merged with traffic, then sent Ted a look through the rear view mirror. "I'm proud of you, dude."

Ted nodded and tried to roll over. "Thanks. Means a lot."

"On to Quinn's!"

"Do we have to?" Ted slumped back onto his back, having a hard time getting comfortable. "I'd rather go home and sleep."

"Did you take some drugs?"

"Yeah."

"They'll be kicking in by the time we get there."

Ted gave the idea some thought. "Okay."

"I'll buy you a big bag of ice, too."

Ted gave Kunal a weak "thumbs up."

KUNAL WAS RIGHT about the drugs. Below the belt, Ted's pain had reduced to a dull ache. The Tylenol 3s were doing their job. The three piled into their regular booth, Kunal and Ray on one side, Ted stretched out taking the other side.

A waitress stepped up to their booth. She looked harried, clearly at the end of her shift. Her hair was pulled up in a messy bun and food remnants were smeared across her apron. She snapped gum between her teeth.

Kunal smiled at her. "Chloe off tonight?"

"She starts her shift in an hour, Romeo, so you're stuck with me." She took out a pad and pen. "What can I get you?"

"Romeo?" Ray exchanged a glance with Ted.

"Tequila shots all around times two," Kunal said.

"And a beer," Ray added.

Kunal looked at Ted. "Oh, and a big bag of ice for my friend here."

The waitress paused for a moment. "Just ice?"

"Yeah, just ice," Ted said.

Ray pointed to his crotch. "It's for his swollen balls."

"Will you *shut up?*" Ted covered his eyes in embarrassment.

The waitress placed one hand on her hip. "You some kind of pervert?"

"No…" Ted sighed. There was no point fighting his current reality. "Look, I had a vasectomy, okay? It hurts. Ice helps."

"I'll have to charge you," the waitress said.

Kunal leaned into the table and caught the waitress's attention. "What's your name?"

"Charlie." The waitress looked annoyed, half-expecting to be hit on.

Kunal pulled out his wallet. "Charlie, here's a twenty. That should cover ice for the night."

Charlie took Kunal's twenty and disappeared into the recesses of the pub.

Ted glared at Ray. "You really need to learn when to keep your mouth shut."

"Chill out," Ray said. "She doesn't give a shit, and neither should you."

"Dudes!" Kunal slapped his hands on the table. "This is supposed to be a celebration of Ted's new sexual freedom." He leaned over the table and clasped his hands, a grin spreading across his face. "Tell us about Casey."

Ray shot confused glances to both Kunal and Ted. "Who's Casey?"

"She was Ted's date last night," Kunal said. "She was also the one you were hitting on at the doctor's office. Or should I say slapping her in the face with your creepy *mojo*."

"Great." Ted pictured Ray in his Fu Manchu putting the moves on Casey. He wanted to reach across the table and smack him upside the head but his groin ached too much. Even sitting was becoming a chore. "Now I got to apologize for you, too."

"You're doing her…and Iris?" Ray slumped against the backrest of the booth. "Lucky bastard."

"I'm not *doing* anybody," Ted said. "Iris and I are taking a break, probably permanently, so I had some innocent fun with someone else."

"You fucked her, didn't you?" When talking about sex, especially other people's sex lives, Ray was like a dog with a bone. "Banged her brains out, I'll bet."

Ted raised his head and stared straight across the table at Ray. "No. I didn't."

"But you wanted to, didn't you?"

Ted ignored the question. "Why do you hit on women, Ray? You know you can never follow through. And one of these days you're going to be charged with sexual harassment."

"I could follow through if I wanted to."

"You'd cheat on Vivian?"

Ray avoided Ted's gaze and lowered his voice. "No."

"Because you love her and respect her, right?"

Ray nodded. "Yes."

"How does Vivian feel about all your flirting?" Ted asked.

"She's fine with it."

"Really?" Ted studied Ray with surprise. "What if she did

the same to you? What if she flirted with all the handsome men she met, especially the ones that *don't* wear coordinated track suits?"

Ray recoiled. Ted's words stung and he knew it. "You need to back off the sleaze a bit, Ray."

"Okay, break it up, you two." Kunal scanned the pub for Charlie. "Our drinks will be here any moment."

Ted sighed. "Sorry, Ray. I've got a short fuse tonight."

Ray nodded, still a little gun shy. "For your information, I wear track suits because they're comfortable."

"And the loose waistband gives you easily accessible man time." Kunal grinned and leaned into Ray's shoulder. "Am I right?"

Ray wasn't one to stay angry for long. He cracked a smile and laughed with Kunal. Ted joined them, offering a brief chuckle. Laughing wasn't comfortable.

"Back to what we were talking about." Kunal looked at Ted. "She's heavy into you, dude."

Ted furrowed his brow. "Who, Casey?"

"Who do you think?" If Kunal could have reached Ted across the table, he would have given his shoulder a playful smack. "Yes. Casey."

"Oh. Great." It was good to hear positive news regarding Casey. Ted might have a second chance after all. But his short-lived excitement was doused by the dull throb below his belt. It had only been a couple of hours since he took his first dose of pain killers, and the pain's edge was returning.

"What? You're not interested?" Kunal cast his mind back. "She's stunning, dude. And those *eyes*."

"Stop it, Kunal," Ray said, his eyes beginning to glass over. "I might have to take advantage of my loose waistband."

"Look. I *am* interested, but I've got other things on my mind." Ted looked down. "I think I should just go."

"Hi Ted."

Ted recognized Ella's sing-song voice immediately. Ray and Kunal would have disagreed, but for Ted, the evening went from bad to worse.

All three guys turned toward the open end of the booth. Ella stood with one hand on her hips and the other propping her sixteen year old body on the front of the table. She was dressed in short denim shorts with the front pockets poking out under the hem, and a crop top exposing her slender midriff, emblazoned with the word "RECKLESS." On her head, barely containing her long blond hair, perched her bright pink baseball cap worn backward.

Ray's eyes bugged out and his Fu Manchu hung listlessly from his face.

Why Ella? Why now? Ted thought. "Uh, Ella. Hi."

Kunal and Ray shared a look as Ella pushed Ted's legs off one half of the booth's bench seat and slid next to him.

She looked at Ted. "You going to introduce me to your friends?"

"What are you doing here?"

"Don't look so surprised." Ella rocked on her hips, pulled out her ID, and handed it to Ted. He examined it and handed it back. Ray sat entranced, watching Ella's every move.

"I look older, don't I?" Ella said, pleased with the photo on her ID. She slid it back into her rear pocket. "So?"

Ted made no attempt to hide his annoyance. "Ella, this is Kunal and Ray."

Ella leaned up onto the table to get closer to Ray. She scanned his features, ending on his Fu Manchu mustache. Beads of sweat formed on Ray's thinning hairline.

"What's with the…mustache?" she asked.

Kunal shook his head. "Don't ask."

Ray tried to smile, but it looked more like he was terrified. "You like it?"

"It's…weird." Ella slid back across the table just as Charlie arrived with a tray holding tequila shots and one beer. In her other hand hung a bag of ice.

Charlie dropped the ice on the table first, then set the tray down, unloading the drinks on the table.

"Thanks, Charlie." Kunal winked at her but it didn't register. Either she didn't see it or she ignored it.

Charlie looked down at Ella. "Anything for you?"

"She's fine," Ted said.

Ella glanced at Ted, surprised. "I'm fine?" She looked back at Charlie and smiled. "I'm fine."

"You're *fine*…," Ray said under his breath but loud enough for Kunal to hear.

"Easy, boy," Kunal whispered back.

Ted grabbed the bag of ice and pulled it across the table and into his lap. "Shouldn't you be somewhere else?"

"My friends won't miss me for a bit." Ella looked at Ted, then at Kunal and Ray. "What are we celebrating?"

Kunal grinned at Ted. "Worry-free sex."

Ray grabbed a shot and raised it, excitement and enthusiasm evident in his voice.

"Here's to Ted's vasectomy." He downed it in one hasty gulp.

Kunal offered a shot to Ella, but Ted intercepted it. "Sorry. Not on my watch." Ted pushed back the tequila.

"You're so lame," Ella said. "For your information, I drink *all* the time."

Ted wasn't budging. "Am I supposed to be impressed?"

Ella rolled her eyes and huffed. "Whatever." She looked at the bag of ice on Ted's crotch. "Aww, you're just like Buster now? Poor baby." She placed her hand on Ted's thigh. "Does it hurt?"

Ted pushed her hand away. "I think you better go."

"Mellow out, dude." Kunal downed his shot of tequila. "The party's just getting started."

"That reminds me…" Ella looked up at Ted. Her eyes were clear and blue. If she had been ten years older, all three guys would have been fighting for her attention. "When do I start work at the shop?"

Ray choked on a mouthful of beer. "You're working for *Ted*?"

"Yeah. Right, Ted?"

"About that…" Ted narrowed his eyes at her. "Turns out I won't be needing you this summer." He saw Charlie standing at the bar and waved her over.

"Is he out of his mind?" Ray whispered to Kunal.

"Really?" Ella's posture straightened as her jovial nature melted away. "I guess I'm just going to have to tell my mom the truth about my missing bikini."

Kunal and Ray turned to each other, flashing recognition and both mouthing the word "bikini."

She looked at Kunal and Ray across the table. Ted could see her devious mind working. Ella returned her fiery, blue-eyed gaze to Ted and continued. "I'll have to tell my mom about how you *fucked* me in your bathroom that day."

Predictable, Ted thought as he gave her a sideways look. "Go ahead."

"I'm serious." Ella stared angrily back at Ted.

"So am I," Ted said. "I'm sure your mom would love to know all about your fake ID, underage drinking, and using blackmail to get a job."

Ella sat, stunned for a moment. "You'd do that?"

"Looks like you're forcing me to fight fire with fire," Ted said, just as Charlie strolled up to the table. "Perfect timing, Charlie. What's Quinn's policy on fake IDs?"

"We usually call the police and let them handle it," Charlie said.

"Must be bad then, huh?"

Charlie shrugged. "You can lose your driver's license for up to a year, as well as face fines and community service."

"Thanks," Ted said.

"Besides wanting answers, do you want to order something?" Charlie looked annoyed.

"I'd love a club soda, please."

Charlie headed back to the bar.

Ted glared at Ella. "I don't appreciate being accused of rape. That shit is serious. It *destroys* lives. Give me your fake ID, right now, or I call the cops."

Ella's jaw dropped.

"If you run, my friends will stop you." Ted looked at Kunal and Ray, who both looked almost as stunned as Ella. "Right, guys?"

Kunal blinked and shook off his surprise. He slid out of the booth and blocked Ella's only escape route. "Right."

"I'll just buy another one," Ella said.

"Your mom will be onto you by then."

Ella scoffed. "She's clueless."

"I'll tell her that, too," Ted said.

Ella saw no choice but to comply. She slipped the fake ID out of her back pocket and handed it to Ted. "I so fucking *hate* you."

"I know." The short-lived excitement had taken Ted's mind off his aching groin. But now he felt the pain's jagged edge returning. He looked at the fake ID. "Now that I have this, I just might hire you this summer. You never know."

"I wouldn't work at your place if it was the last coffee shop on Earth!" Ella scowled at Kunal. "Move, asshole!" Kunal stepped aside and she pushed past him, running toward the exit.

Ella brushed by Charlie, on her way back to the table with Ted's club soda, nearly causing her to spill the drink.

Charlie looked back at Ella's hasty retreat. "Was that the guilty party?" She placed a drink coaster on the table and Ted's club soda on top.

Kunal sat down next to Ray again. "Yeah."

Ted flipped the fake ID around in his fingers. "It's not a bad forgery, but there's no way she'd pass for twenty-four."

"I've seen her in here before," Charlie said. "If I see her again, I'll call the cops right away."

"That'd be a good idea." Ted took a sip from his club soda. "Thanks, Charlie." She nodded and trudged back to the bar.

"Aren't you worried about the whole 'woman scorned' thing?" Kunal appeared genuinely concerned.

Ted shook his head. "It's her word against mine and she has no proof. Plus I got insurance." He tapped the fake ID before slipping it into his back pocket.

Kunal raised another tequila shot. "Here's to Ted. For someone who just got snipped, you sure got balls."

Ray joined the toast, raising his beer and a tequila shot. "To Ted's balls."

"I'll drink to that…and to good drugs." Ted raised his club soda as Kunal and Ray slammed their shots, both well past pleasantly buzzed and heading towards shit-faced.

✂

TED, KUNAL AND Ray stumbled out of Quinn's Cavern. Kunal and Ray were stinking drunk, working against gravity by propping themselves up on each other. Ted walked, bowing his legs and favoring his crotch, the front of his pants wet from melted ice. He held the remnants of the bag of ice in one hand.

Ray pointed at Ted's wet pants, laughing. "He pissed himself! Look!"

"I'm looking." Kunal was snickering as well but not as enthusiastically as Ray.

"You're never going to get a date if you keep pissing yourself." Ray buckled over in hysterics.

"Shut up." Ted spotted Kunal's sedan in the parking lot and made a beeline for it.

Kunal took out his keys and jangled them at Ted. "Looks like you're driving."

"Maybe we should call a cab."

"No way, dude." Kunal tossed the keys to Ted. "I'm not leaving my wheels here. Only degenerates go to Quinn's." He looked at Ray and they both started howling with laughter.

"Degenerates that piss themselves!"

Ted had no desire to drive, but he wasn't impaired like the other two. The Tylenol 3s he had taken a few hours ago had begun to lose their effect. He could dump Kunal and Ray at Kunal's place and be home in less than thirty minutes. A comfortable bed was the only incentive he needed.

"Okay." Ted unlocked the driver's side door. The locks on the other three doors unlocked in unison. "Get in, you degenerates."

"I call shotgun." Kunal scrambled to the passenger side door. "Just don't puke. The seats are genuine leather."

Ray opened the door to the back and crawled in, flopping on his stomach.

Ted jammed the bag of ice into his pants. The initial shock of cold took his mind off the dull ache. He took his time entering the sedan and lowered himself into the bucket seat. Despite his best effort, the raised sides of the seat made his legs naturally slide together, placing unwanted pressure on his sack.

Ted's hand went instinctively to the right side of the steering column, but found no ignition keyhole. Kunal pointed at the dash, close to the navigation screen.

"It's a push button start, dude."

Ted pushed the start button and the sedan's engine roared to life. He held up the keys, which he now noticed looked more like keys to a house than a car. "What do I do with these, then?"

"Don't lose them." Kunal tilted his seat back and closed his eyes. "On second thought, give them to me." Ted gave the keys to Kunal, who pocketed them.

Ted pulled out of the parking lot and began the journey to Kunal's condominium. He looked at the digital dashboard and noticed the gas gauge pointing close to empty. The last thing Ted needed was a stall due to an empty gas tank.

"Did you know you're running on fumes?"

"No worries," Kunal said, his eyes still closed. "I always keep an emergency jerrycan in the trunk."

"Wouldn't it be easier to just fill up the tank more often?"

"Nah." Kunal smiled. "You know me. I'm a lazy fuck."

Ray's voice piped up from the back. "Speaking of fuck, you never did answer my question back at Quinn's."

Ted knew the question before Ray asked it. Ray's one-track mind made predictions easy. But the bag of melted ice in Ted's pants shifted into an uncomfortable position and distracted him from both the conversation and the road. Instead of stopping, he slipped one hand into his pants and began rearranging the bag's chilled contents. He nudged the steering wheel and caused the sedan to weave a little.

Kunal cracked his eyelids. "Watch where you're going, dude."

"I'm on it." Ted returned both hands to the steering wheel, one slicked wet with ice water, and straightened the sedan's path.

"You going to answer my question?" Ray repeated.

"What question is that, Ray?"

"That bikini I found…" Ray rolled onto his back. "You know the one? It was red and white—"

Here it comes, Ted thought. "What about it?"

"Was that…what's her name again?"

"Ella."

"Yeah," Ray said. "Was that Ella's?"

Ted was tired, tired of his balls aching and tired of talking about Ella. "You're obsessing, Ray."

"Just tell me," Ray pleaded from the back seat.

Kunal turned to look at Ted. "Just tell him, for Christ's sake, so we can all move on."

Ted sighed. "Yes. The bikini was Ella's."

"I still remember the smell." Ray slipped into a sensory memory.

"Quit the jizz parade, dude. These seats are genuine leather."

"Do you still have them?"

"What?" Ted turned to glare back at Ray, the steering wheel turning slightly right. "Of course not. I returned them. I'm no pervert." The sedan's right front wheel bumped a sewer grate. Ted faced forward again and corrected left, narrowly missing hitting the curb.

"That stings, Ted," Ray said. "I can't help it if I got a healthy sexual appetite."

Kunal looked back at Ray. "I don't think *healthy* is the right word."

Ray slapped the back of the passenger seat. "Don't you start on me, too."

"Hey." Ted caught Ray's attention in the rear view mirror. "Sorry. I don't know what you are, but you're not a pervert."

Ray belched. "Apology accepted." He placed his hands on his abdomen. "I wonder if Ella's a virgin."

"Give it a rest," Kunal said. "Please."

"Those jean shorts were hot. I wanted to lick her body. Do you think she was wearing panties?" A trail of drool flowed from Ray's mouth and down the back seat.

Ted threw his hands up in the air in exasperation. The sedan drifted a bit. "It's comments like that that make people think you *are* a pervert."

"Besides," Kunal added. "She's *sixteen.*"

Blue and red lights flashed from behind the sedan, reflected in the rear view mirror and onto Ted's face. As if he didn't know it was a police car, he heard a familiar *whoop-whoop* sound.

"Shit," Ted said. He slowed the sedan and pulled to the side of the road.

✄

THE POLICE CRUISER pulled over behind the sedan. Ted watched the red and blue lights in the rear view mirror flash. In a strange way, he found them relaxing. Ray on the other hand lost his shit.

"What the hell is he doing in there?"

"Calm down." Ted kept his eyes glued to the cruiser. "He's probably looking up your plates." He glanced at Kunal. "Anything I should know? You got any outstanding parking tickets?"

Kunal took a moment to think. "No, dude. My driving record is spotless."

Ray looked over the back seat and through the rear window. "He's getting out."

Ted shifted his gaze from the rear view to the side view mirror. "*She's* getting out."

Ray looked back at Ted, confused. "What?"

"*She*. It's a woman officer," Ted said. "Everyone stay cool… and keep it in your pants, Ray."

"Shut up," Ray said as he turned to face forward.

The three guys composed themselves as innocently as possible, but ended up making themselves look guilty as hell.

The officer switched on her flashlight and approached the driver's side door. She tapped the glass.

Ted powered down the window. He noted the officer's name on her uniform, "Adams," but only nodded. Her hair was pulled back into a tight, neat ponytail.

"Shut the car off, please," Officer Adams said.

Ted complied without delay and killed the engine. "Is there a problem?"

Officer Adams bent over slightly and looked in at Ted, then Kunal and Ray, flipping her flashlight between the three of them. "Have you all been drinking tonight?"

Kunal and Ray spoke in unison. "We have."

"They have." Ted remembered the couple of Tylenol 3s he had taken not too long ago.

Officer Adams directed her flashlight beam to Ted and studied him.

Do I look stoned? Are my pupils dilated? Panicked thoughts flew through Ted's head as beads of sweat broke out on his forehead. "I'm the designated driver."

Officer Adams offered a small nod but her face indicated no clues about what she was thinking. "License and registration please."

"Get the registration," Ted said to Kunal as he jammed his hand into his front pocket, bumping one side of his swollen sack. He winced and pulled out his wallet. Officer Adams noticed. Ted slid out his license and handed it to her.

Kunal popped the glove compartment door and a flood of condoms fell out onto his lap and into the footwell, topped by the blue vibrator Ray had discovered earlier. The fall had knocked the switch on and the vibrator buzzed around in Kunal's lap.

"What can I say. I was a Boy Scout," Kunal stammered, offering a weak smile and looking at Ray, then Ted. "Always be prepared."

Expressionless, Officer Adams looked at the vibrator, the condoms, then at Kunal. "Registration somewhere in there, Casanova?"

Kunal switched off the vibrator. He dug through the mountain of sex products and through the emptied glove compartment but couldn't find his registration. "I know it's in here somewhere."

"Check the floor," Ray whispered.

"What, dude?" Kunal said, still searching.

Officer Adams flipped her flashlight beam to Ray's face. "Did you say something, Yosemite Sam?"

"Check the floor," Ray repeated.

Kunal dug around on the floor and under his seat, his hand finally brushing across something familiar. He raised his registration up in its protective plastic cover and glared at Ray.

"Sorry," Ray said. "I forgot to tell you."

Kunal said nothing as he handed the registration papers to Ted, who passed them to Officer Adams. She flipped through the papers, comparing the information there with Ted's license.

"Sir, you're not the registered owner of this car."

"No, officer." Ted hooked a thumb at Kunal. "He is."

"Your license too, please." Officer Adams waited for Kunal to retrieve his license from his wallet and pass it over. With this new information, she returned her attention back to Ted. "Did you know you were driving erratically?"

"No. I'm just tired, I guess."

Officer Adams held her gaze on Ted for a moment, a little too long for Ted's liking. She flicked her flashlight beam from Ted to Ray to Kunal and back. "Please remain in the vehicle."

Ray watched Officer Adams return to her police cruiser. "Who's she calling?"

"Probably checking our records," Kunal said. "She better not figure out you're high on drugs, dude. That's just as bad as drunk driving."

"I'm not high." Ted flipped out the mirror in the sun visor and examined his eyes. "I took those hours ago."

Kunal weighed Ted's chances. "You might be okay. You might not."

"Great." Ted flipped the sun visor back. "Thanks for your support."

"Shut up." Kunal nodded back toward the cruiser. "She's coming back."

Officer Adams shone her light through the driver's side window. "Please step out of the vehicle, sir."

"Okay." Ted shot a quick panicked look at Kunal as he unbuckled his seatbelt. He pushed the sedan door open and gingerly extracted himself from the driver's seat. As he stood, the bag of ice in his pants slid down and to one side. Without thinking, Ted jammed one hand into his pants to adjust it.

Alarmed, Officer Adams drew her gun and aimed it as well as the flashlight at Ted. "Hands above your head! Now!"

"What?" The gravity of what Ted must look like to the police officer dawned on him and his blood ran cold. "Wait, no. No! It's ice—"

"Now!" Officer Adams kept her gun trained on Ted, taking no chances.

Ted extracted his hand from his pants, now soaked with melted ice and placed them behind his head.

"Slowly," she commanded.

Kunal yelled out through the open driver's side door. "He just had a vasectomy—"

"You," Officer Adams motioned at Kunal. "Be quiet." She returned her attention to Ted. "Kneel on the ground."

Ted, hands raised, dropped to his knees, one at a time, legs apart to give his swollen sack some much needed room.

Ray sat in the back of the sedan, mesmerized by the confidence and power of Officer Adams.

"Now lie flat on the pavement, arms out to your sides, palms up."

Ted complied. "But I really have had a vasect—" Officer Adams kneeled on Ted's butt. He winced at the added pressure and groaned. "You don't have to do this."

The officer placed her flashlight on the pavement and holstered her gun. She unhooked a pair of handcuffs off her belt and locked them around Ted's wrists, drawing his arms back one at a time.

Officer Adams pulled Ted up by his belt and slammed him onto the hood of the sedan, his groin taking most of the impact. Eyes watering, pain bloomed in his head and he nearly passed out.

The officer kicked Ted's legs wider and began to frisk him from behind. She pulled out his wallet and tossed it onto the hood. She felt the plastic pill container in his pocket and pulled it out.

"Take two every four hours for post-operative pain as needed," the label read. Officer Adams paused for a moment, then moved her hands further down Ted's pants. She registered the wetness of his pants, then felt the cold, hard bag of ice.

"What's that in your pants, sir?" she asked.

Ted forced his way through the pain. "Ice. Like I told you before."

Officer Adams paused mid-frisk. "Come again?"

"Not likely," Kunal said under his breath, watching Ted rest his head on the hood of the sedan.

"I'm so hard right now," Ray said from the back seat.

"No. Not in my car you're not."

"I know, I know. Genuine leather and all that shit." Ray continued to watch the unfolding action on the hood of the sedan. "But can you imagine her in bed?"

Kunal turned back to Ray. "How about you imagine the pain Ted's in right now."

Ray looked away sheepishly.

"Priorities, Ray." Kunal tapped his temple with his index finger. He called through the windshield. "Is it okay to get out of the vehicle?"

Officer Adams nodded and waved him forward as she unlocked Ted's handcuffs.

"Ted needs our help," Kunal said. "Let's go."

"I can't get out of the car with a boner."

"Not my problem." Kunal opened the passenger door and stepped out, drunk but able to stand.

✄

EVEN THOUGH KUNAL couldn't walk a straight line to save his life, he managed to help Ted back to the driver's side door. Ray slid out of the sedan when they were halfway there and grabbed one of Ted's arms. His gesture didn't impress Kunal.

"What?" Ray said. "Better late than never."

Kunal ignored him as both guys rolled Ted into the driver's bucket seat. Ted winced.

"Maybe we should call a cab." Ray looked at Kunal and Ted. "You know, for all of us."

"And leave my car here, on the side of the road, overnight?" Kunal shook his head. "No fucking way."

"Who's being a good friend now?"

Kunal's eyes narrowed. "Keep talking, Ray. I'd love a reason to beat your ass."

"It's okay," Ted piped up. "I can drive. I just need to sit for a bit."

Officer Adams emerged from her cruiser and walked over to the driver's side door. She handed Ted and Kunal's licenses and the sedan's registration back through the window.

"Hey, sorry for being a little rough with you there," she said. "I thought you had a gun."

Ted nodded. "I understand. You were just doing your job. I shouldn't have stuck my hand down my pants."

"An old partner of mine, his nuts swelled to the size of oranges after his vasectomy." Officer Adams palmed imaginary oranges in her hands. "Wasn't pretty."

"How's he doing now?"

"His nuts are fine, but his wife just had twin girls." The officer laughed, her utility belt jangling. "Go figure, huh? Nothing was going to keep his sperm from busting loose."

What the hell have I done to myself? Ted thought. *And here I am talking about vasectomies and sperm with a female police officer.* "Glad he's okay."

"Well, his nuts are at least. Get yourself home and get more ice on that. And keep your eyes on the road." Officer Adams rapped the side of the sedan and walked back to her cruiser.

Kunal nudged Ted's shoulder. "Get her phone number, dude."

Ted powered up the window and started the engine. "I've had enough excitement for one day, thanks."

As Ted drove away, Ray kept his eyes on the cruiser until it disappeared from view. "Damn, she was hot," he whispered to himself.

Ted tapped his fingers on the steering wheel. "So, who's idea was it to go drinking?"

"Hey, don't put that on me, dude." Kunal paused to belch. "I didn't know this was going to happen."

"It *was* your idea," Ray said.

Annoyed, Kunal turned to face Ray in the back seat. "And I *twisted* your arm, right?"

Ray didn't answer as silence consumed the rest of the trip. Five minutes later, Ted arrived at The Penthouse. He placed the sedan in park and let the engine idle.

Kunal turned to Ted. "I'm proud of you, dude."

"That's the tequila talking."

"The fuck it is." Kunal sat up and straightened his back. "You grabbed both nuts and set them free. Your life changed in a big way today and I think you're going to love it."

Ted smiled and accepted the compliment. "Thanks."

"Okay, jizzmaster, this is our stop."

Ray looked up at the condominium complex from the back window. "This is *your* place."

"You're spending the night to sleep it off." Kunal unbuckled himself. "Call Viv and let her know."

"I don't want to spend the night here."

"Non-negotiable." Kunal stepped out of the sedan and opened the door to the back seat. "Come on. Let's leave Ted to recuperate."

Ray crossed his arms. "No."

"It's okay. I can drive him home," Ted said.

"He's staying here. End of story." Kunal beckoned Ray but he wouldn't budge. "I'll let you watch my porn collection."

That got Ray's attention, but he tried hard not to appear overeager. "Oh, all right."

"Can I help you guys to the door?"

"See that, Ray? Such a gentleman." Ray slid across the back seat and Kunal hoisted him out. "Ted, go home. Get some ice and relax." Kunal closed the car door.

The two guys staggered to the front of the building, fumbled with keys and unlocked the door.

Ted waved, put the sedan into drive and pulled away. He'd be home in ten minutes and imagined stretching out on the couch with an ice pack on his groin.

Southeast Ankeny Street was for the most part straight, and at this time of night, the traffic was sparse. The drive was easy.

After five minutes, the engine began to sputter and the sedan slowed.

"What the hell?" Confused, Ted scanned the dashboard only to see the fuel gauge resting on empty. "Shit."

The vehicle rolled to a stop as Ted pulled over for the second time that night. He turned the ignition off and flipped on the hazard lights, letting out an exasperated breath.

The jerrycan! Ted thought.

He found the trunk release and pulled it. The back popped. He opened the door and carefully made his way to the back of the sedan. Just as Kunal had promised, a jerrycan sat secured to the left side of the trunk with bungee cords. He lifted it out, surprised by its weight.

It's full. Thank God for small miracles.

Ted found the gas tank cover but realized he had no idea how to open it. He returned to the open driver side door and searched for a button or lever, like the one he was used to on his SUV. He turned up nothing.

"This isn't happening." Ted shook his head and moved back to the gas lid and tried to pry it open with his fingers. That didn't work either.

He dug out his phone and called Kunal. The phone rang seven times before he answered. Sounds of porn filtered through the ear piece, making it sound like Ted had interrupted an orgy.

"Guess what? Ran out of gas," Ted said. "How do you open the fucking gas tank?"

"Are the doors to the car unlocked?" Kunal had to talk

louder to rise above the heavy breathing and moaning in the background.

"Yes."

"Push the right side of the gas cover. It should pop open."

"Just a sec." Ted pressed the gas lid and sure enough it popped open just as Kunal said it would. *Fucking luxury cars.* "Great. Thanks." He hung up before Kunal had a chance to say goodbye.

Ted emptied the jerrycan's contents into the tank, replaced the gas cap and closed the cover. He threw the empty jerrycan into the trunk and slammed the trunk closed.

He returned to the driver's side door and slid into the seat again.

"Finally." He pressed the ignition switch, but instead of hearing the engine start, an icon of a key with a slash through it flashed on the dashboard screen, followed by the words, "The remote control cannot be located. Starting the engine may not be possible."

Kunal has the keys. Ted sat and stared in disbelief at the error message on the screen. He pressed the ignition button again even though he knew he would get the same message. And he did.

"Fuck." Annoyed, Ted sat in the sedan, stranded halfway to rest and relaxation. He didn't have the energy to yell or even be angry. Instead he started to laugh. Silently at first, his chuckles built into a full belly laugh until he felt the ache radiating across his groin.

He pulled out his bottle of Tylenol 3s and popped a couple tablets, ignoring their bitter taste. He pulled out his phone and texted Kunal, having no desire to talk to him at this point. "Gas tank refilled, but YOU HAVE THE KEYS. Leaving car on Ankeny, near 25th Ave."

Ted called a cab. It took an hour to get him the five blocks home, most of that time spent waiting, but there was not a chance in hell he was going to walk. He was done.

Ted's day was over, but his nightmare was just beginning.

TED STAGGERED INTO his condo a few minutes after one in the morning. The door was unlocked just as Kunal and Ray had left it. He closed the door and engaged the deadbolt.

The familiar scent of coffee, Columbian mixed with Jinotega, his most recent experiment, filled his nose and helped distract from his pain. The Tylenol 3s that he had taken over an hour earlier had put a small dent in his discomfort, but not enough for his liking.

His stomach rumbled. He hadn't eaten much since the procedure the day before and was ravenous, but he had no energy to make himself something.

Buster jumped up, licking his hands, happy to see him. Ted protected his crotch from the dog's exuberance.

"You hungry, buddy?" Ted stepped to look at Buster's bowl and noticed both compartments were filled with both kibble and water. He cast a curious glance at Buster and the dog returned it with a head tilt.

Someone's been in here, Ted thought. "You feeding yourself now?"

Buster chuffed as if he was answering "yes."

Ted grabbed a bag of frozen vegetable medley from the freezer, a bag of Doritos Roulette chips off the counter and carefully stretched out on his sofa. He placed the frozen vegetables over his crotch and eased himself onto the couch. He flipped on the television and began surfing channels.

Buster walked to the front of the couch and rested his chin on the cushion. He wasn't allowed on the sofa as a rule, but that rule had been created and enforced by Iris.

Ted looked at the dog and the dog looked back, his dark chocolate eyes seeming to reach into Ted's soul. He couldn't deny eyes like that.

"You know what? Come on up, buddy." Ted grinned at Buster as he hopped up onto the couch. "Iris made the rule, but she's…" A flood of memories rose up and almost swallowed him, but he pushed them back.

Buster curled up against one of Ted's legs, as much as a seven month old golden retriever can, and rested his head and BiteNot collar on his right thigh.

"We're one and the same now, you and I." Ted gave Buster an affectionate scratch on his head. "You're a good dog. Don't let anyone tell you anything different." Buster closed his eyes.

Ted flipped through more channels, settling on the WXYZ Thursday Night movie, although technically it was Friday morning. After the commercial break finished up, he realized the movie was *Love, Actually*, one of Iris's favorites.

"You're not making this easy," Ted said to the television as memories of sitting with Iris watching, and sometimes not watching, the movie floated through his mind. This time he was powerless to stop it.

He muted the television and dug his phone out. Ted pulled

up his contacts and scrolled to Iris's number. His thumb hovered over the "call" icon.

"One more voicemail can't hurt." Buster peeked at him through sleepy eyes as Ted touched the call icon. Soon, he heard her phone trilling at the other end.

IRIS HAD CRASHED at her best friend Sara's place and was dead to the world on Sara's couch when her cell phone began to buzz.

Iris and Sara had become fast friends just after Iris had joined the firm. The two of them were both smart, strong women looking to advance their careers and they helped each other out whenever they could, both personally and professionally. The two women had each other's backs.

Three years ago, Sara had stayed with them at Ted's condo for a number of weeks after a bad breakup of her own. So when Iris came knocking several days ago, Sara had welcomed her with open arms.

Her buzzing cell phone pulled Iris from sleep. She was never one to let a call go to voice mail without good reason. But when she grabbed the phone and raised the screen to her sleep-blurred eyes and saw Ted's name displayed, she almost let the call go to voicemail again. Almost.

Annoyed, she pressed the green phone icon to accept the call. "Ted...it's one thirty in the morning."

There was a pause on the line.

Maybe he's cluing in what a bad time to call this is, Iris thought. No such luck.

"Sorry. I can call back later."

Iris rubbed sleep from her eye. "No. I'm already awake. What is it?"

Ted paused again, shorter this time. "I miss you."

What are we, in high school? Iris sighed. This was one thing that she couldn't stand about Ted. He could be such a wuss. *Jesus Ted, why don't you grow a pair?* The words flew through her head so fast that, for a moment, she thought she had said them out loud.

Instead, Iris echoed his sentiment, even though she had already started to forget what she had seen in him. "I miss you, too." She thought she heard a sniffle but couldn't be completely sure. "Is that all you wanted to say?"

"Where are you?"

"Where do you think?"

"Sara's."

"Yeah." Iris searched for tact but came up empty. "Look, it's late. Can this wait until morning?"

Ted either ignored the question or didn't hear it. "I had my vasectomy today," he said. "I mean yesterday."

Shit, Iris thought, closing her eyes in dread. *He went through with it.* The conversation began to feel like she had a sinking anchor tied to her neck. She wasn't looking forward to the rest of it. Avoiding Ted's calls had kept their failing relationship on life support. Talking about it would make it real and part of her, a small part, didn't want things to end.

"When are you coming home?"

"I'm…" Iris hit the point of no return and decided to commit to the decision she had been agonizing about for days. "I'm not coming home, Ted."

"What…? Why?" Ted sounded surprised. *How could he be?*

"I've decided that I want different things than you do," Iris said.

"What things?"

I'm trying to let you down easy, but you're making it really difficult. Iris grew impatient and felt her rage build.

"Iris?"

"I want kids." She knew her words would destroy Ted, but she carried on anyway.

"You want…kids?" Ted took a breath. "But I thought—"

"I want kids, but not with *you*." Iris heard her words knock the wind out of Ted, crushing him with their weight.

"But the vasectomy was your idea!" Iris heard anger rise in Ted's voice and she was glad. "Remember what you said? How great it would be to make love without having to worry? Remember that?"

Iris took a deep breath. "I didn't know for sure until just now. I'm sorry."

"I've lost a piece of me I can't get back. Ever!" Ted was furious. No amount of electronics could hide his anger.

"I never forced you to do anything."

"But you led me on, Iris," Ted said. "You made it seem that what we had was fixable."

"Maybe it was. Before."

"Before what? That thing with Ray?"

"Things were bad long before that."

"And here I thought honesty was important to you." Ted fumed on the other end of the line. "You're such a bitch."

The phone line clicked, followed by a dial tone. Iris sighed, knowing that she hadn't handled the call well, but what was done was done. She dropped her phone back into her purse and rolled on her side. She closed her eyes but sleep eluded her for the rest of the night.

After

TED WOKE EIGHT hours later still sprawled on the couch. His frozen vegetable medley had become soggy mush. He tossed the sodden bag on the coffee table.

Buster still slept on the couch next to him. His presence there was a comfort Ted hadn't entirely appreciated until now. Iris's rules had prevented the joy of owning a dog to fully develop. Ted looked forward to that changing.

He pulled out his phone. The time on the display read 9:46 a.m. He propped himself up on his elbows and slid himself to a sitting position. The pain level seemed about the same as last night, despite the drugs and sleep. Buster opened his eyes and pricked his ears up.

Ted saw a voice message waiting from Kunal. He half expected to see a message from Iris, but the more he thought about it, the more thankful he was that she had moved on. He would too.

Kunal had sent a bunch of texts as well, all concerning his sedan. The first one read, "You abandoned my car??? DUDE!" Kunal had taken a taxi in the middle of the night to retrieve his car from where Ted left it, sending Ted a series of play-by-play texts, nineteen in all, concluding with, "Car's fine. L8R."

Of course the car's fine. Ted read through the texts, amused, and sent one reply back. "Sorry. Couldn't walk. Caught a taxi. BTW you guys have my keys. Drop off at Buster's?"

Just as Ted slid the phone back in his pocket, Kunal texted back a "thumbs up."

Ted eased himself into a standing position and shuffled toward the kitchen. He popped open his container of Tylenol 3s and washed down two tablets with a glass of water. He scooped some kibble into Buster's bowl and topped up his water. The sound of food hitting his bowl roused Buster from the couch. The dog trotted to his dish and began to eat hungrily.

Ted was dying for a shower. He headed to the ensuite bathroom, closed the door and began to undress. He slowed when he reached his black Saxx underwear. For as long as he could remember, his underwear had been black. It hid the stains.

He pulled the waistband out from his abdomen to take a peek. The gauze dressing once held by Blanche's clawed fingers had slid down. His sack was bruised, just as Dr. Palmer had said it would be, but it looked worse than it felt. Ted started the shower, let the water come up to temperature and stepped in, letting the warmth seep into his body. He relaxed and began his cleansing routine, being extra careful around his groin.

Ted could have stood in the shower for an hour but coffee beckoned. *I'll grab a cup at the shop,* he thought.

When Ted stepped out of the tub, Buster was lying on the bath mat waiting. "Hey buddy. Want to go to the shop?" The dog's head popped up and he began wagging his tail. "I'll take that as a 'yes.'"

Ted dried off and pulled on fresh clothes, paying particular attention to his underwear. He packed the front with crumpled toilet paper for extra support. As he left his condo with Buster in tow, he remembered he had no keys to lock up. He also had no keys to his SUV.

A taxi again it is. Ted pulled out his phone and secured a ride.

✂

TED ARRIVED AT Buster's Beans just before eleven o'clock. He requested a stop at a Safeway on the way to pick up a few bags of frozen vegetables.

Ted's mind wandered. *It's always peas* and *carrots. Why not just carrots?* According to Ted, any vegetable that passed through the body undigested, like peas or corn, should be considered useless.

Buster fell into his routine and made a beeline to his dog bed near the entrance. Ted waved at Joe and Danielle as he fumbled his way to the back of the shop and into the small bathroom. He dropped his bag of frozen vegetables into the sink.

The small mirror over the sink did not offer a full body view. He dropped his pants, then dropped his underwear, revealing another pair of Saxx underneath. The extra pair was a last minute brainstorm before leaving the condo.

Ted refreshed the cushioning toilet paper inside the inner pair of Saxx and pulled up the outer pair. Between the two pairs of underwear, he inserted a bag of frozen vegetables into the crotch. He felt the soothing cool seep into his skin exactly where he wanted it to, and didn't have to worry about direct contact with the plastic bag. The outer pair of underwear held the frozen vegetables in place. In his current condition, he thought the idea was brilliant. There was just one problem.

Ted pulled up his pants, buttoned and zipped up. With the added bulk of the vegetables, it was a tight fit within his pants. He couldn't see lower than his chest in the small mirror, but when he looked down at his front, the unnaturally wide bulge in the front of his pants looked strange. He couldn't see his shoes, either.

I don't care, Ted thought. *It feels good.*

He stepped out of the bathroom and wandered back to the front counter. Ted placed his hands on his hips. "What do you think?"

Joe glanced at Danielle. "I don't find the front-butt sexy. Do you?"

Danielle shook her head. "Definitely a turn off."

"But the cold feels good," Ted said. "It's what my body needs right now."

"Staying at home and resting is what your body needs right now." Danielle cocked her head and a visible shiver of repulsion rode up her back. She tossed Ted his apron. "At least cover yourself up."

The apron didn't help. Ted looked like he was double-jointed and at first glance it was difficult to determine if he was coming or going.

Joe leaned over to Danielle and whispered, "I don't think this is going to end well."

Danielle shrugged and began preparations for the lunchtime rush. "All guys are stubborn to the point of stupidity."

"*All* guys?"

"Okay. *Most* guys."

They watched Ted wiping down empty tables.

"*This* guy?" Joe hooked a thumb at Ted.

"Definitely *that* guy."

Soon after the lunchtime rush, which spilled over past one o'clock most days, Ted sat down at one of the tables in the back of the shop and nursed a coffee. He looked pale and sweaty.

Danielle nudged Joe, a concerned expression on her face. "You should talk to him."

Joe nodded and approached Ted's table. "Can I sit?"

"Sure."

"How's the cold pack working out?"

Ted looked down at the bulge under his apron. "Fine. I just refreshed the bags. And the drugs help."

"What do you do with the thawed veggies? You can't freeze them again, can you?"

"Not if you're planning on eating them."

"*Are* you planning on eating them?"

"No. I mean carrots are okay, but I don't like peas." Ted sipped his coffee. "Take note. If you ever get a vasectomy, the double underwear system with a cold pack in-between works great."

Joe cringed like he had just heard nails on a chalkboard. "Nope. A vasectomy is *not* in my future. No one gets close to my junk with sharp objects."

"Never say never," Ted said. "I think for the right woman, you'd do anything." Thoughts of the past five years with Iris swirled in Ted's head. "I did, but as it turned out, it wasn't the right woman."

"So…you and Iris are kaputzville?"

"Yup." Ted managed a weak smile. "I should have seen the writing on the wall months ago. But everything happens for a reason, right?"

Joe clasped his hands together, placed them behind his head and stretched. "Whatever helps you feel better."

Ted's phone rang. He pulled his apron aside and slid it out from his pocket. He looked at the call display, then showed the screen to Joe. "Like maybe this…"

The phone's screen read, "Call from Casey Collins."

"Hello?" Ted showed no hint of nerves, unlike his first coffee "date" with Casey a week ago. The truth was Ted welcomed the distraction. It forced his mind off of the pain and discomfort. "Hi Casey. I'm so glad you called."

"Are you feeling okay?" Casey's voice filtered through the phone's speaker. "When I saw you yesterday, you were a little out of it."

"I'm doing much better now, thanks." Ted hesitated. "Hey, about last time—"

"Like I said last time, I'll give you a second chance." Ted could hear Casey's smile through the phone. "Not many guys get second chances with me, so you made an impression."

I'm one lucky son of a bitch, Ted thought.

Joe watched a wide grin spread across Ted's face, the first sign of genuine happiness he had seen from him since arriving at the shop this morning.

"And that's partly why I'm calling," Casey continued. "My parents are in town. It was a last minute visit and I wanted to take them somewhere special for dinner. Would you like to join us at The Garlic Rose tonight?"

There was no delay answering this time. "Yes. Absolutely," Ted said, even though he felt terrible. All he wanted to do was crawl into bed and sleep. "What time?"

"I was thinking six."

"Six sounds great," Ted lied, his balls screaming at him to hang up the phone. "What's the other part?"

"What do you mean?"

"You said making an impression was *partly* why you called."

"Oh, right." Casey was a smart woman and her response came without delay. "I just wanted to hear your voice again." Ted sensed that smile of hers again and blushed.

"I've missed you, too. Everything, really." Ted pictured Casey playing with a lock of her ginger hair.

"You're sweet," she said.

"I try to be."

"Oh, one more thing."

"Anything."

"You're single…right?"

Again, Ted made sure he answered promptly. "Yes, I'm single."

Joe nodded and gave Ted a "thumbs up."

"Promise?" Casey smiled.

"I promise." Officially calling it quits with Iris couldn't have come at a better time, and he didn't have to lie either.

"I'm excited to see you again, Ted."

"Me, too, Casey."

"I got to go. Blanche is giving me the stink-eye, even though I'm technically on my break."

"Okay. I'll see you at six. Bye."

"Bye, Ted."

The call ended and Ted looked at the phone's screen for a moment before placing it back in his pocket.

Joe crossed his arms in front of his chest. "Another date, huh? Impressive."

"Her parents are in town."

Joe nearly fell off his chair. "*And* meeting the parents? You move fast. Maybe I should start taking dating tips from you."

"It's not like that," Ted said.

"Oh yeah, I forgot. It's not a 'date.' " Joe air-quoted the word. "Have you checked yourself in a mirror lately? You don't look so good."

Ted raised his head to look at Joe, then turned his eyes on himself for a cursory once-over. His skin was pale and had a clammy sheen to it.

"I'm not going to miss this dinner," Ted said. "It's my last chance with Casey."

"But you're a train wreck, Ted," Joe countered. "What kind of first impression are you going to give her parents looking like shit?"

Danielle had been standing at the counter, tending to the odd customer and monitoring Ted and Joe's conversation as best she could. She grabbed a rag and walked towards them.

"He's got a point," she said as she wiped down a nearby table. "Looking like death warmed over doesn't get you any brownie points." Danielle surveyed a slouching Ted with an icy cold front bum and shook her head. "You should have stayed home today. That's what you would have told Joe to do if this situation was reversed."

"Don't tell me what I should have done." Ted took a deep breath and examined the state of his cold pack.

Danielle shook her head and crossed her arms. "Stubborn."

Joe shot a quick look at Danielle, then settled back on Ted. "Let me help you get cleaned up…"

"No. It's okay. I—"

"What'd I tell you?" Danielle said. "Stubborn to the point of stupidity."

"At least let me drive you," Joe said.

Ted cast a thankful glance at Joe. "Okay."

Joe looked at the clock hanging above the front entrance. "It's almost two o'clock…and dinner's at six." He rubbed his beard and did some quick math in his head. "That leaves us about three hours to get there."

Ted scrunched his brows. "Three hours?"

"Yup. Get your stuff and I'll get Buster."

"Are you okay to lock up?" Ted said to Danielle. "You can close the shop early if you want."

"I'll be fine," Danielle said. "Oh, I almost forgot." She dug around in her pocket and pulled out Ted's keys. "Your friend Kunal was by this morning, about half an hour before you arrived. He left these for you."

She tossed the keys over the counter. Ted followed the keys through the air with his eyes, but his reflexes, addled by pain and drugs, couldn't keep up. The keys hit him squarely in the crotch and dropped to the floor.

Eyes wide, Danielle placed her hand to her mouth. "Oh shit. I'm sorry. Are you okay?"

Ted nodded. "Didn't feel a thing." He crouched to pick up the keys but Danielle had rushed over and beat him to it. She picked up the keys and handed them to him.

"Sorry."

"No worries," Ted said, winking at her. "Frozen veggies for the win."

For a brief instant, Danielle understood the attraction Casey must have felt towards Ted. His wink, his smile, an all-around gentleman. She smiled back.

"What's the holdup?" Joe called from the front of the shop. He kneeled and fluffed Buster's fur. "We got a schedule to keep."

Ted removed his apron and hung it behind the counter. "Wish me luck."

"I would but you won't need it."

"I don't know," Ted said as he shuffled to meet Joe and Buster waiting for him at the front entrance. "I think I'll need all the luck I can get."

"Okay. Break a leg, then." Danielle waved as Ted, Joe, and Buster left the shop.

Ted had plenty of luck coming, just not the good kind.

"How's condo life?" Joe looked up at Ted's building towering ahead.

"Great. When I bought in, I could have snagged a unit higher up, but I couldn't justify the cost. The view isn't much different."

"Impressive." Joe turned left onto NE Davis Street to access the building's underground parking. Ted handed Joe his parking card.

"You don't need to do this, you know."

"What do you mean?" Joe activated the gate, handed the

card back and drove his Corolla into the parkade. He glanced at Ted as he looked for the visitor parking.

"This. Helping me out." Ted pointed at the parkade elevators. "You can drop me off. I'll be fine."

"I'm on the clock until seven." Joe threw the Corolla into park, killed the engine and stepped out of the car. "You're a good man and a good boss. I'm not taking no for an answer." He opened the back door and helped Buster out.

"Okay, okay." Ted unbuckled his seatbelt and exited the vehicle.

When the three of them stepped inside Ted's condo, Buster sauntered over to his food dish, sniffed its empty contents and chuffed.

"Buster's hungry. I can throw some kibble into his dish."

"Buster tries that with everyone new to the condo. He's already eaten." Ted walked down the hallway to his bedroom. "I'm going to pull out some clothing options."

Joe scanned the condo unit with appreciation. "You weren't kidding about the view."

"Yeah, nice huh?" Ted called out from the bedroom as he began the slow process of trying on clothes.

Ted walked out into the kitchen and held up a pair of khakis and a white button-up shirt.

Joe gave him a thumbs up. "You going tie-less?"

"That was my plan. I can't stand ties. It would just be one more aggravation." Ted walked back to the bedroom.

"A tie might go over well with the future father-in-law."

"It's just a dinner," Ted called back.

"It's just your future."

Silence, then Ted said, "Damn. You're right."

"That's why you pay me the big bucks." Joe chuckled, knowing that he was getting under Ted's skin. It wasn't very often that he had an opportunity like this.

Ted poked his head back into the kitchen, a look of serious concern on his face. "Do I pay you enough?"

"Yes. Go." Joe waved him away. "I was joking."

Ted disappeared back into the bedroom.

"Although I wouldn't say no to a raise, but you'd have to give it to Danielle, too."

"I'll think about it," Ted said.

Joe's stomach rumbled and he opened Ted's fridge. It was almost bare. Since Iris had moved out, Ted hadn't done much grocery shopping. The basics were there, bread, cheese, bacon and milk, plus beer and some assorted condiments. There were no fruits or vegetables, unless you counted the frozen vegetables in Ted's pants. The freezer was equally barren. Joe's appetite vanished.

Ted stepped out from the bedroom and into the living room. "What do you think?"

The bulge from the frozen vegetables drew Joe's eye like a magnet. He grimaced. "You sure you can't do without the veg?"

"I'll try something else." Ted walked back to his bedroom. "Fix yourself a coffee if you want."

"Nah," Joe said. "I get enough of that at work."

The process of trying on different clothes continued, but an hour later, Ted was no closer to finding a workable ensemble and the clock was ticking.

Joe walked to Ted's bedroom and knocked on the door.

"Come in." Ted sat on the edge of the bed, looking uncomfortable, pale and depressed.

"You've tried on twice as many clothes as I own," Joe said. "It's nice stuff, but you've got to decide."

"It's the damn frozen vegetables. The bag's too big."

"Maybe you should embrace the size of the package," Joe said with a hint of a smile. "Treat it as an asset."

"Would you be serious?" Ted selected a neck tie, held it up to his chest, and began to tie it on.

"Okay. Go without the cold pack," Joe said. "Problem solved."

"No. It keeps the swelling down."

"Do you have a smaller bag of vegetables?"

"Did you look in my fridge?"

"Right." The image of Ted's barren fridge and freezer was still fresh in Joe's mind. "We could buy another package."

Ted didn't like the tie and removed it. "I'm running out of time."

"I know this flies in the face of sexiness, but what about sweatpants?"

Ted pulled the tie from around his neck and held it taut, like a choke rope. "Do you have a girlfriend?"

"Yeah. Who can resist this body?" Joe struck a pose.

Ted threw the tie on the bed and picked another. "Did you wear sweatpants on your first date?"

"No, but this isn't your first date," Joe said. "It's not a date at all…*or is it?*"

"This is the first date with the parents. It's more important than the first date."

"So relax." Joe crossed his arms. "It's not like you're asking permission to marry Casey, are you?"

Ted busied himself tying the new tie around his collar. He didn't like it as well and removed it.

"Are you?" Joe repeated.

"No."

Joe stepped into the room to get a better look at Ted's current ensemble. The frozen vegetable front bum blew the image again.

Ted watched Joe's scrutinizing eyes. "I can fire you, you know."

"You're not going to fire me. I'm indispensable."

"No one's indispensable."

"Shut up." Joe looked around the room at all the clothes strewn on the bed and floor. "Here's what you're going to do."

✂

JOE CROSSED THE Willamette River on the Burnside Bridge, heading toward downtown Portland. It wasn't far to The Garlic Rose, but traffic was heavier on Fridays.

"It's probably best that we left your car at your place. Then your options are open," Joe said.

"Yeah, maybe I can get hammered in front of Casey's parents." Ted entertained the thought for a second before casting it away. "That'd go over well."

"When was the last time you took your meds?"

Ted's short term memory was a little muddled and he shook his head. "No clue. A couple hours?"

"Another good reason I'm driving." The two continued in silence for a moment until Joe spoke up again. "Want some music?"

Ted never heard the question. "Are you sure I look okay?"

Joe took his eyes off the road for a second and gave Ted a quick once-over. "You look good. Casual, yet respectable."

Ted had taken Joe's advice and worn khakis with a button-up shirt, but untucked. The look worked, plus the shirt tail helped cover his frozen veggie front bum bulge.

"Thanks."

"Except for the sweaty, pallid skin…but you can't do much about that."

"Asshole," Ted grumbled as he flipped down the passenger side visor and appraised himself. "You don't know when to shut your mouth, do you?"

Joe shrugged, a subtle grin under his beard. "Just being honest."

Ted dug into his front pocket and pulled out his vial of Tylenol 3s. He popped the lid and swallowed two.

"You better take it easy on those. You don't know what the future holds for you tonight."

"Whatever happens, it'll be better on drugs." Ted closed his eyes and rested his head on the Corolla's head rest.

Joe signaled and turned left onto Southwest 2nd Avenue. No matter how many years he'd spent living in Portland, he continued to see the city as vibrant and full of life, and even more so on Friday nights. "Can I ask you something personal?"

"Yeah. Go ahead."

"Does Casey know about the vasectomy?"

"It never came up." Ted cracked his eyelids enough to look at Joe, expecting a cross examination from him that only Joe could deliver. "We've only had one date."

"Ah, hah!" Joe raised an index finger. "It *was* a date."

"Really?" Ted gave Joe an unimpressed sideways look. "Let it go."

"Alright. But seriously…does she like kids?"

"I don't know." The thought had wandered through Ted's head a few times in the days between booking the vasectomy and the actual procedure. He may have reconsidered going through with it if he had not blown his first date with Casey. He never thought he'd get another chance. A sinking feeling began to seep into his gut, one of remorse and regret. "She has a lot of brothers and sisters."

"So, she probably likes kids."

"I can't think about that right now." Ted could feel the warmth of the Tylenol 3s float through his bloodstream, waking up all his extremities, yet making him feel sleepy at the same time. The drugs did a lot to mask the pain, but he still felt a dull ache radiate from his groin.

"All I know is I really like her," Ted continued. "I want to have a lot of fun with her and not have to worry."

"Fun…meaning sex."

"Not just sex, but yeah." Ted pictured Casey in his mind, skating circles around him at Jay Jay's. The image brought a smile to his face. "The spontaneity of it all. Everything with Iris was always so planned out."

"And if Casey wants kids?"

Joe's question popped Ted's memory like a bubble. "Obviously that's not going to happen."

"Hmm." Joe stroked his manscaped beard. "It's funny. I always pegged you as a family man." He pulled up to the curb in front of The Garlic Rose.

Maybe I am…or was *a family man,* thought Ted.

Damn you, Joe.

THE GARLIC ROSE was packed with patrons. Casey had called ahead and made a reservation for a table for four near the window. The table sat crammed in the far corner of the restaurant, and did share a window on one side, but it wasn't as nice a spot as when she had come here last week with Ted.

Casey's parents, Fiona and Liam, were both in their sixties. Fiona had free-flowing ginger hair like Casey, but it was lightening and developing touches of gray. She had the same slim body type, although the years had begun to leave their mark. Still, Fiona looked damn good for her age and she knew it.

Liam's balding pate had a patch of graying hair growing ear to ear around the back of his head, and what hair he had lost up top was more than made up for with a healthy beard below, mottled with tones of ginger, salt and pepper. His protruding stomach indicated a love for food, alcohol and as little exercise as possible.

Fiona and Liam sat closest to the window, opposite each other at the table. They made quick work of the first bottle of wine, Liam dividing the remnants of the bottle between Fiona and himself.

Casey hadn't drunk any wine from her glass. Instead, she sat fidgeting. She looked at her watch, an elegant and classy Daniel Wellington with a red, white, and blue striped band.

"So, where is this mystery man you've been raving about?" Fiona drank an ample sip of her wine.

Please don't embarrass me, mother. Both Casey's parents were lushes. If pressed, she would have described them as alcoholics, a title Fiona would deny. Liam would laugh and pour himself another drink. But here her mother sat, well on her way to shitfaceville. It took Liam a little longer.

Casey looked around the restaurant, then back at her watch. "He should be here by now…and I haven't been *raving* about him, Mom."

"Really?" Fiona sipped her Valpolicella. "Could've fooled me."

"Give the man a break." Liam's voice thundered at the best of times. The man had no volume control. "He's still fashionably late."

"Ten minutes?" Fiona scoffed. "That's pushing it."

As if Fiona's voice had magic in it, Ted appeared from around the partition separating the front entrance reception and the main dining area.

✄

TED SPOTTED CASEY at a table in the corner. He offered a weak smile and walked with care toward her, bowing his legs a bit to allow room for the cold pack of vegetables. His hair was plastered to his forehead with sweat.

Casey stood up and walked toward him. "You made it." She gave him a quick hug and whispered in his ear, "I missed you."

Ted moved his hips back for the hug, to hide the cold, unnatural prominence in his pants. "Missed you too," he whispered back, planting a light kiss on Casey's cheek. He stepped to the table and extended his hand to Fiona.

She shook Ted's clammy hand, and didn't try to hide the unpleasant experience, wiping her hand on her napkin.

"Hi, I'm Ted." He presented his hand to Liam.

"Good to meet you, Ted. My name's Liam, and this is my lovely wife Fiona." Liam extended his strong hand towards Ted's and shook with a firm grasp. "Jesus, you alright, boy? Looks like you've been wrapped more times than a bad Christmas present."

"I'm just hungry." Ted pulled out Casey's chair and only sat after everyone else at the table had seated themselves. Even half bombed, Fiona noticed the gesture. "Sorry I'm late. Traffic was insane."

Ted grabbed the glass of water at his place setting and downed it in several large gulps.

Fiona raised an eyebrow and sent a look of suspicion at Casey. "A gentleman would have called." Fiona punctuated the barb with a sip of wine.

"Mom!" Casey returned fire with a look of her own.

Fiona shrugged. "It's common courtesy."

"You're right, Mrs. Collins," Ted said. "I should have called. Won't happen again."

Unconvinced, Fiona's lips tightened. "I should hope not."

"Well, you're here now, my boy," Liam said. "What's your poison? I can vouch for this…what is it again?"

"Valpolicella," Casey said.

"Actually, cold water would be great." Ted looked at Casey across the table, then pointed at her water. "Are you going to drink that?"

"Um, no. Go ahead."

Ted grabbed Casey's glass of water and chugged it in the same fashion as the first. This time Casey caught both her parents' stares and tried to dismiss them.

Casey leaned forward over the table. "Are you feeling okay?"

"I'm fine." Ted wiped beads of sweat from his brow. "Maybe a little nervous." But it wasn't Ted's nerves. His anxiety and pain mixed with painkillers had caused his heart rate to soar. The beads of sweat on his brow were the least of his worries. His vision started to swim.

"No need to be nervous, lad." Liam downed the last gulp of wine. "Hey, what about a photo? Fi, where's the camera?"

Fiona dug around in her purse without success. "I think I left it at the hotel."

"That's a fine place for it, isn't it?" Annoyed, Liam crossed his arms over his ample gut.

Ted pulled his cell phone out of his pocket and presented it to Liam. "Here. Use mine."

Liam grinned at Ted beside him, then at Casey across the table. "Your man saves the day. These flippin' phones, savage, eh?" He raised his hand and flagged down a waiter. "Could you take our picture, lad?"

The waiter took the phone and framed up everyone at the table. Ted tried his best but his smile felt forced.

The waiter returned the phone to Liam.

"Another bottle of that val-polly-whatsit." Liam admired the photo. "That's one for the family album…if there's room!" He presented the image on the screen to Fiona and Casey before handing the phone back to Ted. "A big family means a lot of grandchildren and I love the little buggers. I can spoil the lot and send them back to their mommies and daddies." Liam reached out and placed his hand on Casey's, tapping it gently. "But we're still waiting on beautiful Casey here. All her brothers and sisters have fallen in line."

Ted was coherent enough to see Casey's cheeks turn a light shade of pink as she sent a daggered look at her father. The corners of his mouth curled into a subtle grin.

"It's hard to find a good man when you spend all your time in a cave," Fiona said.

"Mom!" The shade of pink on Casey's cheeks deepened.

"Well, it's true, honey."

"This is only our second date, Mom." Casey flicked her eyes at Ted, cast him a nervous smile, and settled back on Fiona. "Did you know you were going to marry Dad after your first date?"

Liam and Fiona locked each other in a warm gaze. "I seem to remember your mother and I knowing…pretty quickly."

"Oh." Fiona bit her lower lip and her gaze slid into seduction. "Those were *quite* the days." She flashed her eyebrows at Liam and he blew her a kiss.

Her parents' sensual gestures toward each other pushed Casey over the top. "I think we should order."

"Maybe Ted's the one?" Liam nudged Ted's shoulder. "You like kids, Ted?"

Sweat beaded down Ted's forehead and his vision blurred, distracting him. He gripped his phone with a slippery hand.

"You don't have to answer that, Ted," Casey said. "Don't let him bully you."

Liam grunted. "I'm not bullying the lad. It's just a simple question."

Casey focused on Ted's eyes. His pupils were large, inky black, and vacant. "Ted?"

"What?" Ted faced Casey. "Oh, yeah. I'm glad you asked. I love kids. I think they're…" He trailed off as his vision refocused but split into double vision.

Casey moved around the table and felt Ted's forehead. "Oh my God, he's burning up. Ted?"

Ted tried to wave away Casey's attending, but he looked like he was drunk. "I'm fine. So thirsty…where was I?"

Fiona gave Ted a sideways look and her brows furrowed. "You were saying you love kids."

"You want my water?" Liam presented his untouched tumbler.

Ted's double vision blurred out of focus again. "I need to…go to the bathroom." He stood up and took two steps forward before his body shut down. His vision went black as he passed out cold, face-planting the floor. The impact sent frozen peas and carrots exploding out from the waistband of his pants. His phone jettisoned from his hand and sailed across the restaurant's tiled floor.

Conversation in the restaurant hushed to whispers as everyone stared at Ted, unmoving and prone on the floor.

"Ted!" Casey ran to his side and rolled him over. She shook him but Ted was unresponsive. "Someone call nine-one-one!"

Liam leaned over the table, concerned but also confused. "Are those…peas and carrots?"

Casey leaned close to Ted's mouth and felt his warm breath, his chest rising and falling in a slow and gentle cadence. She pulled him close, up onto her lap, and rocked him.

Fiona stepped beside Casey and placed her hand on her shoulder. Casey looked up at her, working hard to hold back her tears. They shared a look of understanding and Fiona kissed the top of her head.

Fiona stepped over Ted's motionless legs to Liam. He took her in her arms and kissed her forehead.

Casey couldn't hold her tears back any longer. They flowed down her cheeks, some falling on Ted's face, others absorbed by her ginger hair that shrouded their faces from onlookers.

The oscillation of an ambulance siren rose in the distance, getting louder with each agonizing second.

"Excuse me, miss?"

Casey looked up at a waitress from the restaurant. She handed Ted's phone to Casey. "Your husband dropped this."

The phone displayed an image, but it wasn't of the four of them taken minutes ago. It was an image of something quite different.

Truth

THE TAXI PULLED up in front of Portland Metro Hospital. Casey emerged from the passenger seat, followed by Fiona and Liam from the back.

"Give us a moment," Liam said to the taxi driver, who nodded in acknowledgment.

Fiona approached Casey and opened her arms to offer a hug. Casey accepted, wrapping her arms tight around Fiona and taking in her essence.

Cinnamon. For as long as Casey could remember Fiona smelled like cinnamon. It was a comfort, and even though she had recurring issues with her mother, they always managed to work it out, or at least apologize for recent indiscretions. They never parted angry. With her parents now living in New York, Casey didn't see them often, and wanted to end this short visit on the right note.

Fiona pulled back, but held Casey's shoulders firmly in her hands. "Are you going to be alright? Is there anything we can do?"

Casey wiped a tear away and shook her head. "No, I'll be fine."

"Yes, I believe you will. But I'll always worry about my

youngest." Fiona offered a pensive smile. "I think I was a little hard on Ted…I'm sorry. I look forward to meeting him again, in better circumstances."

Casey hugged Fiona again. "Thanks, Mom." Her voice was quiet and raspy with emotion. Casey transferred her arms to Liam and embraced him just as tight.

"Love you to pieces, Bug," Liam said. "You got a good lad, that Ted. I can feel it in my bones."

"I hope so." Casey stood back from her parents and took a mental snapshot of them both, standing hand-in-hand after forty-one years of marriage. She wanted that kind of relationship and hoped it would be with Ted. "Love you both. Have a safe flight."

"Don't be a stranger," Liam said as his escorted Fiona back into the taxi, closing the door behind him. Casey watched the taxi pull away from the curb until it disappeared from sight.

Casey turned, looked up at the hospital looming above her, and headed for the entrance. After a quick elevator ride to the fifth floor, she stepped out into the Urological Surgery department and confirmed Ted's room number at the nurses' desk.

Ted shared his room with an old man in his eighties, who had the Sunday edition of the Portland Tribune sprawled across his lap. As Casey stepped into the room, the old man looked over his reading glasses, smiled and winked at her before going back to his paper. She didn't return his gesture and the man didn't seem to mind.

Casey stood at the foot of the hospital bed as Ted slept. She picked up his chart that hung off the bed and scanned it, zeroing in on the admitting diagnosis.

Complications from vasectomy.

She rehung the chart and sat on the edge of Ted's bed.

It wasn't his prostate at all, Casey thought. His friends had fed her a story. Anger began to simmer in the back of her mind but she kept it in check as she worked through past events in her head, trying to sort them out. She should have known. Looking back, everything seemed so obvious.

A nurse entered the room pushing a wheelchair. "Good afternoon, Mr. Humphrey. Ready for your test?"

Mr. Humphrey shuffled the newspaper together and refolded it. "You're darn tootin', I am. I got to piss some-thin' fierce."

The nurse helped Mr. Humphrey into the wheelchair. "Having a full bladder is part of the test. You can visit the lavatory afterward."

"How long is this test gonna to take?"

"It will be over before you know it." The nurse wheeled Mr. Humphrey toward the door.

"Wait." The nurse stopped and Mr. Humphrey turned to Casey sitting on the bed. "That fella must really love you."

Casey looked up at the old man. "What?"

"I'd bet the farm that your name's Casey."

Casey's eyes went wide with surprise, diffusing her anger more. "Yes. How did you—"

"He talks in his sleep. A lot. Bloody annoying." Mr. Humphrey pointed at Ted. "But whatever he did, he's sorry about it."

"Okay, time to go, Mr. Humphrey," the nurse said. "We can't be late for your test." She pushed the wheelchair toward the door to the room and out into the hall.

Before the old man was out of sight, he called back, "Forgive him so I can get a good night's sleep."

Forgive him for what, exactly? Casey thought. There were too many questions and not enough answers. She took Ted's hand in hers, feeling its warmth. The image of matching wedding bands on their ring fingers popped into her head. Casey was surprised at how easily she saw married life with Ted, but she always saw a future with children around her. Ted had removed that option from the table. Sadness overtook her. Could she live her life without children in it? Adoption was an answer but Casey was so far from that solution that it didn't feel like a solution at all. She wanted children with her eyes, her husband's eyes.

Casey's thoughts ran away from her. She could feel hot tears trying to rise to the surface. She stood to leave as Ted stirred and opened his eyes.

"Hey, you." Ted's voice cracked.

"Hey."

Ted reached for a cup of water on the bedside table. Casey reached the cup first and handed it to him. "Thanks." He looked over at Mr. Humphrey's empty bed. "Good. He's gone."

"Mr. Humphrey. They took him away for tests."

"You know his name?"

Casey shrugged. "We talked."

"Well, he snores like a goat." Ted took another sip of water and handed the cup back to Casey. She returned it to the bedside table. "Barely slept at all."

"He said you talk in your sleep, so I guess the feeling is mutual."

"Oh yeah?" Ted's lips curled to a grin. "What did I say?"

Casey ignored the question. "Do you remember anything about last night?"

"Sort of." Ted closed his eyes in thought. "I remember your mom and dad, Fiona and…"

"Liam."

"Right, Liam." Ted looked at her, trying unsuccessfully to sort out her state of mind. "I think your mom hates me."

"She doesn't hate you." Casey picked up Ted's phone. "Pull up the camera app for me?" Ted keyed in his passcode, opened the camera app, and handed the phone back. Casey pulled up the group photo that had been taken at The Garlic Rose.

Ted looked at the phone's display and nodded. "Yup. I remember that. Look at your mom's face. She hates me."

"I rode with you in the ambulance. I was so worried." Casey swiped through a few photos. "What I really want to know is who's *this?*"

The photo on the phone's display captured Ella, flowing blond hair under a pink baseball cap and wearing her red and white striped bikini. She lay with her head resting in Ted's crotch, laughing like she was having the time of her life.

"She's practically naked, in *your* lap, in *your* car." An edge of anger sharpened Casey's words. "Were you driving?"

Ted swallowed hard, his throat clicking and drying up all at once. He looked at the cup of water by the bed, but this time Casey made no move to get it for him.

"I know. It looks bad."

"What is she, a teenager?"

Ted fell silent.

"The bathing suit I found, in *your* couch…It was hers, wasn't it?" Casey's face hardened.

"The guys came over and—"

"I don't want to know." Casey looked toward the window and beyond. The sky was brooding in an overcast gunmetal gray.

"Casey…" Ted looked up, embarrassment burning hot on his cheeks. "Casey, look at me."

She did and Ted's blue eyes chipped away at her resolve, ever so slightly, but not enough to sway her.

"Nothing happened," Ted said. "I swear."

"Okay." Casey dropped the phone on Ted's chest, the photo of Ella still full screen on the phone's display. "Since we're being honest, could you please tell me why you're here?"

Ted began to open his mouth, then closed it. Words evaded him.

"That's what I thought." Casey sighed. "Why did you even get a vasectomy in the first place?" Ted looked up at her astonished. "Don't look so surprised. I read your chart."

"Okay." Ted pushed himself up to a sitting position and took a deep breath. "I got snipped to try and win Iris back. But it turns out she wants kids after all, so she dumped me. Looking back on it now, I was just going through the motions. I should have broken up with Iris a long time ago."

"But you went through with it *after* our first date," Casey said.

"Our first date ended badly," Ted continued. "Even though you said I would, I didn't believe I'd get a second chance with you, so I carried on with my plan…Iris dumped me *after* I was snipped." He spread his legs a bit and adjusted his sitting position. "Then you called about dinner with your parents and I wasn't going to pass that up."

"So I was your consolation prize?"

"No, you were my first choice. But only if I was single, you said. And suddenly I was."

Casey clasped her hands on her lap. Ted's story sounded plausible. Lying now would seal his fate as far as she was concerned.

"Ironically, I would have never met you if I hadn't had a vasectomy," Ted said.

She turned and looked at him, locking her emerald eyes with his.

"Something in me just felt right when I met you," Casey said. "It's been a long time since I felt that way about a guy. And *if* we ever got married, and that's a *big* 'if', I'd want kids." Ted could see a tremble in Casey's lips. "So, where do we go from here? Seems kind of pointless, don't you think?"

Ted dropped his gaze. "I'm sorry. I've totally screwed things up…but I guess we could adopt."

Casey could no longer contain her anger and stood. "You don't get it, do you? I saw myself having kids with you, Ted!" She paced back and forth. "I feel like such a fool. You surprised me and I'm so mad at myself for falling for it." She turned and stormed toward the door.

"Casey!" Ted made a move to follow her, but his swollen groin stopped him in his tracks.

Kunal entered Ted's room just as Casey flew by. "Hey, Casey," he said.

"Fuck off, you prick."

Kunal raised his hands defensively, palms out. "Whoa. What the hell was that, dude?"

"I'll give you one guess."

"It's hard to keep a secret like that in here." Kunal wandered through the hospital room and picked up Mr. Humphrey's newspaper. He flipped through it and tossed it aside.

Ted looked deflated. "I screwed up, Kunal. Big time." He held up his phone with the picture of Ella on it.

"Oh, shit, dude." Kunal tilted his head to properly take in all of the picture's details. "She's *hawt*."

"She's sixteen."

"Wait." The shoe dropped for Kunal. "The one from Quinn's? Ella?"

"Yep."

"Damn." Kunal took an extra moment to study the image before handing the phone back to Ted. "Don't show this to Ray."

"Hell no," Ted said, swiping at the phone's display. "I'm going to delete the photo."

Kunal picked up a homemade get well card from Mr. Humphrey's bedside table. It looked like it had been made by a child. "You'll meet someone else."

Ted shook his head. "I don't want someone else. Casey's the one. I know it."

Kunal put the card down. "How do you know?"

Ted shrugged. "I just do."

"I wish I could do that." Kunal sat on the edge of Ted's bed. "It would make my life so much simpler."

"Then stop being afraid," Ted said.

"Afraid?" Kunal scoffed. "Of what?"

"Romance. Making a connection with someone." Ted picked up his phone and swiped back to the photo of himself, Casey and her parents. "Falling in love."

Kunal shook his head. "I'm not afraid."

"Yeah, you are."

"No." Kunal stood and wandered the room. "I'm not. I just don't want those things."

"You'd rather have one night stands for the rest of your life with people you rarely see again?"

Kunal stood at the window. "It's working for me so far."

"You're going to have to move to a bigger city. You're running out of women."

Kunal laughed. "You're funny, dude."

"Look. I've taken your advice and look where it got me." Ted raised his hands like he was pointing out features of the hospital room. "Maybe you should take my advice for a change."

"You got here because you tried to do too much too fast."

Ted shook his head. "Kunal, you're my friend and I want the best for you. My wish is for you to meet a woman that blows your mind in every way, not just sexually."

Kunal crossed his arms and looked at Ted eye to eye.

"Then you can come to me and say, 'Ted, you were right all along.' " Ted grinned.

"Okay." Kunal walked to the bed and gave Ted as much of a bro hug as he could manage leaning over the mattress. "I'll give it some thought."

"Good." Ted's grin melted away. "Damn. Can you swing by my place and check on Buster? Poor dog. I bet he's feeling like he's been abandoned. The keys—"

"Got it," Kunal said. "Has he ever shit on the floor?"

"Not since he was a puppy. Maybe take him for a walk?"

Kunal balked. "I'll try. I'm pretty busy today as it is."

"I've been told a man with an adorable dog is very appealing to women." Ted's smile crept back.

"Who told you that?"

"I think it was you."

Kunal chuckled. "Touché, dude."

Just as Kunal grabbed the keys from the bedside table, Ray walked into the room wearing a bright orange track suit that shimmered even under the fluorescent lights.

"Five bucks to park? For thirty minutes!" Ray scowled. "That's bullshit, man."

Ted looked at him and was thrown for a moment, not knowing what was different. Then it clicked. "Ray! Your beard!"

"Hey, Ted." Ray stepped to the bed and lifted up the sheets covering Ted's groin, playfully trying to get a look. "How's your balls?"

Ted pushed his hand away. "Hanging in there." He studied Ray's face. "I don't think I've ever seen you beardless."

"It's a good look, dude," Kunal said.

Ray waved him off. "It's temporary. My supplier is back-ordered on Star Trek styles."

Ted touched the sleeve of Ray's track suit. "What is that, silk?"

"Damn straight, baby." Ray beamed. "Feels great, huh?"

"That's not silk." Kunal walked around the bed, stopping next to Ray.

"What do you know?"

"I know silk, dude. And I know how to read tags." Kunal twirled his index finger. "Turn around."

"Shit…" Ray presented his back to Kunal.

Kunal pulled the manufacturing tag out from the collar of the suit. "One hundred percent rayon."

"Rayon?" Ted raised his eyebrows. "Sounds like science fiction to me. Right up your alley, Ray."

"Whatever. Don't care," Ray said, pushing a grinning Kunal away. "It feels great on my skin. I have to wear underwear though, or I get a raging hard-on."

Ted cringed. "Too much information."

"Viv loves it, but the kids started asking questions."

"Stop," Ted said. "My imagination needs a break."

"So, you coming to the party?"

"What?" Ted looked at Kunal, then back at Ray. "Did I miss something?"

"Angie's birthday, remember?" A look of concern flashed across Ray's face. "I told you about it a while ago. She'd love to see her 'Uncle Ted.' "

"Depends on what the doctor says. I'm going to listen this time."

"You better show up," Ray said. "Or I'll kick your ass."

"Okay. Okay." Ted watched Ray relax. "I'll do everything in my power to be there." His words were sincere, but Ted had trouble picturing the reality.

Somehow, he had to make it work.

AFTER VISITING HOURS were over, Ted tried to sleep, but either the antiseptic smell invading his nose or the ambient hospital noise kept him awake. It didn't help that Mr. Humphrey had returned from his tests and had easily slipped into a deep slumber, accompanied by an annoying phlegm-rattling snore. The nurse on shift said he had been given a sedative during the tests and might be out for a while.

Lucky bastard, Ted thought.

An orderly brought meals through the ward promptly at six o'clock. Ted sat up as the orderly pulled a rolling table over to the bed. He placed a covered tray with Salisbury steak, mashed potatoes, peas and orange Jello onto the table. The color of the Jello reminded Ted of Ray's track suit.

Ted found his appetite awakening and he wolfed down the steak and potato, even though both were overcooked. The Jello was passable but he couldn't get past the peas. Depressed, he pushed the remainder around his plate with his fork.

Mr. Humphrey let loose a loud grunting snore. After listening to the old man sleep this afternoon, Ted had learned to expect a "mega-snore" every five or six minutes.

Ted looked over at Mr. Humphrey in his bed, mouth agape, and saw an opportunity too tempting to resist. He placed a pea from his plate onto his spoon, and catapulted it across the room. The first volley came within inches of the old man's open cavern of a mouth.

Ted reloaded, this time filling his spoon to capacity. He pulled back and released. The peas flew across the room in random directions and bounced off Mr. Humphrey's face and pillow. He awoke, blinked wearily, and rolled over. His snoring stopped.

There's a use for peas after all, Ted thought.

A nurse entered the room and right away spotted the peas scattered across Mr. Humphrey's bed and floor.

"I know hospital food can be bad," she said, "but it's not *that* bad."

"Not hungry anymore." Ted set his spoon on his plate. "Besides, I've reconfirmed my dislike for peas."

The nurse pulled out a portable electronic thermometer and pointed it at Ted's forehead. After the device beeped, she recorded the results on his chart, then sat at the edge of the bed.

Mr. Humphrey began to snore again. Ted sighed in despair, as he anticipated a sleepless night.

The name tag affixed to her hospital blues read "Melissa." She regarded Ted with intelligent eyes. "Lots of guys feel depressed, or even regret, after vasectomy."

"I'm not depressed," Ted said.

Melissa held Ted's gaze. "Are you happy?"

"Not exactly."

"What you're feeling is pretty common." Melissa rested her hands in her lap. "You're mourning, in a way. You chose to remove your ability to create life."

Ted looked up at the ceiling tiles, now that the fluorescent lights had been turned off. "Thanks. I feel so much better. I think I'll go hang myself now."

"It's no joking matter," Melissa said. "You made a life-altering decision."

An especially loud, guttural snore rose up from Mr. Humphrey's side of the room.

"Jesus." Ted looked over at the sleeping man. "How is it that he hasn't swallowed his tongue yet?"

"You can't swallow your tongue."

"You can't?" Ted couldn't hide his disappointment.

"It's impossible," Melissa confirmed. "A myth."

The snoring from Mr. Humphrey stopped all at once. Ted looked at Melissa, across to Mr. Humphrey, and back.

"Is he dead?" Ted raised his brows and listened closely.

Melissa shook her head. "He's not dead. And you'd be lucky to live that long." The old man's snoring resumed.

"I guess."

Melissa took Ted's wrist and measured his pulse. "Look at it this way. You've learned something really important about yourself."

"What would that be?" Ted said. "That my balls can swell to the size of oranges?"

"You're lucky it didn't come to that, but my point is maybe vasectomy isn't for you." Melissa released Ted's wrist and noted his pulse on his chart.

"A little late to learn that lesson." Ted slumped against his pillow.

"Maybe not," Melissa said.

"Wait." The record player of Ted's life scratched off its grooves. "What?"

"Get some sleep. You're getting discharged tomorrow." Melissa rehung Ted's chart and walked out of the room.

Can't leave me hanging like that! Ted grabbed his phone and called up his Internet browser. Into the search field he typed "vasectomy reversal."

As he read, a plan began to percolate in his brain, one that might fix this whole mess he'd gotten himself into.

THE MORNING COULDN'T have come soon enough. It had been a busy night at the hospital. Between the sirens outside, the explosive snoring from the next bed, and the hubbub from the hallway, Ted got very little sleep. Visions of shoving a sock into his bedmate's mouth crossed Ted's mind more than once.

By eight in the morning, he was out of bed. The swelling and pain between his legs had eased to a mild annoyance. He walked out of the room's shared bathroom, dressed and cleaned up, ready to go.

Mr. Humphrey sat up in his bed. "Good mornin'," he said.

Ted offered a nod to the old man. "Morning."

"Do yah mind?" Mr. Humphrey pointed to the Monday edition of the Portland Tribune, folded and placed in a plastic bag at the foot of his bed, just out of reach.

Ted grabbed the newspaper and handed it to him.

"Thanks." Mr. Humphrey opened the bag and extracted his paper. "Hope my snoring didn't keep yah up."

"Well, actually…" Ted's tone of voice did his talking for him.

"Sorry 'bout that. My wife…" Mr. Humphrey broke off his reply with a wet cough that sounded more solid than not. Ted shuddered and distracted himself by collecting his belongings.

"My wife keeps me in line with that elbow o' hers." Mr. Humphrey's eyes went almost misty. "Don't know what I'd do without 'er."

Ted was half-listening. He grabbed his phone and un-locked it. He launched the photo app and was met with the photo of Ella in her bikini. He deleted the photo with an emphatic finger, then swiped through his photos, finding a second photo of Ella. This one was even more suggestive, with Ted's arm outstretched over Ella's body and making it look like he was touching her inappropriately. Ted thought of Casey seeing this photo and groaned. She had to have seen it.

"Bye-bye." He deleted the photo and swiped through the rest of his recent photos to make sure he hadn't missed anything.

"What'd ya say?" Mr. Humphrey said, flipping through his newspaper.

"Nothing." Ted found Casey's phone number in his contacts. His thumb hovered over the telephone icon. *What if she doesn't answer?* he thought. *What if she does? What am I going to say?*

"Fuck it," Ted said and dialed. Mr. Humphrey looked up from his paper and watched Ted pace around the room.

The call went to voice mail and Ted listened to Casey's outgoing message before hanging up. Hearing her voice, and knowing how he had hurt her, made his heart ache.

Ted dialed Kunal. "Hey…I'm good to go. Can you swing by and pick me up? Like after one? I'm stuck here until then." He paused to listen to Kunal's reply. "Thanks. See you later." As Ted ended the call, a wistful smile formed on his lips. He may have been talking to Kunal, but he was still thinking about Casey.

"That yer wife?"

"Huh?" Ted turned around to find Mr. Humphrey addressing him. "No. Just a friend."

The old man's eyes narrowed. "Yah got kids?"

"No."

Mr. Humphrey nodded to himself, like he was understanding the final piece of a puzzle. "So, yah don't *want* kids, is that it?"

"What's with the questions all of a sudden?" Ted walked around his bed, looking for any items he'd missed, then sat on the bed. He didn't want to overdo it again.

"Look. Yah talk in yer sleep," Mr. Humphrey said. "I feel like I know yah."

"I don't talk in my sleep."

"Well, yah do here, let me tell yah." Mr. Humphrey pointed a finger at Ted. "Yah know, I can't understand why guys yer age get yer nuts cut off."

"It was a vasectomy," Ted said. "I still got my *nuts*, thanks."

"Whatever." Mr. Humphrey swished at him with his hand. "Family's everything, through thick and thin. Don't yah want to pass yer knowledge on to the next generation before yah die?"

Ted regarded Mr. Humphrey with understanding he hadn't expected.

"Raising a child builds character." The old man's eyes burned bright blue. "Being a father makes a man *a man*."

"I hadn't thought about that."

"Sounds like yah haven't thought about a lot o' things."

If only you knew the whole story, Ted thought. *Then again, maybe you do.* "What about you? Where's your family?"

Mr. Humphrey sat back, his face softening a bit. "Tabby's back at the home. We don't get out much anymore..." He pointed at his crotch. "Except when the plumbing needs work. But I see my three kids, eight grandkids, and one great grandkid every Christmas. We look forward to that visit all year."

Ted sighed. "You're pretty cool, Mr., uh—"

"Humphrey." The old man thrust his hand forward. Ted accepted the gesture and shook it. He hoped his handshake would be that strong when he was Mr. Humphrey's age.

"Thanks, Mr. Humphrey," Ted said. "You've given me a lot to think about." In a moment of clarity, an image of Casey returned to his mind, accompanied by the answer he was looking for.

Ted knew what he had to do.

KUNAL ARRIVED AT the hospital at quarter past one. He transported Ted via wheelchair to his sedan and helped him into the front passenger seat. Twenty minutes later they pulled up close to Ray's modest two-story home in Northeast Portland. Close to schools and playgrounds, and featuring unique restaurants and stores (including Ray's Tronikusu), the diverse cultural community of Northeast Portland was a great area to raise a family.

Since the birthday party had begun at one o'clock, vehicles belonging to other party-goers already lined the curb. When Ray's kids had a birthday party, he made it a family affair. Everyone was welcome.

Kunal killed the sedan's engine. "You sure you're up for this, dude?"

There was no hesitation to Ted's nod. He held a giant stuffed bear in front of him that he had bought at the hospital gift shop. "A little girl is counting on me."

They both stepped out of the sedan and Kunal hooked his

arm around Ted's, like he was escorting his grandmother. Ted accepted the gesture without question.

Kunal and Ted pushed through the side gate and stepped into the back yard. Angie's birthday was in full swing. Groups of parents stood socializing, nursing cold drinks. Kids, what seemed like a hundred of them, ran around the back yard, laughing and squealing, some using the swing set, others playing hide and seek around a small vibrantly colored plastic house. Children's music, indiscernible over the laughter, played in the background and helium balloons floated everywhere, tied with ribbons to any available piece of lawn furniture. Ray and Vivian knew how to host a kid's party.

Ted watched Ray play with Angie and some of her friends. They chased him around the back yard, laughing and squealing with delight. Occasionally, Ray would feign a stumble and let the kids overtake him. They'd clamber over his back until he would roar, stand up, and become the pursuer, tickling any child that was within reach. The sight of this happy gathering of family and friends made Ted's heart ache with longing, and his thoughts began to stray toward Casey again and the mistakes he had made.

Angie spotted Ted and scrambled away from Ray's tickling fingers. "Uncle Teddy! You made it!" Her brothers, sisters and friends followed Angie's beeline to Ted as she crushed herself into the side of his leg and wrapped her arms around his waist. Ted held the stuffed bear in front of his crotch to protect it as other kids jumped, reached and hugged him, even though they had no idea who he was. If it was okay for Angie to hug Ted, it was fine for everyone else too. Ray sat on the grass and caught his breath. He sent Kunal and Ted an exhausted but contented wave.

Ted presented the bear to Angie. "This is for you. Happy birthday, sweetie."

Angie held the large bear in front of her, its brown plush body almost obscuring her from sight. "What's his name?" she asked, suddenly concerned.

"I don't know." Ted thought for a moment. "How about…"

"How about Woody?" Kunal chuckled. "Or Harry Johnson?" Ted shot him a look. "Claude Balls?" Kunal flashed his brows.

"Enough." Ted looked at Angie, her clear, vibrant eyes looking back at him expectantly. "How about you choose a name for him…or her."

"Okay." Angie gave the bear a tight hug. "Uncle Teddy?"

"Yes?"

"Who kicked you in the balls?"

"Boy, she gets right to the point," Kunal said.

Ted crouched to Angie's level, even though it ached to do so. "Your daddy tell you that?"

Angie nodded. "He said someone kicked you in the balls and you had to go to the hospital."

I did. I kicked myself in the balls, Ted thought. "It doesn't matter who kicked me. What matters is I'm feeling better now."

"Okay." Angie held the bear up over her head. "Super Mystery Bear, blast off!" She rejoined the party, running toward the back yard, flying the bear through the air. Her young entourage followed close behind, giggling and jumping, trying to grab the gigantic stuffie.

Ted stood up, steadying himself on Kunal's shoulder. A

hint of a smile crossed his lips. Watching these kids play with abandon nourished his soul. The feeling was unexpected and welcome.

✂

TED AND KUNAL stretched out on aluminum loungers in the middle of the back yard, underneath a clear and warm evening sky. Kunal cradled a beer in his lap and Ted held a water and an ice pack. The aftermath of Angie's party surrounded them, like they had been at the epicenter of an explosion at a Fisher Price factory.

"It's always good to see Ray in his element." Kunal sipped his beer. "He throws a good party. I wish he did it more often…but maybe with a little less neon plastic."

"Goes with the territory, I guess." Ted stared at the evening sky shifting from oranges and reds to blues and purples. "His kids had a blast."

Kunal looked at Ted. "I knew it…I *knew* it!"

Ted looked at him, confused. "What?"

"Fuck, am I dumb."

"What the hell are you talking about?"

"I knew vasectomy wasn't right for you, dude." Kunal sighed and swatted away a mosquito. "I guess I just wanted a brother in arms, or *balls* in this case. I should have tried harder to stop you."

Ted shook his head. "Not your fault. It's not like you forced me to do it."

"I still feel shitty about it."

Before Ted could answer, Ray stepped through the sliding

door at the back of his house, a beer in one hand, and pulled a folding chair next to Kunal. He sported a mustache and goatee combination. "What's happening, bitches?"

Ted looked at Ray's fake facial hair and smiled. "There's the Ray we know and love."

Kunal offered Ray a casual glance. "Evil Spock."

"Bingo!" Ray snapped his fingers, ending with his index fingers pointing at his mustache and goatee. "Evil Spock rocks. It's a classic, am I right?"

Kunal swigged from his beer. "That's one of the better ones. The Fu Manchu was the creepiest so far."

"You got that right." Ted turned toward Ray. "So, what's with the fake beards all the time?"

"We've been through this." Ray twisted off the cap of his beer. "I feel I've been very clear about it."

"Humor me."

Ray sucked back a couple gulps of beer. His eyes glazed over and his body slid into relaxation. "I can't grow a beard to save my life. It's my stupid genetics…Look, how often do you guys shave?"

"Once a day," both Ted and Kunal said in unison. They laughed and clinked bottles.

"See?" Ray stared at the two men like he had already proved his point. "It's once a week for me, if I'm lucky. And it's patchy as fuck."

"The fake facial hair makes Ray feel *sexy*." Kunal thumped his chest. "Me, Ray. Beard help me fuck good. Arr."

Ray picked up a plastic bowling pin and threw it at Kunal. "Shut up."

Kunal ducked the pin. "Well? Am I wrong?"

Ray paused, then a little sheepish grin spread across his face. "Viv likes it, so…"

"See?" Kunal reached out with his fist, bumping it with Ray's. "I think part of 'The Secret of Ray' has just been unlocked."

"But why Star Trek?" Ted said.

"Are you kidding me?" Ray looked at Ted, eyes wide and shaking his head in surprise. "Star Trek is, like, the best thing ever. Well, except for Viv and the kids…and you guys."

"I'll drink to that." Ted raised his bottle and all three guys clinked necks. "So what's next for facial hair?" Ted said.

"Harry Mudd," Ray said.

"Who?"

Kunal sat up on the lounger. "Harcourt Fenton Mudd."

Ted had no idea who Kunal and Ray were talking about.

"I think we got to school this bitch." Ray hooked a thumb at Ted.

Kunal nodded. "Binge watch The Original Series?"

"Yep. Eight weeks?"

"Better make it twelve." Kunal turned to Ted. "When do you want to start?"

"Look guys, no offense but how about just sending me a bunch of pictures?" Ted shifted his eyes between Kunal and Ray as they both considered the option.

"Okay," Kunal said. "But you can't avoid it forever."

You can't avoid it forever. The words took on a different meaning as Ted's brain returned to the plan that was percolating in the back of his mind. Time was his enemy.

✄

KUNAL DROPPED TED off at his condo. "Need any help?"

Ted shook his head as he closed the sedan's passenger door. "Nope. Feeling pretty good now."

"I'm glad you came out. Angie seemed pretty stoked. Ray too, for that matter."

"Me, too." Ted slapped the roof of the sedan. "Later, man."

As Kunal began to drive out of the roundabout drop off area, Ted felt his pockets. *No keys.*

Ted turned back toward Kunal's tail lights. "Kunal! Wait!"

Kunal was taking his time leaving, making sure Ted got inside okay. He stopped and reversed toward Ted as Ted hobbled toward him, meeting him in the middle.

Kunal rolled down the passenger door window. "What's up, dude?"

"Keys," Ted said.

Kunal snapped his fingers. "Shit, right!" He placed the sedan into park and reached to the glove compartment. He pulled out Ted's keys and handed them over. "It's good you remembered these. My brain's a little foggy."

"You okay to drive? You can crash here if you want."

"No worries," Kunal said. "It's been more than an hour since my last beer. I think I'm tired more than anything."

"Okay." Ted hooked a finger through one of the key rings, jangling the keys. "Drive safe."

Kunal pulled out of the roundabout, then turned right onto NE 2nd Avenue and disappeared into the night.

Ted let himself into the building. He checked his mail, grabbing a handful of envelopes, and meandered to the elevators. On any other day, he would have taken the stairs for a little extra cardio workout, but he'd learned his lesson.

Recuperation was forefront in his mind. He even had arranged with Danielle and Joe to cover the shop for him for a few days. Whether they chose overtime or reduced hours, it didn't matter to Ted as long as they were happy.

The elevator doors opened onto the fourth floor and Ted shuffled out. As he walked toward his suite, he flipped through his keys. He isolated the one to his door and unlocked it. He threw his keys and mail onto the counter as Buster trotted over to greet him.

"Hey, Buster," he said as he gave the dog's head and ears an affectionate scratch. "Did you miss me? I missed you. I bet you're—" Ted reached into the cupboard for Buster's food, but stopped cold when he heard a noise from the far side of the room.

He looked toward the television and couch and spotted a human figure. A chill ripped up his back. Before words could escape Ted's lips, the figure turned on the lamp next to the couch. Iris's face and the curve of her body lit up under the lamp's warm glow.

"Hi, Ted." Iris sat reclined on the couch. She wore an overcoat and held a glass of wine in one hand, the remnants of the bottle in the other.

Ted's fear willingly stepped aside to make way for anger, and he stepped into the living area. "What are you doing here?" It took every ounce of will to keep his voice calm, yet he couldn't completely hide its angry edge.

"I wanted to see you." Iris sipped wine from her glass.

"Sorry, but you don't *get* everything you want anymore." Buster whined.

"Did you feed Buster?" Ted didn't give Iris time to respond. "Did you walk him? Oh yeah. That's right. You don't live here anymore."

"He's fine," Iris said.

"He's not fine. He's hungry." Ted grabbed Buster's food dish and walked back to the kitchen, the dog right on his heels. "Come on, buddy, I'll get you something to eat."

Iris placed the wine bottle on the coffee table and stumbled off the couch, already drunk, following Ted toward the kitchen.

He filled Buster's bowl and set it on the floor. Buster began to wolf down his kibble. "I've got to get the locks changed, eh boy?"

Iris held up Ted's post-vasectomy specimen cup, rolling it between her fingers. "Would you like me to help you fill this?"

Ted looked daggers at Iris. "I'd like you to leave. *Now.*"

"Oh, Teddy. A vasectomy was what we both needed." She placed the specimen cup on the counter, then traced her finger tip around the rim of her wine glass. "It solves all our problems."

"You're drunk. Why are you here?"

Iris placed her wine glass down on the counter. Ted half expected her to spill it, but she steadied herself and didn't spill a drop. She sauntered toward Ted, her hips swaying in the same seductive way he remembered, yet slightly unstable due to the wine. Ted backed up, avoiding her approach until he had no more room to move.

She planted her lips full on his mouth, leaving red lipstick smudges on his face. Ted turned his head and wiped his face with the back of his hand, smearing the lipstick.

"Fuck me, Ted." Iris bit her lower lip. "Now. Right here." She placed her hand on Ted's crotch.

"Don't do that." Ted pushed her hand away. "I'm still sore."

"I know what you need."

Ted pushed past Iris, breaking free from her drunken grasp. "You haven't got the slightest idea."

Iris followed his retreat. "Oh, yes I do."

"*You* dumped *me,* remember?"

"We all make mistakes." Iris licked her lips. She untied the belt on her overcoat as she strolled toward Ted's new position against the front door. The coat fell open revealing nothing but sexy red lingerie underneath.

"That's not going to work. I'm seeing someone else." Despite his anger, Ted could feel arousal stirring deep inside him. It had a mind of its own and it wasn't going to listen to reason.

Iris boxed Ted in with her arms and pressed her body against him. He could feel the warmth from the swell of her breasts and her skin through his shirt. He forced his mind elsewhere, into the financials of the coffee shop, Buster, Angie's party, anything to distract him from Iris's advances.

"You've never been able to resist the overcoat, Ted," she whispered into his ear as she leaned in to kiss him again. Ted turned his head at the last moment, Iris's lips missing their mark and instead leaving red lip prints smeared all down his neck.

A knock sounded through the door.

"You expecting someone? That *someone else* you're talking about?" Iris sent him a sly look.

Ted's mind raced. *Who could it be? Kunal? Ray? Yeah, please let it be Ray. He's a definite turn off for Iris.*

"Want to make it a threesome?" she added.

A threesome? With Ray? Ted's stomach did a back flip as he shook his head in horror. He looked through the peephole. The person he saw standing in the hallway both surprised him and scared the hell out of him.

"Shit." Ted's life was about to get worse.

IT HAD ACTUALLY been her mom's idea. Fiona had called early that morning to let Casey know they had arrived safely back at home in New York. Trying to be supportive of Casey's choice in men, Fiona casually asked about Ted.

"I'm not talking to you about him, Mom," Casey said.

"Well, I'm just trying to be interested in your life."

Through the phone's receiver Casey could hear ice cubes clinking in a tumbler, likely half full with vodka. Fiona was well on her way to Blitzville. Casey knew from experience that conversations with her drunken mother were pointless. Still, she listened.

"Don't give up on love, honey," Fiona said. "It's what's kept your dad and I together all these years. That and all the sex."

It was the way Fiona said the word "sex" that sent Casey around the bend. "Ew, Mom! Gross." But despite the alcohol cruising through her brain, odd occasions such as this saw Fiona come up with simple and profound ideas.

Don't give up on love. The idea reverberated and repeated in her mind. *But is it love?* Casey thought. *Does Ted love me?* She thought he did, but after everything that had happened at dinner and at the hospital, doubts crept in. But she returned to their first date and how it felt so right. Casey decided to give Ted another chance.

She pulled on some form fitting jeans, a black tank top and her favorite asymmetric hoodie from Rotita. She took a chance on Ted being discharged from the hospital already and called a cab. In less than thirty minutes she was on her way to Ted's building. From the cab's back seat, she caught glimpses of the sunset sliding into night behind Portland's cityscape across the Willamette River. The beauty of the city had a hard time competing with her excitement.

Casey paid the cab driver and stepped toward the front entrance of the building, just as a young couple stepped out. She ran towards them and they held the door for her. Instead of buzzing up, Casey now had the option to surprise Ted, and the thought ramped up her nervous energy. She smiled to herself and stepped into the elevator.

She stepped off at the fourth floor and approached suite 408. Casey stopped herself an inch away from knocking when she heard noises behind the door.

Voices? Maybe he has friends over, she thought, and resumed her knock on the door.

"Shit," someone said, their voice filtered through the thickness of the door.

Casey thought the voice belonged to was Ted, but wasn't one hundred percent sure. "Ted?"

"Uh, yeah." Scuffling sounds traveled across the door. "One moment."

Casey tilted her ear toward the door. "Are you okay?" She caught sounds of whispering as the door cracked open.

Ted poked his head out, blocking the rest of the open door with his body.

"Did I come at a bad time?" Casey craned her neck to get a look inside.

"Kind of." Ted looked like he was struggling with something behind the door. "Can I meet you somewhere, like, in ten minutes?"

"Um, sure. Where?"

Ted struggled against the door, but it swung open wide despite his opposition. He closed his eyes and sighed.

Iris stood in the doorway, her overcoat hanging open, her scanty lingerie in full view. Casey's eyes, with her excitement fading fast, traveled down Iris's body and back, settling on her face.

Iris gave Casey a once-over, but with a scowl that morphed into a sly grin. She closed her overcoat with slow, measured movement and tied the belt.

Ted looked at Casey, saw her crushed before him but maintaining her composure, then turned to Iris. "Aw Jesus, don't do this."

Iris turned to him, still wearing that grin, a grin that said *I win again.* "I know we can make this work, Ted." She tried to kiss Ted on the lips but he turned his head. She left another lip print on his cheek and she made a half-hearted attempt to wipe it away with her thumb.

"Call me later, okay, lover boy?" Iris slinked by Casey, a red wine haze following her toward the elevators down the hallway. Both Ted and Casey watched her drunken exit.

Casey turned to Ted, her eyes blazing and wet with tears that refused to fall. "You're *single*, huh?"

"Nothing happened, Casey," Ted pleaded. "I swear!" He pointed down the hallway. "She's drunk."

Ella opened the door to her unit, with a bag of garbage in her hand. Casey caught sight of her and recognized her face immediately. Images of a bikini-clad teenager in Ted's lap flashed through her head, enraging her more. Ella beat a hasty retreat back into her suite.

Casey turned back to Ted. "Why should I believe you?"

"Because it's you I want, not her." Ted pointed at the elevators where Iris had just stood.

"Could have fooled me." Casey uttered a scream of anguish and frustration. "I knew I shouldn't have come here." She stormed toward the stairwell, but stopped at Ella's door. "And fuck you, you little *bitch*!" She slammed her hand on the door and continued her angry exit toward the stairwell.

Ted tried to run after Casey, but he was still too sore to move that fast. "Casey, wait! I can explain."

Casey reached the stairwell, daggered a look at Ted, and headed down the stairs. Her furious steps down the stairs echoed back up the stairwell as the door closed in a slow arc.

"This is all your fault, Mom," she yelled. Tears breached her eyelids and Casey sobbed as she descended the stairs.

TED WATCHED THE stairwell door latch close and sighed. The door to Ella's suite cracked open. She emerged with the garbage again.

"Is it safe?" she asked.

Ted nodded.

"Man, she's pissed." Ella glanced back at the stairwell exit, then back at Ted.

"She has every right to be." Ted stared vacantly down the hallway.

"What did you do?"

Ted shook his head. "Never mind. No point rehashing it."

Ella took in this shell of a man standing before her, and even with their spotty recent history, couldn't help but feel some sympathy toward him. And a little guilt. "You really like her, don't you? And by 'like', I mean 'like-like.'"

Ted looked up at her, his eyes weary with pain and sorrow. "Yeah, I do."

Gears started to turn in Ella's head. "You want me to talk to her? If she's not gone already?"

"You?" Ted huffed, more in pain than amusement. "She'll probably rip your head off. What could you tell her that she doesn't already know?"

Ella shrugged. "Since she *doesn't* know me, I could—"

"Oh, she knows you," Ted said, his voice barely a whisper.

Ella's eyes narrowed. "What did you say?"

"Forget it."

She gave him a sideways look and sighed. "Look. I tried to blackmail you…in the worst way possible." Ella locked gaze with Ted, her eyes sincere. "Consider this my good deed for the day."

Ted nodded. "Okay. Thanks."

Ella turned and walked to the stairwell, garbage in tow. Ted watched the door close again, then stood in silence, propped up against the wall. He heard Buster scratch at the door and bark. Ted shuffled back inside, gave Buster a head scratch, and closed the door behind him. The sound of his deadbolt engaging echoed through the empty hallway.

Ted made his way to the couch and sat, shrouded by the darkness of the condo, drained physically and emotionally, his face still covered with smeared lipstick.

Buster walked over to where Ted sat, his claws clacking on the hardwood floor. He placed his head on Ted's thigh and looked up at him with his big brown puppy dog eyes.

"You've had enough? You and me, both." Ted placed his hands on both sides of Buster's head. "Okay, buddy. Let's get the collar off you." He rotated the collar until he found the Velcro seam and separated it. The collar slid off easily, leaving the fur underneath matted and flat. Ted ran his fingers through it, fluffing it back up.

Ted held the dog's head in his hands. "I know it's going to be difficult, but try not to lick yourself, okay?"

Buster chuffed back at him.

"Okay." Ted eased his legs onto the couch and patted the cushion beside him. Buster hopped up, traced a circle before settling down beside him. "You're sure getting big."

Buster let out a sigh and was already half asleep. Ted was soon to follow.

CASEY SAT ON the back steps of the building. She dragged a wrist across her face, wiping her tears away. A path flanked by small shrubs led to a bank of dumpsters a short distance away, but far enough that she wasn't assaulted by the smell.

Ella emerged from the building. She looked at Casey, giving her a wide berth, and walked to the dumpsters. She could feel Casey's angry stare follow her all the way there and back.

Ella held her hands up. "Truce? If I had a white flag, I'd wave it, but I'm not sure why."

Casey kept her eyes on the teen as she approached. *It couldn't hurt to hear her side of things,* she thought. *How much worse could it get?*

"I'm Ella." She began to extend her hand, hesitated for a moment, then fully presented her gesture of goodwill. Casey ignored it. "I live beside Ted in the next unit down... with my mom."

"I've seen you before," Casey clasped her hands on her lap. "You're the bikini girl. I've seen the photos."

Ted's earlier comment about Casey knowing her flew to the forefront of her mind. Ella stood motionless, feeling heat rise on her cheeks.

"In fact, I was the one who I found your bikini bottoms." Casey looked at her. "In the *couch*. It was a real laugh riot."

"Shit. Sorry," Ella said. "And I thought he'd deleted those pictures."

"Well I guess he forgot."

Ella sat down on the steps next to Casey, but made a point to give her space. "I can be a little rowdy sometimes." Ella shook her head in recollection. "He was so mad at me that day."

Casey looked at her.

"He was driving Buster home from the vet and offered me a ride home from the pool." Ella spotted a hangnail on her thumb and bit at it. "I started playing around with his phone. He tried to grab it, we swerved, and we almost crashed." Ella fell silent for a moment. "Later, I changed at his place and left my bottoms behind. I don't know why…I was being stupid."

"Why are you telling me this?" Casey said.

Ella faced Casey, her eyes sincere, just as they had been with Ted earlier. "Because as guys go these days, you could do a lot worse."

"You're an expert, are you?"

"Just a good judge of character, I guess."

Casey opened her mouth to say something, hesitated, then continued anyway. "You two didn't…you know…"

"What?" Ella's eyes went wide. "No! He's old enough to be my dad…Eww. Gross."

"Sorry."

"By the way…" A sheepish look crossed Ella's face. "I stashed some of my underwear under Ted's mattress."

It was Casey's turn to be surprised. "What's with you and the underwear? And…how did you get in?"

"It must have been when he was going to have his surgery," Ella said. "His friends carried him away and left the door unlocked. He looked drunk. I was angry at him…so I let myself in."

"Why were you angry at him?"

"He offered me a job, then changed his mind."

Casey shook her head. "Even you knew about the vasectomy before me."

"I didn't until I left my underwear there that last time." Ella picked at her hangnail. "There was a post-op checklist in his bathroom."

Casey fell silent, lost in thought.

"He like-likes you, you know."

Casey scrunched her brow. "Like-like?"

"You know, more than like and less than love. Or maybe it *is* love. I don't know." Casey could see that Ella was trying to be an expert on this subject. "Way heavier than a crush, that's for sure."

"Do adults get crushes?"

Ella shrugged. "I don't see why not." She looked at Casey with her vibrant blue eyes and teenage eagerness. "So, are you going to talk to him?"

Casey studied her face. "Ted put you up to this, didn't he."

"To talk to you?" Ella shook her head. "No. That was my idea." She was either a very good actress, or being completely sincere. Casey chose the latter and believed her.

"He's blown it three times now." She looked at Ella. "You're suggesting I should give him *another* chance?"

"They say fourth time's a charm."

"Really? They say that?"

"Whatever. He's a good guy, and you seem like a nice person. I mean, you didn't rip my head off...so..." Ella smiled.

"What about his ex?"

"You mean Iris?"

Casey shrugged. "I guess. I don't know what her name is."

"Personally, I think she's a skanky bitch," Ella said. "I barely know you and I already like you better. Ever since I met her, she's barely acknowledged me. It's been, like..." Ella counted in her head. "...six years. Who does that? And besides, she doesn't like Buster."

Casey looked at her. "That is bad. Buster's adorable."

"I know, right?" Ella shrugged. "So, what have you got to lose?"

What have I got to lose? Casey thought. *If Ted's the one, perhaps everything.*

Casey pulled out her phone and called a cab. She stood up and extended her hand. Ella took it and the two women shared a firm handshake.

"Thanks," Casey said. "It seems I have some thinking to do." She headed toward the front of the building to wait for her ride. Ella unlocked the stairwell door and headed back to the fourth floor.

Don't give up on love, Casey thought as she walked to the building's front roundabout. *Thanks, Mom.*

Apology

TED WADDLED INTO the coffee shop shortly after ten in the morning, Buster close on his heels. The tables were all occupied with paying customers as were the two tables out front. The morning sun streamed through the front window, boosting the ambiance to match the warm essence of coffee.

Danielle and Joe busied themselves serving customers. Ted paused at the door to the small stock room and hooked his finger at Joe.

Ted was able to crouch now, so he got down to Buster's level. "You be a good dog, huh?"

Buster chuffed and Ted scratched him behind the ears.

"Hey Boss." Joe stepped up beside Buster.

"I got to take care of something." Ted stood up and motioned at Danielle. "You two'll be okay by yourselves for a while?"

Joe gave Ted a slightly annoyed look. "You've been gone for a few days already. What's another couple of hours?"

Danielle called across the counter, "We'll be fine, *Dad*."

Ted pulled Joe aside and handed him Buster's BiteNot collar. "If he starts licking himself, put this back on, okay?"

Joe lowered himself to one knee, ruffling Buster's fur. The dog licked his face. "No tea-bagging for Buster. Got it."

"I'll be back as soon as I can." Ted turned to head out the way he came.

"What's going on, Boss," Joe said, "if you don't mind me asking?"

"Damage control," Ted said without looking back.

Buster trudged over to his dog bed near the door, like he was on autopilot. The dog knew what his job was: official snoozer and greeter, with an emphasis on snoozing. And he was eager to get back to work.

Joe stepped back behind the counter and washed his hands.

Danielle handed a coffee and a home-style rice crispy treat to a customer in exchange for several bills. "Did Ted say where he was going?" she asked as she made change.

"No, but I have my suspicions." Joe retied his apron strings and grinned as he watched Ted walk up the street and beyond the shop's front window. "It took a vasectomy for him to grow some balls," he said to himself. "Good luck, Boss."

✁

CASEY SAT AT her desk completing patient paperwork, but her mind was elsewhere, trying to imagine the future and forget the past. Three times today she had failed to see a waiting patient before hearing them rap their knuckles on her desk.

She pictured Ted at his condo door, pleading with her. His pain and sorrow looked sincere. After talking to Ella, Casey was certain that Ted had been truthful with her the previous night. But she was still conflicted. Part of her wanted to throw caution to the wind and forgive him. She had forgiven past boyfriends too quickly before, and it had never ended well.

"Learn from your mistakes, Bug," she heard her father say in her head.

But maybe Ted isn't like those other guys, Casey thought. *But how will I know for sure?*

As if she had summoned him with some inexplicable power, Ted rounded the corner and entered the medical office holding a bouquet of roses in a crystal vase. He placed the flowers on Casey's desk and waited for her reaction.

Casey ignored him. She placed her paperwork into several file folders, stepped to a filing cabinet and inserted the folders in their appropriate spots.

Ted leaned over the desk so he could lower his voice. "Give me another chance, Casey? Please?"

She returned to her task chair and continued with her work. *I think I'll let him sweat for a while,* she thought, a small grin escaping at the corner of her mouth.

"Come on, Casey." Ted raised his voice a little. "Please?"

Without looking at him, she said, "You're disturbing the other patients…and I'm not talking to you."

"You just did. Good." Ted rubbed his hands together. "We're making progress."

"I'll call security."

"Look, about last night…" Ted looked around at the other patients in the waiting room and leaned closer to Casey. "Iris is the last person I want to see. I haven't changed the locks yet and she just let herself in."

Casey let out an exasperated sigh. "Is that why *your* face was covered with *her* lipstick?"

"She forced herself on me," Ted said.

Casey gave Ted a sideways look. "*Oh, please.*" She reached for the phone and began dialing. "I'm calling security."

Ted raised his hands, palms up. "Okay. I'm going." He backed up and left the office.

Casey began to second-guess herself. *Did I go too far? What if I never see him again?* She looked at the vase with the beautiful arrangement of roses in them and softened a little. She wanted to run after Ted and throw her arms around him, but she stopped herself. *Not yet,* she thought. *I have to be sure.*

Casey's desk phone rang. She picked it up, expecting Ted's voice on the other end. Instead it was the voice of her nemesis, Blanche, cackling through the receiver like a witch.

Blanche sat at her desk with her hand cupped over the phone. "You'll *always* be a trollop," her voice rasped in Casey's ear. "All the flowers in the world won't change that unless you *repent* your sins and *accept* the teachings of Jesus Christ."

Casey said nothing and stared straight back at Blanche with such intensity that Blanche hung up the phone. She picked up the vase of roses and walked calmly to Blanche's desk.

Blanche began to cower as Casey approached her, raising one arm in expectation of Casey throwing the vase at her. Instead, Casey placed the vase down on Blanche's desk.

"You know, Blanche," Casey said in as cool a voice as she could muster. "You'd have more friends if you learned to live and let live." She plucked the little card from Ted out of the bouquet, shoved it into her pocket and walked back to her desk. A stunned Blanche watched her go.

Casey couldn't swear to it, but she thought she heard a smattering of applause as she returned to her desk. Her heart pounded in her chest but she was pleased she had remained in control.

My random act of kindness is done for the day, Casey thought as she went back to her duties. And her thoughts led back to Ted. She pulled out the little card that had been included with the bouquet and opened it

The card read, "Jay Jay's tonight? XO T."

Casey smiled and a flood of good memories overtook her. Ted was chipping away at her resolve even when he wasn't around.

✄

THIS IS CRAZY, thought Ted. *I'm going to break my neck…or my nuts, or worse.*

Ted stood outside the front entrance of East Portland Medical Center, holding one rose and wearing an old pair of roller skates. He maintained his balance as best he could, faltering at random moments but remaining upright. That was the important part.

The overcast sky had darkened in roiling patches. The forecast called for rain, but so far not a drop had fallen. Office staff left the building in scattered groups. Many cast him strange looks and Ted was sure those looks accompanied strange thoughts.

"Just waiting for someone," he said, trying to look casual. It didn't work. Ted looked odd.

The first raindrop that he noticed landed on his nose and

splashed his face. Ted groaned as he wiped the raindrop away and almost lost his balance.

Casey appeared just inside the main doors to the medical center. She looked up at the sky and dug a red umbrella from her purse. She stepped outside and popped it open. She headed left toward the bus stop.

Okay, it's now or never, Ted thought. *Slow and easy.* He pushed with each foot, one at a time just as Casey had taught him at Jay Jay's, moving forward in the same direction Casey was walking.

"Casey! Wait!" Ted pumped his legs, one hand cupping his crotch, and the other holding the rose.

Upon hearing her name, Casey looked behind her and did a double take at Ted's rickety approach. To everyone else, Ted looked like some kind of deranged stalker. The wheels on his feet didn't help with that perception.

"Please, Casey." Ted missed grabbing her shoulder by inches and spun himself to a stop, miraculously staying on his feet. "Hear me out, okay?"

Casey looked him over and Ted thought he saw a small smile pass across her face.

"You have one minute," she said, resting the shaft of her umbrella on her shoulder.

Ted collected himself and cleared his throat. He realized the hand not holding the rose was still hovering over his crotch, and he let it drop to his side.

He held the rose out, his earnest eyes connecting with hers. Casey looked at the red petals dotted with raindrops, then back at Ted. She accepted the rose, but pricked her finger on a thorn. The rose fell to the ground as she placed her thumb in her mouth.

Ted reached out to catch the flower and lost his balance. His butt landed on the concrete and the impact reverberated through his groin and up his spine.

"Oh my God, Ted. Are you alright?" Casey began to kneel when he waved her off. Instead she picked up the rose, avoiding the thorns this time.

"I'm okay. I got this." He struggled to his knees, gritting his teeth through the dull pain, and stood. His feet rolled back and forth as he found his balance again.

Ted took a deep breath and closed his eyes. *It's now or never,* he thought.

"Casey, I'm sorry," Ted began. "I've made mistakes. Too many recently. But I've realized I want a future with kids in it, and with you in it too, if possible...I've discovered I'm a family man, and that's more important than a lifetime of mind-blowing, worry-free sex."

A crowd of onlookers began to gather around the two. Casey felt their prying eyes and resumed her walk toward the bus.

Casey shook her head. "Ted..."

"Wait." Ted rolled with her, his arms and legs moving awkwardly to maintain forward momentum and balance. "Everything else...it's a huge misunderstanding that I can't reliably explain." Ted grabbed the shoulder of Casey's coat with one hand to steady himself and cupped his crotch with the other as his body swung around wildly and came to a stop.

Casey turned toward him.

"One thing I can say is my world shifted the moment I met you," Ted said, "I knew you were the one, and I know in my heart that we can be great together."

Casey took one of Ted's hands and looked down at it. She was about to say something when Ted continued.

"That's why I've decided to have my vasectomy reversed. I should have listened to my heart instead of my…" Again, Ted realized where his hand was and moved it away from his nether region. "Can we have a do-over?"

Casey looked up at Ted, then spotted her bus pulling up to the stop. "I don't know. That's a pretty big do-over." She stepped up to the bus as its door opened, then found a seat at the back.

Ted watched her go. Soaked to the skin and a dull ache in both his butt and his groin, he had given his all. Casey sat and looked out the window at him as the bus began to pull away.

No, this isn't the way this is supposed to end, Ted thought, and began to skate after the bus. "Casey! Wait!"

Casey's eyes lit up and she slid the bus window open. "Want to go roller skating?" she called out.

"Yes!" Ted yelled back, breathless but smiling.

"Okay! Call me later." Casey smiled and waved back as the bus accelerated down the street, far faster than Ted could keep up with.

"I will!" Ted slowed himself down enough to grab a lamp standard. His legs flew around it as he came to a stop.

Phase one of his plan was complete, but phase two was still an unknown.

Phase Two

A WEEK LATER, TED found himself back in Dr. Palmer's office. This time around, Casey knew about the appointment and had wished him luck beforehand. Everything about the office had remained the same, not that Ted had expected things to change. However, the songs were different.

Just a different place in the playlist, Ted thought. The dulcet melody of "Red Rubber Ball" by The Cyrkle crooned out of the small speakers.

"I heard about your little misadventure, or should I say *Miss Adventure*," Dr. Palmer said. "Neandross's receptionist! Score!" He held up the hand that wasn't in a sling for a high-five but Ted just looked at him, unamused. "Although, I'm a little disappointed. I thought my instructions were very clear. You didn't ice your balls as I instructed, did you?"

"I didn't come here to rehash the past," Ted said flatly.

Dr. Palmer cocked his ear to the music, drawing inspiration from it. "I guess you're past the worst of it now, eh? Did you learn your lesson well?"

"Yeah. I learned that I should never have gotten a vasectomy in the first place," Ted said. "I want it reversed."

"Ooo." Dr. Palmer shook his head and crossed his arms. "That ain't cheap."

"How much are we talking about?"

Dr. Palmer leaned forward, his eyes narrowed and a sly grin spread across his lips. "How much you got?"

"Can you be serious for one second?" Ted said, annoyed. "This is my future."

Dr. Palmer sat back. "Twenty-K."

Ted choked a bit on his words. "Twenty thousand dollars? You're joking."

"For once, I'm not. I never joke about money."

The enormity of Ted's misguided decision came crashing down around him. "Holy shit," he said quietly to himself.

"Look, this kind of thing isn't covered by insurance," Dr. Palmer said. "You've got to pay for the anesthetist, the hospital stay, the operating room. Then, of course, you have to pay for *my* expertise. Lucky for you, this won't be complicated."

"But twenty thousand?"

"Sometimes more. But it's undoing my own handiwork after what...a week or two? It'll be like untying a pair of shoes." Dr. Palmer chuckled. "You poor bastard. You didn't even get to experience the genius that is 'Lone Wolf.' "

Ted's brain was running mental calculations to see if the shop's cash flow could handle the hit.

"Anyway," Dr. Palmer continued, "I think the cost will be closer to ten. That's kind of why I told you that vasectomies were *permanent*. Remember me telling you that?"

"Can you guarantee that it will work?"

"Typical success rates are over ninety percent within three years of getting snipped." Dr. Palmer grabbed his own crotch and Ted couldn't tell if he did it instinctively or on purpose. "I'd take that bet in a heartbeat."

The upbeat melody sung by The Cyrkle was coming to an end. Dr. Palmer thrummed his fingers on his legs in time with the music.

"So what's it going to be, Ted? Are we going to get your red rubber balls bouncing again?" Dr. Palmer watched Ted's brain work. "I've got my eyes on a new set of golf clubs *and* a golf cart."

Ted took a moment to think, but there was only one answer that made sense.

TED STOOD IN his kitchen, making coffee in his French press. He still had a little Jinotega left and wanted to use it up before the beans became stale. He filled the kettle and set it to boil as he ground the required amount of beans. Placing his nose close to the freshly ground coffee beans, he inhaled their rich aroma. A wave of calm flowed through his body. His life was beginning to feel normal again.

Ted felt a warm pair of hands slide around his waist from behind and up his chest. The fingernails were painted in a French manicure, with a small black Mickey Mouse icon on each ring finger.

Casey turned her head and set her ear into the hollow between Ted's shoulder blades. She sighed, content, and closed her eyes. "I can hear you breathing, Mr. Barista."

"Your body feels good on mine," Ted said.

"Mmm hmm."

Ted removed the kettle from its electric base. "You sure you don't want a coffee?"

"On second thought, yeah, a small one." Casey kissed Ted's back through his shirt. "When's the next siesta?"

"Any time's a good time for me."

Casey kissed his shoulder. "I can't wait until you're back in commission." She turned and walked out of the kitchen, around the end of the counter and down the hallway to the bedroom.

Ted watched her go. Her fiery ginger hair fell loosely around her shoulders and her only article of clothing, an old and well-worn sweatshirt of his, hung down just low enough to cover up her behind.

Lord have mercy, Ted thought, feeling amorous stirrings below, ones that he had to quell. He still felt a little discomfort from his vasectomy.

He poured the boiling water into the French press and set the timer for four minutes.

"Ted?" Casey's voice floated back from the bedroom. "What are these?"

"What?"

Casey appeared from the hallway on the opposite side of the counter, with a pair of girl's underwear hanging off each index finger. "These aren't mine and they're *definitely* not yours."

Flashbacks ripped through Ted's mind, clashing with questions and nonexistent explanations. "I…ah…I have no idea."

Casey smiled, stood up on tippy-toes, and leaned over the counter. She beckoned him with her index finger, the underwear still hanging by its waistband. Ted moved closer, bewildered, until Casey kissed him on the lips.

"Of course you don't," she said, dropping the underwear on the counter. "They're Ella's. Could you return them to her before we go?"

Um, what? Ella's underwear? How? Ted dismissed the thought as quickly as it arrived. He didn't want to know. Been there, done that too many times.

Ted took the underwear, placed them in a sealed baggie, and headed for the door. Buster snoozed in his dog bed, having just wolfed down an enormous bowl of kibble.

He walked down the hallway to Ella's suite. He knocked on the door and waited. Ted was just about to knock again when Ella opened the door.

"Hey." Ella looked surprised to see Ted.

"Hey."

"What's up?"

Ted pulled the baggie out of his pocket and presented the underwear. "These are yours, apparently."

Ella smiled, nodded, and stifled a laugh. She took the baggie and jammed it into her front pocket. Both Ted and Ella experienced their own feelings of déjà vu at the same moment.

"I'm not going to ask why or how, but…is that it?" Ted said. "I'm not going to find any more of your *underthings* in my apartment, am I?"

"No," Ella said.

"Good." Ted cleared his throat. "Now that that's out of the way, I wanted to thank you…for the other night."

Ella shrugged. "No bigs."

"It is…bigs," Ted said. "Definitely bigs."

"Did it help?"

Casey stepped through the door to Ted's condo holding a travel mug of coffee. Ted looked at her and smiled warmly.

"Yes, it did," he said.

Ella beamed. "Good. I figured I owed you one. And that random act of kindness stuff feels pretty good."

Casey locked the door and walked towards Ted and Ella.

"Hi, Casey."

"Hey." Casey planted a kiss on Ted's cheek, leaving behind a red lip print. Both women grinned. "Did you get your *scanties* back?"

"Yup." Ella tapped her front pocket with her hand.

Ted felt heat rise on the back of his neck as he tried to ignore their conversation. Never would he have predicted Casey and Ella talking about skimpy underwear in front of him, especially after all the recent misunderstandings. Ted took comfort knowing this conversation would never have happened with Iris.

"Ella!" Sheridan called out from somewhere inside the suite. "Who's at the door?"

"Ted...I mean Mr. Cooper," Ella said.

"Ask him about the job!"

Ella faced Ted and Casey, and rolled her eyes. "Sorry, she's a little relentless."

"And subtle." Ted smiled.

"I know, right? I think she wants the summer to herself."

"The job's yours, if you're still interested. I could use the help." Ted looked at Casey. "I like the idea of working a little less this summer." Casey returned his gaze.

"Seriously?" Ella's eyes bugged out with excitement. On any other day, Ted and Casey's public display of affection

would have made her gag with embarrassment, but all Ella
heard was "the job's yours."

"For reals," Ted said.

Ella let out a little squeal, and before Ted could react, she
wrapped her arms around his neck and gave him a quick hug
and a kiss on the opposite cheek.

"Oops." She observed Ted now had lip prints bookend-
ing both cheeks and let out a small giggle. "Sorry. Kind
of a habit."

"I'll take a handshake next time, okay?"

" 'Kay." Ella was vibrating with excitement. "So when
do I start?"

"If it's okay with your mom," Ted said, "how about
next week?"

Ella squealed again and almost hugged Ted once more,
but stopped herself. Instead, she bounced on her tiptoes.
"Thank you, Mr. Cooper!"

"You're welcome." Ted looked at Casey. "Shall we?"

"Yes. I think so."

Ella closed her door, and as Ted and Casey walked toward
the elevator they heard her excited voice through the wall.
"Mom! I got it! I got the job!"

"You did a good thing back there," Casey said. "Especially
after everything that's happened."

"I think a job will do her some good." Casey handed Ted
the travel mug of coffee. "Thanks, but where's yours?"

"I thought I'd steal a sip from yours." Casey gazed at him.
Ted felt her emerald eyes look into his soul.

He stopped, kissed her, and said, "Drink as much as
you want."

Ted pressed the elevator call button and the two of them kissed until the doors opened to the fourth floor. They stepped inside and began their second official date. Jay Jay's Crystal Palace would become a regular destination in their courtship.

TED DISCOVERED THAT scheduling a vasectomy reversal took a lot longer than the original procedure. The earliest appointment he could get was in three months. The wheels of medical bureaucracy turned slowly, especially for elective surgery.

In the weeks leading up to the reversal, Ted and Casey spent every spare waking moment with each other. They both knew things were getting serious when Casey surprised Ted with a new pair of roller skates. She also bought Buster a dog bed for her place, which he preferred over the one back at Ted's.

Over the summer, Casey shared some of her favorite caving spots with Ted. He had never gone spelunking before meeting Casey, and central Oregon was blessed to have a sprawling system of caves. Most were clustered around Bend, a three and a half hour drive from Portland. They made weekend trips, leaving Friday after work and arriving back home Sunday evening.

Ted discovered that Buster loved to travel, but the caves were off limits for dogs. For the few caving weekends, Joe offered to take Buster. Ted wanted to pay him the equivalent of a kennel fee, but Joe declined, having taken a shine to the dog. He liked to think of himself as Buster's honorary uncle.

Ella worked out fine at Buster's Beans over the summer, so much so that Ted offered her a permanent part-time position so it wouldn't interfere with school. She made fast friends with Danielle, taking a keen interest in her hair and piercings. One week before her senior year of school started, Ella arrived at the shop with her hair dyed jet black with purple highlights. Of course, Danielle approved.

When the day of the procedure arrived, Casey offered to drive Ted to the hospital. He accepted without question.

"How are you feeling?" Casey stole a glance at Ted as she navigated the parking lot at Portland Metro Hospital. "Any second thoughts?"

"None." Ted looked at her. "I was a basket case before, but there's no stress, no worries. It's the right thing to do."

Casey pulled into a stall and shifted the SUV into park. She turned to Ted, her eyes just a little misty. "I love you, Ted Cooper."

Ted leaned across the divide between seats. "I love you too, Casey Collins." They kissed until the windows began to fog up. He drew a heart on the window with his finger. "Let's do this."

Once out of the vehicle, Ted placed one arm around Casey's shoulder as hers snaked around his waist. Together they headed for the front entrance.

"How long does recovery take?"

"One or two weeks, according to Palmer," Ted said.

"I'm not sure I can wait that long." Casey looked up at him, a little devious grin on her lips.

And those eyes. I'll never tire of them, thought Ted as he kissed her hair, always fragrant with hyacinth. "We'll figure something out," he said with a smile.

Ted and Casey emerged on the fifth floor to be greeted by Ray, Kunal and an unfamiliar woman. She was taller than Kunal by an inch or two, and wore a white tunic dress with denim-patterned leggings and white Skechers over bare feet. Her dark hair was styled in a short pixie cut. She and Kunal were holding hands. Ray sported a full, well manicured black beard that framed his face well. For once, it was a good look.

"You must be getting used to this place by now, eh dude?" Kunal said.

"I'll never get used to hospitals." Ted looked around the nexus of three hallways. "Something about the smell."

"And the gowns," Ray said. "I've seen more butt crack in five minutes than during bath night at my place. Maybe that's what you're smelling."

Ted smiled at the woman next to Kunal and presented his hand. "My name is Ted. I've known these misfits for years." He motioned beside him. "And this is Casey, the love of my life."

"Boy, he's got it bad," Ray whispered to Kunal.

Kunal ignored Ray and took Ted's cue. "This is Rebecca. We met a few days ago at a hot yoga class."

Rebecca shook Ted's, then Casey's hand. "Nice to meet you."

"I figured this would be a great place for our third date," Kunal said. "The institutional tile really seals the deal." Everyone shared a short laugh.

Ted raised his brow and gave Kunal a sideways look. "*Third* date?"

The panicked look that drifted over Kunal's face was priceless. He tried to shake his head subtly and even raised his hand and wagged it to his neck a little, as if to say "stop" or "cut."

He doesn't know what I'm going to say, Ted thought, grinning.

"You sound surprised," Rebecca said.

"No. It's just that…" Ted paused for effect. He wanted to make Kunal sweat a little. "It's just that Kunal went through quite a dry spell recently. I'm glad it's working out."

Kunal heaved a sigh of relief and gave Ted an "OK" symbol with this hand.

Rebecca looked at Kunal and smiled. "Thanks. He's quite the gentleman."

"Ahead warp factor one, Mr. Sulu," the ring tone played from Ray's pocket. All eyes were on him as he dug into his pocket and pulled out his phone.

"It's Viv." Ray keyed in his passcode and pulled up his text messenger application. Ray's eyes went wide as saucers. "Holy shit."

Ted didn't know if he should be concerned or intrigued. "You okay, Ray?"

"No! I mean yeah…" Ray's hand holding the phone trembled and his eyes misted over. "Viv just went into labor."

Ted clapped his hands and gave Ray a hug, patting his back. "Congratulations, man. That's great news."

Kunal followed Ted. "That's awesome, man, really."

Then subtle panic set in. "Oh, shit. I got to go! Good luck with your balls, Ted." Ray jammed his phone back in his pocket and ran to the elevator, pressing the down call button

like a mad man. When the elevator doors didn't open immediately, Ray ran to the stairwell door and pushed it open.
"Number five has arrived!" His victory yell echoed as he flew
down the concrete steps.

"That's our Ray," Ted said. "If I can be half as good a
father as him, I'll be set." Casey wrapped her arms around
Ted's waist and gave him a squeeze.

Dr. Palmer burst through the double doors that led to the
operating rooms. His braced wrist still hung in a sling.

"There you are, Ted, my man," he said.

"Hey."

Dr. Palmer leered at Casey. "Zelda?"

"Casey."

"Right. You work for Neandross, don't you?"

Casey gritted her teeth and managed a smile.

"That lucky son-of-a-bitch." Dr. Palmer's eyes lingered
on Casey as he turned to Rebecca. "And who's this vision
of beauty?"

Kunal stepped forward. "This is Rebecca. She's with me."

Dr. Palmer dismissed Kunal. "Jealousy doesn't look good
on you, my friend." He extended his hand towards Rebecca. "Dr. Palmer, at your service…well at his service really."
The doctor hooked a thumb at Ted. "But everyone calls me
'Lone Wolf.' "

Rebecca took Dr. Palmer's hand and offered a limp "Hello."

"So, Ted." Dr. Palmer flashed his brows and grinned. "Are
you ready for me to go nuts on your nuts?" The doctor was
met with looks of embarrassment from the rest of the group.
"Tough crowd. That one usually gets a few laughs."

Ted looked into Casey's eyes. "I'm ready, Doc." He took

Casey's face in his hands and kissed her, long and deep. "I'll see you in a few hours."

"I'll be here." Casey wrapped her arms around her chest and tried to hide her concern.

"Don't worry. I'll be fine." Ted smiled, content that his decision was the right one.

Casey nodded.

Ted waved goodbye. "Thanks, Kunal. Nice to meet you Rebecca." He followed Dr. Palmer through the double doors, down the hallway and into a small operating theater. A couple of hospital staff were busy preparing the table and laying out the necessary surgical utensils.

Dr. Palmer pointed to a small change room to the left of operating theater's entrance. "I want you to get naked and put on that sexy paper gown over there. A nurse will be by in a few minutes to get you…and no hard-ons, please." The doctor disappeared into another adjoining room. Ted could hear his cackling laughter long after he disappeared from sight.

In a few hours, everything would be right with the world again, Ted thought as he began to undress.

The gown ended up being well laundered cotton instead of scratchy paper and Ted wondered how many people had worn it before him.

Ray had been right about visible butt crack. The tie at the back was just long enough to secure the gown around his body, but the sides barely covered his butt cheeks.

They're operating on my balls, Ted thought. *I guess it's time to throw modesty to the wind.*

A knock on the door. "Mr. Cooper?"

"Yes?"

A female nurse opened the door. "Dr. Palmer is ready for you. Follow me, please."

"Sorry about the gown." Ted followed the nurse into the operating theater.

"It's one size fits all."

"More like one size fits *small*."

The nurse took Ted aside. "Don't worry. I've seen it all before, and some things that would turn your hair white."

Dr. Palmer stood next to the operating table. "You've met Andrea already and your anesthetist today is Rachel." Both women nodded at Ted, their cheeks indicating a smile under their surgical masks. "Let's get this show on the road, Ted. Hop on up and lie down for me." He cued Andrea and she pressed play on the portable desktop stereo system. "Big Balls" by AC/DC rocked out of the speakers.

Ted shook his head and smiled as he slid up onto the operating table. "Subtle, doc."

"What can I say?" Dr. Palmer said. "Today, you've got the biggest balls in the room."

"Well, go easy on me." Ted laid back, squinting at the bright operating room lights.

" 'Lone Wolf' wouldn't have it any other way." Dr. Palmer nodded at Rachel. She placed a mask over Ted's nose and mouth. "Count how many times Bon Scott says 'big balls.' "

Ted got as far as three before blackness overtook him.

Life

TED'S EYES CRACKED open a few minutes before his 6 a.m. alarm. The morning sun slid across the bedroom wall in orange slashes. He turned on his side to watch Casey sleep. Her ginger hair flowed across her pillow, framing her clear and peaceful face. She wore her favorite night shirt, one covered in cartoon-style illustrations of bears engaged in various antics: riding bikes, playing baseball, hang gliding, parachuting. Across the chest were the hand-written words "Bearly Sleeping."

I'm the luckiest son of a bitch on the planet, Ted thought, as he considered waking her up with a blanket of kisses.

His phone, which doubled as his alarm, sounded off by playing a track from his Crystal Palace playlist. This morning it was "September" by Earth, Wind and Fire, and the song brought with it a flood of good memories. He rolled over to turn the volume down and closed his eyes, reliving five year old memories as if they were yesterday.

And a lot had happened in those five years since Ted reversed his vasectomy. Kunal and Rebecca dated for three months before parting ways, but instead of falling back into his familiar pattern of one night stands, Kunal's goals changed. He was now looking for his one and only. He had come close a few times, but hadn't found her yet.

After her fifth child, Vivian informed Ray that her child-bearing days were over and that he was to have a vasectomy. After a small private meltdown, he accepted his fate graciously, and both Ted and Kunal made sure Ray had no complications due to "uncontrollable urges." He still wore Star Trek-inspired facial hair.

After a year of dating, Ted had asked Casey to marry him on bended knee in the middle of Jay Jay's roller skating rink, "The Time of My Life" by Jennifer Warnes and Bill Medley playing in the background. Casey wasted no time saying yes. They held the ceremony and reception at Jay Jay's as well, and together with a hundred twenty-eight friends and family skated and danced the night away. They spent their honeymoon at Disneyland and a year later, Casey gave birth to twins, a boy and a girl. Ted sold his condo and the family moved into a two-story character house in Northeast Portland, not too far from where Ray and his family lived.

Casey stirred and snuggled up to his back. She was so warm. Ted loved the feeling of her body next to his. From another room, Ted heard the sounds of waking giggles. He'd just pretend to sleep in on this Saturday morning. That would be a fun start to the day.

The wood floors in their house were sturdy, but they creaked unpredictably and usually betrayed the location of any attempted stealth attack. But that didn't matter because that's how the game was played.

Ted heard whispers from the doorway, and a familiar clacking of canine claws on the floor. Buster jumped up, front paws on the mattress, and licked Ted's face.

"Good morning to you, Buster, now shoo." He ruffled Buster's fur. The dog hopped down and trotted back to the bedroom doorway and chuffed.

"Shhh, Buster!" a child's hushed voice said.

More whispers mixed with the sounds of shuffling and giggling. Ted kept his eyes closed as the sounds drew nearer. A pair of three year old hands, with index fingers extended, raised up past the edge of the mattress. The wiggling fingers targeted his nose.

Ted opened his eyes, feigning fear and surprise. Saoirse and Finn gazed up at him from the floor, with their ginger hair and twin smiles a mile wide. They sat wiggling their fingers and giggling.

"Wake up, Daddy," Finn said.

"Time to play," Saoirse said, "or we'll pick your nose."

Ted narrowed his eyes, grinned and reached over the side of the bed, grabbing both kids and raising them up with a playful growl. "The tickle monster eats nose pickers for breakfast!"

"Mommy, help!" Finn said between laughing snorts.

"The tickle monster's got us." Saoirse squirmed under Ted's wriggling fingers.

Buster jumped up onto the bed, hopping on his front paws and barking.

"I'd better save you then." Casey propped herself up on one elbow and ran her right hand down Ted's side, then spread her fingers out across his ribs and abdomen.

Ted moved his tickle fingers to Casey's stomach and the

twins scrambled onto his back. The bedroom woke up to playful giggles, barking, and laughter, one Saturday of many to come.

March 15, 2017- March 6, 2018
Victoria, BC

If you like this book, please leave a review. I must manage my time and since I write in multiple genres, I will pay more attention to the books/genres with the most reviews. What I focus on next depends on you, the reader. Help me make the most of my time.

Titles by Lee Gabel

Detest-A-Pest Series
Arachnid 2.0 (Coming 2019)
Vermin 2.0

Standalone
Snipped
David's Summer
Tied

Afterword

Like it? Rate it. Share it.

If you enjoyed *Snipped*, please rate it and spread the word. With your rating, you take part in this book's success. If you're interested in joining my Reader Group for updates and advance notice of upcoming releases, please sign up by going to LeeGabel.com.

Note from the author

Thank you for reading my fourth novel. The seed of the idea spawned from my own experiences undergoing "the procedure." I felt there was untapped comedy potential and my searches for equivalent stories came up dry. I wanted to see this story on the big screen as a romantic comedy. The story began as a screenplay but that medium only allowed me to go so deep. My characters spoke to me (as they so often do) and told me they wanted more. I obliged. The screenplay became my outline and the book was born from that.

I enjoy writing about real places. As with my previous novels so far, I have used real street names where appropriate, but have changed addresses and made up most locations and businesses.

I believe comedy to be one of the most difficult genres to write and I hope I have succeeded. My Advance Reader Team has been immensely helpful for letting me know what worked and what didn't. Their insightful comments helped shape the story before this book was published. I am thankful for their candor.

Many thanks go to my wife and editor Sheila. I couldn't do this without her, nor would I want to. I owe a debt of gratitude to David Hoselton for his early feedback on the screenplay that this novel is based on. Watch David's work on *The Good Doctor*, which airs on ABC. And to my family and friends who supported my decision to quit my job to write full time, you were right. I am *your* number one fan now.

About the author

Since 1992, Lee has worked within the visual and dramatic arts landscape as a graphic designer, illustrator, visual effects artist, animator, screenwriter and author. He's contributed to an Emmy award and once walked 63.5 kilometers in 13 hours. Traditionally trained as a screenwriter, Lee has moved to writing books in order to share his stories.

Lee has spent most of his life living on an island in the Pacific Northwest and he writes in multiple genres that interest him. Why? In his own words: "Writing is magic. I'll never understand how it works the way it does, but I do know if I put energy into writing, it rewards me in strange and wonderful ways. Even if I know where I'm going in a story, often I'll end up being pulled in directions by my characters that I least expect. What ends up on the page never ceases to surprise me, and that's super cool. Writing continues to be one of the most difficult and most rewarding aspects of my life."

Find Lee on the Internet:

Want to join Lee's Reader Group or find out more about Lee and the books he writes? Please go to:

LeeGabel.com

LeeGabel.com/facebook

LeeGabel.com/twitter

Or follow Lee at BookBub - LeeGabel.com/bookbub